MR. CARTER'S SWORD
Ken Webb

ISBN: 978-1494249410

Book designed by MCWriting.com

IN MEMORY

Brady Herring, the skinny kid with thick glasses who got me through Lutheran Confirmation Class, then years later was posthumously decorated for his Vietnam service. Brady held them off in his downed chopper as long as he could.

Mark Taylor, who gave up a two-run homer to me in Little League, who became my friend and fraternity brother, but died a non-combat death while serving in the Vietnam War.

Jack Truluck, who had a Higgins boat shot out from under him in the First Wave at Omaha Beach and lived to tell about it—my mentor and the best and most fearless news reporter I ever knew.

and

Ginger Webb, the love of my life who believed in me and this story, but did not live to see it finished.

MR.
CARTER'S
SWORD

To: Kingsley —
Thanks for your Service &
Best of Luck!

KEN WEBB

Ken Webb

CONTENTS

CHAPTER ONE:
CONFESSIONS

Hey Shooter?" Buddy Carter spoke in a whisper, taking short, labored breaths as he leaned on the golf cart armrest. "Even with my coaching, you still can't hit a seven iron. What happens when I'm gone?"

"Won't have a coach," Shooter Lee said, never looking up as he followed his errant shot with a relaxed practice swing.

"Wish you'd hit a good iron shot—just once—before I go." Carter's big smile looked out of place on a gaunt face with sagging eyes. A Summerville Country Club cap covered a bald head that, only months ago, was thick with salt and pepper hair. The red knit golf shirt that had fit perfectly at Christmas was now a full size too large.

"I'm hitting my irons better each time we go out." Lee took another practice swing and grinned. "Besides, you're not going anywhere."

"I wish you were right, Shooter, but I'm getting weaker. Blood work shows it, too. I'm not just slipping. It's more like falling off a cliff." Then he found the smile again. "But, I can't tell you how inspiring it's been, watching you hack up this golf course this afternoon."

Lee managed to chuckle, and that was exactly what Carter wanted. Years ago, they had agreed that the golf course was sacred ground—a haven from work and other woes. For the last six months, it had been a special place where Carter's illness had been ruled out of bounds. They had talked, prayed and cried many times in recent months, but not on these fairways and greens until this March afternoon.

"I've got a favor to ask—while I've still got my wits about me." Carter reached for a plastic bag on the back of the golf cart.

"Sure," Lee said, still struggling with his grip on a seven iron.

"See this?" Carter pulled a blue metal box from the bag. "Some insurance guy gave it to me years ago. He fixed the combination lock where my initials—WMC—would open it. There's a note for you inside. It'll tell you what to do with the rest of the stuff."

"That's the favor?"

"That's it," Carter said. "Open it after I die, but before the funeral. Promise you'll follow my instructions to the letter. It's got nothing to do with Marie or the family. Don't discuss it with her, either."

"You don't want to talk about it now?"

"Nope." Carter's voice was firm. "I don't."

"Okay." Lee turned away, skimming the seven iron over the thick Bermuda turf. "You've got my word."

—⁂—

Three weeks later Lee sat on a weathered bench under an old magnolia outside St. Timothy's Lutheran Church. For years, the shady spot had been a favorite of parishioners with proposals or confessions to make. Lee was no stranger to the old bench, but his quiet moments there this April afternoon were intensely personal. He was mourning the loss of Buddy Carter, his best friend who had died during the night, and he was keeping a promise. Carter's words on the golf course had proved painfully prophetic. He did not slip away. It was a free fall over a cliff into that abyss, about which so much is written, hoped and feared, but, in truth, nothing is known.

"Thank you, Father, for taking Buddy home." Lee sat on the bench, resting his forehead against his open palm. He had been praying for days, begging God to put an end to Carter's suffering, and it was finally over. "Please, Father, welcome his soul. Grant him peace. He accepted your son as his savior. He believed in your forgiveness. Please gather him into your eternal arms. Amen."

After his prayers, Lee looked up at the white frame church and its rows of stained glass windows. The way they diffused the light gave the little church in the "Flower Town" a special notoriety, and their beauty had spread far beyond Summerville, South Carolina. As Lee gazed at the windows, depicting Biblical scenes, his thoughts drifted back decades when he first met Carter—the new kid in town. Lee invited him over and to bring his new air rifle. The timing was perfect for young Lee. His father, who disapproved of BB guns, was in Charleston for the day. It was a special helping of forbidden fruit for David, sitting on the side porch of the church parsonage with his new friend and playing with an air rifle. He eased the brown stock up to his shoulder, squeezed his left eye shut, and took careful aim at a moss green seedpod on the churchyard magnolia.

"Better watch it," Buddy warned. "I think that thing's loaded."

Seconds later the airgun fired. David's heart nearly stopped as the copper BB sailed over the seedpod, slamming into an emerald green leaf in the Garden of Eden window. It had been the pride of three generations of McCrearys, memorializing their dear departed who had served in the War Between the States. (They had been quick to tell anyone there was nothing civil about that conflict.) In an instant, a boy's finger had done what Mother Nature had not done in nearly a century.

"An accident." David's voice trembled. "It was an accident. How could I? I was just aiming. I swear!" His mind ran wild. There would be a trial before the church council. His father, the Rev. Dr. David Lee Sr., would preside. A guilty verdict was certain. He would be humiliated before the full congregation—probably on Easter Sunday. Even the much-maligned backsliders would be there.

"Calm down." Buddy pulled the rifle from David's shaking hands. "Can't be that bad."

Buddy looked for witnesses—down the walkway to the parish house then back to the street. Seeing none, he slipped the rifle behind the porch steps. The two scampered across the lawn and ducked into the thick green ligustrum hedge under the Garden of Eden window. Buddy shinnied up the downspout for a closer look.

"Just a nick," Buddy whispered and slid back down. "Nobody'll see it." His voice was firm, suggesting he was a veteran of such incidents. "Just remember." He looked his new friend in the eyes. "I'll never tell. I swear to God." Buddy kept his promise, and the perpetrator never confessed except to God Almighty from whom he sought forgiveness. He also prayed that he not be found out.

Whether or not it was divine intervention, the shooting was never discovered. Surprisingly, the pre-pubescent youngsters of the parish even missed it. It was a congregational right of passage for them to sneak a peak at near-naked Adam and Even in the stained glass window.

—※—

Now, after all these years, under the old magnolia across from the church window with the nick in it, sat the man the shooter had become—the Rev. David Martin Lee, Jr. Not only had he followed his father into the ministry, he had accepted a call to the church where his father had been a pastoral legend. On this day, like his father before him, Lee was dealing with the death of a parishioner who happened to be his best friend.

The pastor shook his head, looking down at the blue metal box. He fumbled with the combination until he lined up Carter's initials—WMC—and it popped open. Inside were faded Airborne Ranger patches and a yellowed snapshot. It was a young Carter with five other soldiers in Vietnam. There was a sealed manila envelope; "SSG Boggs" was written on the front. The pastor smiled when he recognized Buddy's handwriting on folded sheets torn from a legal pad. It said "Shooter Lee." Buddy had given him the nickname after the air rifle incident, and it stuck until the day Carter died.

Pastor Lee was staring at pieces of paper containing a dead man's message, and he was uncomfortable. He was dressed in the golf clothes he had worn to the driving range at daylight to swing away at frustration and pain. For a moment, he thought about going to his study to deal with the contents of the box.

"He's probably laughing at me," the pastor said, trying to smile as he unfolded the yellow sheets. After all, the two men had talked for hours during Carter's last days. There should be no surprises, he thought, and he began to read.

"You're my best friend, Shooter. Sorry we couldn't go a little farther together. Please thank everybody who prayed and helped Marie and the girls. Thanks to you, they'll be fine. We've talked about life and death and beyond, but we didn't talk much about Vietnam. It might've helped, but I couldn't face the guys who survived. Anyway, God's probably tired of hearing my confessions on that subject. Maybe he'll forgive me. Sorry to dump this on you, but it's something I had to do…"

The pastor read on, trying to absorb a tale of suffering and betrayal that followed, wondering how Carter had kept the secret for decades. The last paragraph was puzzling as well. "If a man named Boggs comes to my funeral, share this letter with him, and give him the box. If he doesn't come, destroy everything, forget you ever saw it, and say one last prayer for my soul."

Pastor Lee was shaken by Carter's story. He looked at the photograph again, turned it over and read the note on the back. "Left to right: Boggs, Richardson, Vasquez, Johnson, Calloway and Carter."

"Oh Lord." The minister bowed his head. "Give our brother Buddy relief from the burden he carried all those years. Take him into your fold where he will be safe from the horrors that haunted him. Guide me, Father, as I struggle with this revelation Buddy has laid upon my shoulders. Now, Heavenly Father, what would you have me do?"

K E N   W E B B

CHAPTER TWO:
THE PHONE CALL

"THIS IS BERTHA RICHARDSON." THE VOICE on the telephone was gentle and polite. "May I please speak to Mr. Boggs? I hope this is the right number."

"Miss Bertha." There was a smile in Boggs's voice. "This is Barry. How's everybody down in Pomaria?"

"Bad news." Her voice trembled. "With you living up in North Carolina, I didn't know if you'd see the obituary."

"What's happened?" Boggs asked. "Who died?"

"It's Mr. Carter—Buddy Carter of Summerville," she said. "He passed away yesterday."

"Carter? Was it an accident—a heart attack?"

"Oh, no, sir," she replied. "He'd been sick with cancer for some time. Got real bad since March—least that's what his wife, Miss Marie, said. He was so concerned about my Danny all these years, and now Mr. Carter the one that's gone. My boy's still struggling with his condition."

"Danny's the same?" Boggs knew the answer, but had to ask.

"Yes, sir, the same," she said. "But we're a hopin' some day—some way—he'll snap out of it." There was silence. "Seems like a lifetime since y'all got hurt in the war."

"Time flies," Boggs said, thinking it had not flown far enough from December of 1970.

"Anyway, we're taking Danny to Mr. Carter's funeral," she said. "I understand some veterans plan to attend. Since you were their leader, and all ... well, I was a hopin' you'd come, too."

For years, Boggs had kept Vietnam tucked away in the back of his mind. There had been a flare up with the dedication of the Vietnam Memorial—the great black wall in Washington, DC. He had not visited the monument, but his failure to make the pilgrimage was not a matter of indifference. He had deep feelings for the men with whom he served and, even more, the ones who died, but he was simply not willing to expose those emotions in front of The Wall. For Boggs, having been in the war and living with the memories seemed more than enough.

"Don't think I can make it, Miss Bertha." Boggs paused. "To be honest, I wasn't that close to Carter. He was with my team for a short time. I doubt his family would know who I am."

"Well," she said. "He always asked about you when he'd come up to visit Danny. Kept up with the families of those boys who died, too. Said he even called Bobby Vasquez every now and again."

"I didn't know Carter was close to you folks." Boggs was polite, making small talk, but had no desire to delve into the past.

"Oh, yes," she said. "It was a chance meeting—at The Wall in Washington—where we first met Mr. Carter. We were tracing names. Mr. Carter realized we were tracing the same ones—the boys who died on that patrol with you and Danny."

Boggs closed his eyes and sighed.

"When Mr. Carter recognized Danny, he put his arms around my boy and cried like a baby. All he could say was 'I'm sorry, so sorry.' Danny just kept looking at The Wall. He didn't say anything. When Mr. Carter got himself together, he said he felt bad about what happened to y'all. Said he was up at The Wall a lookin' for forgiveness."

"Forgiveness?" Boggs raised his eyebrows. "For what?"

"I didn't know what he meant. I just patted him on the arm. Told him there wasn't nothing to forgive, as far as I knew. I said I was there just a lookin' for a miracle—anything to help get my boy's mind back.

"I thought I saw a tear fall from Danny's eye, but my other son, Billy—he drove us up to Washington—said it was just the March wind. Said I was crazy like Danny. He still wants to put my sweet boy in a VA home.

"Anyway, Mr. Carter kept up with us ever since. Came to see us several times. Seems to pick Danny up when you boys come 'round. Oh. I'm sorry. I should be calling y'all men now."

"It's all right, Miss Bertha." Boggs smiled, speaking for the first time in minutes. "We'd love to be boys again."

"I'm sure the Carters would be honored if you came." Mrs. Richardson continued to sell Boggs on attending the funeral. "We'd love to see you, too. Would you be driving down?"

Boggs knew this lady would not take no for an answer. And why should she? It had been Danny who had pulled Boggs and Vasquez to safety those many years ago. Danny saved their lives, even if he had never told anyone how he did it.

"No ma'am. I'll fly." Boggs surrendered. "I believe Charleston is the closest airport."

"Can you get a flight?"

"Someone at the airport up here can help me," Boggs said. There was no need to mention he would be flying his own plane. Besides, he might be able to mix a little business with this solemn obligation.

"It'll mean so much, if you come," Mrs. Richardson said. "Wait till I tell Danny and Herbert!"

"How is your husband?"

"Fairly well," she said. "A life of farming's taken its toll, but he's content. His faith is strong."

Boggs smiled. "Give him my best."

"Jackson's Funeral Home is in charge," Mrs. Richardson said. "The service will be at the Carters' church—St. Timothy's—right in Summerville. Saturday at two o'clock."

"It was kind of your to call," Boggs said.

"Thank you, Mr. Boggs. Goodbye, now."

Boggs sighed as he sank into the leather sofa centered on a huge stone fireplace. Before the phone call, he had been enjoying a fire he built at sundown. The calendar said April, but a cold front had drifted across the Blue Ridge Mountains near Blowing Rock. Temperatures were falling into the low forties. For Boggs, the chill cut deeper after Bertha Richardson's call. Now he sat in silence, watching red coals slip through the iron grate, disappearing in a bed of white ash. A trip to South Carolina would mark the first veteran's funeral he had attended—at least one who had died of natural causes. There had been many battlefield services for fallen soldiers in Vietnam, but that was years ago. The services had been simple. The chaplains had been sincere; some kind words and prayers then back to the business of dodging bullets. At Carter's funeral, Boggs could face memories that had taken years to isolate. He was not looking forward to their escape, confident though he was of their recapture. Boggs's ill-fated Ranger patrol and his near maniacal approach to soldiering that followed had been filed away, but never forgotten. Now the old, memory-filled file drawers had been tossed by a well-intended phone call, and the musty contents scattered through his mind.

Boggs would never forget the story of Danny Richardson stumbling out of a Vietnamese jungle in December of 1970—a poster boy for the Medal of Honor. He carried the near lifeless body of Corporal Bobby Vasquez over his left shoulder. With his right hand, Richardson had a vice-like grip on the web gear of Staff Sergeant Barry Boggs and was dragging him along. Richardson was covered with mud and blood. None of the blood was his, but his 19-year-old baby face wore that blank, troubled stare so common after combat. Soldiers debriefing him got nothing but a dazed empty look. Psychiatrists treating him months and years later got the same thing. Richardson would never speak of what happened during the 36 horrible hours after the Rangers lost radio contact. And he had said little to anyone since.

Neither Vasquez nor Boggs could add much. They were the first wounded when North Vietnamese regulars stumbled over their Ranger team. Both were unconscious or in shock during the firefight in which the Rangers had been flushed like a covey of quail. Four other Rangers were of no help at all. They were missing and presumed dead. Their stripped and battered bodies were found the next day when a U.S. Army rifle platoon swept the area after an artillery barrage.

Vasquez lost his right arm just below the elbow. A rifle round shattered his left knee. He would wear a brace and walk with a limp forever. Army doctors credited Richardson with applying tourniquets to Vasquez's wounds and saving his life in the process. After months of hospitalization, he was sent home with a handful of medals and disability benefits. His hopes for a military career had been dashed.

Boggs fared better—physically at least. He got four deep cuts on his back and a concussion courtesy of an enemy grenade. He lived to fight another day and did it with distinction. Some said he did it with a vengeance, giving the enemy a bitter dose of their own guerilla medicine. Boggs and his buddies had business cards printed with their unit crest and pinned them to the uniforms of enemy soldiers they killed. They wanted them to know who had come calling. As a grim memorial and a deadly warning, Boggs wrote a letter to the North Vietnamese listing the names of the four soldiers who died on the December patrol. He left it on the chest of an enemy officer he killed in an ambush. Ironically, it was about two miles from where Richardson had dragged him out of the jungle. In that morbid epistle, Boggs swore to avenge the loss of his friends ten times over. By the time he finished his tour in Vietnam, he had nearly fulfilled his gruesome vow.

"You will rue the day you desecrated the bodies of Rangers Brown, Sigwald, Sciavo and Washington. Pray that you don't walk into my gun sights before my tour is up. I will kill 50 of you to avenge the loss of my brothers. —Staff Sergeant Barry Boggs."

The Army pinned medals on Danny during a ceremony at a VA hospital in California some six months after the mission. His visitors included another survivor of that firefight—Vasquez of Apple Valley, California. Boggs was still serving in South Vietnam, but he wrote a letter thanking Richardson for what he had done. Boggs and Vasquez never forgot Danny's heroics and stayed in touch. Time and again, they tried to reconstruct what happened during those thirty-six hours in the jungle, finally declaring it a waste of time and emotions. Richardson was the only soldier who knew, but his story seemed hidden forever.

After months in a VA hospital, Richardson was released to his parents in Pomaria, South Carolina. He had lived there ever since in his own little world. There were private doctors and government shrinks, but they all reached the same conclusion: Danny had been traumatized by the horror of a firefight years ago and would never break free.

—⁓—

Boggs drifted in and out of a restless sleep on the sofa in front of the fireplace as the old memories returned. He got up several times, pacing along the wall facing the gorge, stopping at each window to brood about the funeral and the flashbacks already tumbling through his mind. It was 3 a.m. The split oak had gone from flame to glowing coals, then white ash. The gas furnace came on, warming the spacious living room, but did little for the psychological chill gripping Boggs.

"Jesus," he moaned. He should have gone to bed hours ago. But he pulled a heavy cotton throw around his shoulders and rested one foot on the raised hearth. He found three pieces of pine from a kindling box and stirred the ashes until he found red coals glowing in the fireplace. He tossed crumpled newspaper in with the kindling and stacked pieces of oak on top. Boggs leaned against the mantelpiece, watching the coals ignite the paper and kindling, then the oak. The gentle fire reached out to him, bringing a small measure of peace to his troubled mind. He knew the flames would not last, but they would keep him company in the dark, lonely hours before dawn.

Boggs finally dozed off about 3:30 a.m. When the antique mantel clock chimed six times, he sat up as first light crept over the mountains. He stretched and yawned, but his eyelids shut tight, resisting the new day and reminding a tired, aging body it needed more rest. Then he leaned forward, elbows resting on his knees and cupping his face in both hands. Amid the overnight anguish and dozing, he had managed to sort things out. At least, he believed he had.

"I'm not ready for this," he muttered, reversing his commitment to attend Carter's funeral. "I can't go. Just can't."

CHAPTER THREE:
GRAVESIDE SERVICE

"**B**LESSED ARE THEY…THAT MOURN." FOR THE first time on an emotion-filled April day, Pastor David Lee's voice cracked. He paused to wipe the tears away, then he continued reading Christ's words from the gospel of St. Matthew: "For they shall be comforted."

Just thirty minutes earlier in St. Timothy's sanctuary, he had delivered an eloquent message of consolation and peace to Carter's family and friends. Now he stood before the casket at the graveside, struggling with the personal grief of his own. By the time he finished reading The Beatitudes, the pastor had regained his composure, and concluded with the Twenty-third Psalm and a special prayer for his close friend.

When the service ended, mourners stepped under the gray canvas canopy, offering condolences to Marie Carter and her two daughters. Others tiptoed around headstones in superstitious fashion, scurrying to their cars to stay ahead of a spring storm. Only his minister, in whom Carter had confided, knew that a storm of a different nature could spring from this solemn afternoon. And, in his heart, the pastor prayed to God that a man named Boggs was not somewhere in the gathering.

As Carter's family walked toward the polished, black funeral cars, three men stepped inside the tent. Silent, with heads bowed, they stood on the bright green artificial grass covering freshly turned earth. They had served with Carter in Vietnam. Today they were his honorary pallbearers. Each man touched the casket in a farewell gesture. One of them placed silver U.S. Army Airborne wings on the corner of the coffin. For a few emotional moments, their minds drifted back decades when boyhood innocence ended on missions ordained by powerful, older men.

This was not the first time these veterans had mourned the loss of one of their own, but the circumstances were different. Unlike those who died in battle, Carter had dodged enough bullets in Vietnam to live and love a family back home and die in his own bed.

Robert Johnson of Columbus, Ga., was the tall, thin black man who had placed the jump wings on the casket. Bobby Vasquez of Apple Valley, Ca., leaned against an aluminum cane he gripped with his left hand. A flesh-colored prosthesis hung almost naturally from the right sleeve of his black suit coat. Mike Calloway of Orangeburg, S.C. was the third man— red-faced with thick white hair, neatly trimmed beard, flashy clothes and expensive jewelry.

Pastor Lee always greeted the honorary pallbearers before a service, but the practice had taken on added significance today. With head bowed and a Bible against his chest, the pastor whispered a private prayer. "Thank you, Father, for sending Buddy's secret to the grave." When he opened his eyes, he breathed a sigh of relief, confident a heavy burden had been lifted from his shoulders.

As the pastor walked toward the veterans to say good bye, he caught a glimpse of another man—someone he had not met—standing alone beneath a tall pine not far from the gravesite. He was impeccably dressed— dark tailored suit, white shirt with French cuffs and gold cuff links. He wore a striped silk tie of blue, olive and gold. He stood ramrod-straight, looking beyond the casket to the thunderheads building in the west.

"Excuse me, sir." The pastor spoke in a soft, consoling voice as he stepped toward the man. As the minister moved closer, he could see the small black and gold lapel pin with "Ranger" emblazoned on it. "Are you a friend of the Carter family?"

"A fellow veteran," the man said, turning away from the thunderclouds closing on the cemetery at the edge of a huge soybean field. "Carter and I served together briefly in Vietnam. He was close to some of my men.

"Please excuse my manners, Reverend." The man smiled as he extended his hand. "I don't believe we've met. I'm Barry Boggs."

"No, no, Mr. Boggs, we have not." The minister swallowed hard, and at that moment, he knew Carter's secret would never rest in this peaceful place. "I'm Pastor David Lee. Buddy hoped you'd come. Before he died, he asked me to give you something."

"Give *me* something?" Boggs furrowed his brow. He had worked with Carter on a few missions in Vietnam, but not on the ill-fated December patrol. Carter had been recovering from a shoulder wound and assigned to light duty.

"You've got my curiosity up, Reverend." Boggs smiled again. "Can we talk as we walk to the cars?"

"The box Buddy left you is back at the church," the Rev. Lee said politely.

"A box?"

"Some pictures, notes—things like that, I suppose. It'll just take a few minutes. You do know your way back to the church?"

"I'll find it," Boggs said.

"Just follow the walkway between the parsonage and the old magnolia. It leads to the parish house. My study's on the left—inside the front door."

"I've got to say hello to those old Rangers before I leave." Boggs nodded toward the honorary pallbearers. By now they had stepped away from the casket and dried their tears. They were smiling, trying to cram decades of post-war life into a few brief moments.

"I'll need a little time with the Richardsons, too," Boggs said.

"Oh, yes," the pastor said. "I met them today for the first time."

"Danny saved my life in Vietnam," Boggs said. "Lost his on that battlefield—the mental part, anyway. But his mother won't give up on him. A true believer, Reverend Lee—a real saint. She's tried everything to bring him back." Boggs waved his hand in the direction of an elderly woman standing patiently in front of an old Chevy van. Patience had never been in short supply with Bertha Richardson.

"Well, then." Boggs cut the conversation short. "Let's meet at the church—say in a half hour or so?"

"Certainly, Mr. Boggs. "I'll be waiting."

—⁓—

Boggs spent a few minutes with the veterans, making plans to join them later that afternoon. Then he walked toward the station wagon parked in the gravel driveway about fifty paces from the gravesite. Carter's wife had arranged for the Richardsons' car to be parked close enough to hear the service without putting Danny in a crowd of strangers. Boggs smiled as he reached the gray-haired lady dressed in a blue print dress. Her white collar was neatly pressed. She held a navy blue pocketbook in one hand and her son's hand in the other.

Danny wore a navy blazer with wider than stylish lapels, and his gray double-knit slacks were flared at the bottom. His wine and navy tie was a bit wide for the times. His clothes may have labeled him a refugee from the Seventies, but he was neat as a pin. A loving mother saw to that. Then there was the medal suspended from a light blue ribbon around his neck. It spoke directly to the character of this incredibly shy and troubled man. "Valor" was the simple inscription on Danny's Medal of Honor.

Boggs hugged Mrs. Richardson like a favorite aunt. "Sorry to meet on such a sad day, Miss Bertha, but it's good to see you.

"Ranger Richardson." Boggs's lip quivered as he took Danny's hand. "You're still my hero."

Danny stared straight through Boggs into the seemingly endless bean field beyond the cemetery.

"Mr. Herbert," Boggs said, leaning into the van. "Good to see you, Sir." Danny's father nodded and smiled.

"You're handsome as ever, Sergeant Boggs," Mrs. Richardson said.

"Thank you, ma'am, but you missed my wrinkles and all this gray hair. I see Danny's getting a little gray, too. And please, call me Barry. Those 'sergeant' days were a lifetime ago."

"It's real sad about Mr. Carter," she said. "He was so nice to Danny. They must've been right close in Vietnam. After we met him at The Wall up in Washington, he called us a lot. Come up to see us, too. He always talked about that mission, wishing he'd been with y'all."

"Carter had a lovely family," Boggs said, guiding the conversation away from old war stories. "I know they'll miss him. He'd be pleased you're here, too."

"Oh, he knows we're here. Mr. Carter had accepted the Lord. He told me so sometime before he died. He's up there." She looked skyward. "He's aware of all this. Yes sir. Mr. Carter's spiritual life was in order. You can't have peace without that. Don't you agree, Mr. Boggs?"

"Yes ma'am," Boggs said. He was uncomfortable talking about faith and religion. "Now," he said, patting Danny's shoulder, "tell me how this guy's doing."

In a rare, clear moment, Danny turned to Boggs and looked him in the eye. "Sergeant," he said, without emotion.

"I can't remember the last time he spoke to me." Boggs was surprised, but his efforts to continue the dialogue failed miserably. He got nothing else from Danny, just his lonely brown eyes gazing aimlessly across the bean field.

"He'll say something now and again." Mrs. Richardson sighed. "Keeps to himself, mostly. Takes care of his cats and dogs—chickens and guinea hens, too—but he don't talk much. Still, we try to help him remember, you know, people and things."

Boggs telephoned the family at least once a year, but it had been five years since he had visited the Richardson farm. Danny looked a little older, but the years had taken a toll on his parents. Boggs wondered where Danny would live if something happened to them, but now was not the time to discuss it.

"Wish you'd visit more," Mrs. Richardson said. She was always glad to see Boggs. He was Danny's closest link to the days in Vietnam and the incident that changed his life forever. She prayed that a visit from Boggs—from anyone—might free her son from that dark and distant prison where damaged minds are held.

Mrs. Richardson believed Boggs was a wealthy, aristocratic southerner, but she did not know he spent his childhood running wild and barefoot on a Kershaw County farm. Even with his education and worldly charm, he never lost his love of country life and those who lived it. Perfect manners and expensive clothes might have suggested otherwise, but he could sit in a front porch swing for hours listening to country folks. He loved to hear them talk about their lives and marvel at city dwellers—living in concrete and steel with no trees and so close to each other.

"I want to thank you and your mother for calling me about Carter." Boggs spoke to Danny as if he had good sense, but Danny had spoken his one word for the day.

"He still singing at Christmas?" Boggs asked.

"That's a puzzlement to us all," Mrs. Richardson said, shaking her head. "He still sings carols at our church up on the Broad River. The doctors are right dumbfounded by it. Except for that singing, it's just a word or two here and there.

"It's been good visiting with you," she said, "but we'd better go. We like to be home by dark. Herbert don't like night driving, and I don't drive that much myself."

"I've got to spend some time with those old Rangers," Boggs said. "I better get moving, too."

"We enjoyed our visit with Mr. Vasquez and the others before the service," she said, nodding toward the veterans.

Boggs reached inside the car to shake hands with Mr. Herbert, then turned to Danny whose mind was God knows where. "See you soon, pal." He gave Mrs. Richardson a hug, promised to visit more often, and walked down the driveway to the rented Ford. As he fumbled for his keys, he looked up to see the black-suited funeral director signal his men to close the grave.

Fearing rain, the other mourners had left the cemetery. Although Mrs. Richardson wanted to get home before dark, she observed the tradition from her own community by staying until the grave was closed.

Boggs got into the rental car and adjusted the unfamiliar seat controls. It was nothing fancy, he thought, but more than adequate for the short trip from Charleston and back. Then he chuckled. How spoiled he had become. He could remember times when a farmer, pulling a flat bed trailer behind a tractor, would stop on a blistering tar and gravel road and pick him up. He smiled as he whispered his grandfather's words: "Po' ride's better'n a proud walk." He watched the Richardsons in his rear view mirror, wondering what, if anything, was going on in Danny's head. As he eased the car down the driveway, the tires pressed the loose gravel into the roadbed, sounding like a muffled drum roll. Boggs put his foot on the brake and glanced back toward the gravesite. He forced a tight-lipped smile and gave Carter a final salute as the work crew lowered the casket.

The funeral was sure to unwind unwanted memories, but Boggs felt he handled it well—almost therapeutic, he thought. Maybe it would help him put the darker side of Vietnam further behind him. He would see the pastor and graciously accept whatever Carter left behind—pictures or something from Vietnam, he guessed. He would smile through the impromptu reunion of old Army friends then fly home to the mountains a little more at peace, and, possibly, a better man for having come.

CHAPTER FOUR:
THE BLUE BOX

W HEN BOGGS'S CAR ROLLED TO A stop at St. Timothy's, the pall cast by Carter's funeral was gone, save mortuary workers loading funeral parking signs into a black station wagon. As he left the car, he inhaled the sweet fragrance of lavender wisteria cascading down tall pines like candle wax. He marveled at the ancient oaks, streaked with Spanish moss in shades of gray. The little church was a fitting subject for watercolorists, and, for a moment, Boggs had forgotten why he was here.

"Found your way back, I see." Pastor Lee was waiting on the parish house steps. He had shed his black suit coat, enjoying the unexpected sunshine.

"No trouble, Reverend." Boggs walked slowly toward him. "I took the scenic route. The flowers are beautiful here."

"They are, indeed, but you should've seen it before Hurricane Hugo."

"Camden took quite a shot from the same storm."

"You live in Camden?" the pastor asked.

"Grew up ten miles from there, out in the country. I live in the North Carolina mountains now. After the war and a failed marriage, I took refuge up there for good."

"Interesting. Interesting, indeed."

The pastor's uneasiness did not escape his visitor.

Reverend Lee opened the parish house door. "Please, come into my study." The hallway was stark white—cold in comparison to the minister's office. It was paneled in cypress with bookcases on three walls. Dusty volumes of *The Pulpit Commentary* filled the top shelves. Scores of texts by famous theologians packed the shelves below—all Greek to Boggs, even those written in English. He shook his head, wondering if this man had read them all. The pastor's family portrait was on one end of a glass-topped credenza behind his desk. At the other end was an old photograph of a gray-haired minister in his robe and vestments.

"My father."

"You look a lot like him." Boggs smiled, continuing his unguided, visual tour of the room until his eyes stopped at a brass wall plaque. "Summerville's Worst Iron Shot" was the inscription. A golf ball, club head of a seven iron, and the three-pointed hood ornament from a Mercedes Benz were mounted on the plaque. Boggs chuckled as he read it.

"That's from my golfing buddies. Ten years ago." The pastor gently rubbed the club head with his thumb and forefinger. "Buddy was the instigator. They presented it to me at a church supper. I sliced a shot across the fourth fairway to Country Club Drive. The ball shattered the windshield of a big Mercedes. That lady driver taught us some new words that day.

"Please sit down, Mr. Boggs." The pastor pointed to an upholstered armchair in front of a desk covered with books, papers, and a coffee cup stuffed with pens and pencils. Pastor Lee sighed as he sank into a well-worn black swivel chair behind his desk. He fumbled with his reading glasses, cleaning them twice before draping them across his narrow nose. Then he reached inside an old leather satchel and produced a blue metal box. He sat quietly for a few moments then lined up the initials WMC on the combination lock, and it popped open. He removed sheets that had been torn from a legal pad, four faded photographs and a manila envelope with Boggs's hand-written name on the front.

"This," the minister said, spreading his hands over the box, "is why I asked you to stop by. Buddy left this behind. I was to give it to you if—and only if—you came to the funeral. Better read these pages first.

"And let me caution you, Mr. Boggs." The pastor held the pages close to his chest, looking wide-eyed over his reading glasses. "This may be disturbing for you. It was for me, and the closest I got to the Vietnam War was the television news."

"Let's have a look," Boggs said as he took the pages from the minister and began to read.

"The first couple of paragraphs are to me," the minister said.

Boggs glanced up, acknowledging the pastor's footnote, but had already skipped past Carter's kind words and prayer requests. He focused on the lines about the mission—the one that had haunted Boggs for decades. He sat quietly, reading without emotion.

Carter's letter told, in general terms, why the orders were changed for Boggs's patrol in December of 1970. It was detailed enough for the pastor to know something had gone terribly wrong, but Carter had not named the soldiers he accused.

Uncovering this old, dirty secret was a revelation and a curse for Boggs. A letter from a dead man had done more than open old wounds; it had created new ones. The more he read, the more it hurt. He had hoped the gulf of time was wide enough to keep these horrors far beyond the horizon, and, just maybe, God would help him make some sense of it. But he knew it would have to be a god who listened to one whose prayers were infrequent, if not afterthoughts.

Just when Boggs was sure decades had softened a hardened heart and dulled the memories, they were back—vivid as ever—but this was no nightmare. He was not piled up in bed covers writhing in a cold sweat. He was wide-awake, sitting before an unwitting messenger delivering the worst news imaginable. At that moment, he felt like he was *in country* again.

Riding the wild currents of his emotions into the past, Boggs gripped the clammy sheet metal door of the Huey. His leg muscles tensed as they had years ago when planting jungle boots against helicopter skids, holding on for dear life. His tearing eyes squinted against the rushing wind. It was all there—the thick smell of aircraft fuel, whirring rotor blades, and crackling radio traffic. Weapons were locked and loaded. Fearful boyish faces were camouflaged in swirls of olive, black and gold. Boggs could feel their hot breath on the back of his sweaty neck, and he strained under the weight of their lives resting precariously on his shoulders. He was a war-rior—their leader—once again, and they were going in.

"Oh, God!" Boggs called out to that deity with whom he rarely com-muned. "*You* could have saved them! I failed them, and I carry it every day of my life. Why this? Why now?"

"Are you okay, Mr. Boggs?" Pastor Lee could see the beads of sweat on Boggs's forehead.

Boggs's eyes had drifted away from Carter's letter, staring blankly through the double windows into the churchyard. He was no longer the stoic figure at the cemetery watching distant storm clouds gather. A differ-ent and more dangerous storm had struck here.

"Mr. Boggs?"

"Oh…Reverend…" Boggs stumbled back to the present. "I'm sorry. This letter. The memories. Things happened over there—horrible things. But now this, after all these years. It's just a lot to take in."

The minister struggled, too. He searched for comforting words that would not come—an uncomfortable dilemma for a man of the cloth. This was not a domestic squabble, a runaway teenager or a scared office clerk whose skimming had been found out. Lives were lost in an alien world, in another time, with which the minister had no frame of reference.

"I wasn't in the war," the pastor said after a long pause. "Maybe I'm not the one to tell you what to think or do. I feel I don't have the right, if you can understand that."

"Thank you, Reverend." Boggs tried to smile. He knew what the pastor was trying to say. "Don't feel bad. Maybe you had to be there to under-stand it. It's just sad so many suffered for so long before the healing started.

"I'm sure you anguished over Carter's letter," Boggs said. "I've got some thinking to do myself."

"I'm sorry—so sorry—to be the messenger," the pastor said. "Truth is, I almost threw that box away. I think everyone would be better off if it had gone to the grave with Buddy. Still, I can't understand how an American could sacrifice his own men for personal gain."

"A lot happened that didn't make sense," Boggs said. "I took it hard back then—used it as an excuse to kill every enemy soldier I could. But this is really personal. It'll take some time, but I'll sort out my feelings."

Boggs regained his stoic expression as he looked out the windows. Then he turned to the minister and spoke in a calm voice: "I assume no one else knows about this?"

"The box was locked when Buddy put it in my hands. No one else has seen it." Then he looked Boggs straight in the eye. "I'm just keeping my promise to Buddy. This is the end of it for me, thank the Lord. All I can do is pray for you."

"Thank you, Reverend." Boggs put everything back in the box, stood, and extended his hand to the pastor. "No reason upsetting Carter's family—anyone else, for that matter."

"Don't forget the combination—Buddy's initials—WMC."

"I guess this is goodbye, sir. Your service was a fine tribute. It was kind of you to mention the Richardsons in your sermon. Didn't know Carter was close to them."

"He was," the pastor replied. "Buddy drove up to their farm several times a year to check on that poor man. He'd get choked up when we talked about Danny, you know, the way the war left him."

"Carter knew something the rest of us didn't," Boggs said. "Funny thing, too. I wouldn't be here if it hadn't been for Mrs. Richardson. She called—practically shamed me into coming. I just couldn't say no to that lady."

"God bless you," the minister said. "May He help you sort this out."

The stunned visitor managed a weak smile, nodding as he left the pastor's study and holding his emotions in check as he walked out of the parish building. The rain clouds that threatened to pour at the graveside were gone, and the warm sun encouraged him to remove his suit coat. He folded it neatly over his arm while glancing up at the little white church and its brilliant stained glass. Then he spotted a bench beneath the old magnolia. He was tired from traveling, not to mention the havoc Carter's revelation had produced. No one was around, and the old bench looked like a good place to sit and collect his thoughts. He would not be the first person to sit there and try to sort out troubling news. Unlike those who preceded him, Boggs's mind was spinning in a direction away from comfort and consolation. His thoughts were drifting through dangerous currents of revenge. Then he looked at the metal box. He wanted to study the contents before meeting his old Rangers. He placed his coat on the bench beside him, set the box on his lap and clicked in the combination. He pulled a silver penknife from his pants pocket and slipped the sharp blade under the flap of the manila envelope, carefully slicing along the fold. As he emptied the contents, he was surprised to find a smaller envelope and a single sheet of legal paper with another note from Carter. Pencil tracings of four names were paper-clipped to the note. Boggs recognized each one.

"Somehow, I knew you'd come," Carter's letter began. "I'm sorry if this seems like spy stuff, but I want to thank you for talking with Pastor Lee and for looking at what I've put together. You've probably figured out that Capt. James B. Cain got your orders switched. The ARVN liaison officer was Nguyen Ha. They were in a smuggling partnership. It was drugs and stolen military equipment. Some of it even went to the Viet Cong.

"I was asleep on a cot at headquarters when they walked in around midnight. I ducked behind some filing cabinets so they couldn't see me. I was surprised anybody was there, much less a couple of officers from Brigade. It was the day you got overrun, and it didn't take long for me to figure out why they were out in the field. They were whispering, but I heard every word. They talked about how Cain changed the orders based on some phony intelligence and diverted your team and SGT Fort's team away from one of their smuggling deal. Cain bragged about it, and they laughed. I guess they were making tons of money. The information I got indicates that they parlayed that smuggling money into a fortune. It includes some nice legal businesses, but I understand Ha has dabbled in the drug trade. Seems he stays in Europe or Asia most of the time. He's had to buy his way out of trouble a couple of times. The bastard's in his late sixties. You'd think he'd sit back and try to keep things legal. Cain retired from the Army as a Lieutenant Colonel. Then he hooked up with Ha in M&H International in England. Cain keeps his stuff clean or at least covered up pretty good.

He's been a big contributor to both political parties and is well known in Washington, DC. That's one reason I couldn't go to the authorities with this. Plus, the charges are so old. The Army wouldn't want to see somebody dig up stuff like this.

"I thought about killing Cain myself. M&H owns a villa at Hilton Head Island. I even went down there, but I didn't see them. I poked around pretending to be a tourist, asking about villa rentals. But the M&H place was not for rent. The real estate guy said it sits empty most of the year, but the owners always come down in mid-October and stay a few of weeks. You could probably hit both of them then."

"Hit?" Boggs looked up from the letter. Maybe the cancer got to Carter's brain long before he died.

"There's a report in a safe deposit box in Columbia that will give you the details about their activities and where you can find them. The key's in the little envelope with the bank's address. I couldn't risk putting that stuff in the letter my pastor gave you. You'll know why when you see the report and find out who helped me. That person would be in a tight spot if somebody found out.

"I can't tell you how sorry I am for keeping this quiet all these years. I was just a scared kid who didn't think anybody would take my word against two officers. I tried to put it out of my mind for a long time. I was doing pretty well until I went to the Vietnam Memorial in Washington. That's when I saw Richardson for the first time since the war. After that I couldn't stop thinking about it and picked up little bits of information here and there. Once I got everything together, I was too sick to do anything. I'm real sorry to dump this in your lap. I'm sure you've got a nice life and don't need it. But some good boys died for nothing because of those two. Danny's messed up for life, and look at Vasquez. All the others got were holes in the ground and their names on The Wall.

"I understand why I couldn't go on the patrol, but I'll never get over it. I probably would have been killed with the rest of them, but I might have helped, too. I think I found out about all this for a reason. And just when I thought I was getting to a point where I could do something, I got sick. It looks like this old Ranger is going to miss the action again.

"God bless you, Sergeant Boggs. I'm not sure where I'm going. Maybe I'll get lucky and I'll find some peaceful place on the high ground. I'll never forget all you guys. I just hope you can forgive me and get some revenge for our brothers."

"Good God." Boggs whispered, wiping tears from his eyes. "What the hell am I supposed to do now?"

CHAPTER FIVE:
OLD GUYS, NEW TIMES

BY THE TIME BOGGS WALKED INTO the Pinckney Inn on I-26 east of Summerville, his old Rangers had found the bar and were a couple of drinks ahead of him.

"Come on over Sergeant Boggs," Calloway said, still loud and gregarious as ever. Each man stood to shake hands with their former leader. Except for the brief moments at the cemetery, it was the first time they had been together since the war.

"Thanks for coming," Johnson said. "It's been a long, long time."

"Too long, but drop the 'Sergeant' stuff. It's just Barry Boggs now."

"Still got the *bracelets.*" Johnson smiled, showing Boggs scars that circled his wrists. Johnson had been with Sergeant William Fort on a mission that paralleled Boggs's ill-fated December patrol. Fort's men had also taken a pounding during the surprise encounter with the North Vietnamese. All members of the six-man team lived to tell about it, including Calloway and Johnson. Johnson's story was a hair-raising tale of capture, escape and evasion. After a two-day forced march with the NVA, he freed himself during the night and killed both of his guards while they slept. Three days later he walked into the Rangers' base camp—scratched, beaten, and bug-bitten, but alive. To this day, he wears scars around both wrists where the NVA lashed his hands together with telephone wire.

"How are you, Barry?" Vasquez asked. He had been Boggs's RTO during the patrol disaster. The two had talked many times over the years.

"Fine. Just fine." Boggs put up a good front while Carter's revelation banged around in his head. One thing for sure, he would not share the story at this little gathering. He was inclined to keep the secret forever. Except for Vasquez, he had not laid eyes on these men in more than four decades. Even then, they had been thrown together by fate.

"How 'bout a drink, Barry?" Calloway raised his hand, giving the barmaid the high sign. A diamond-encrusted signet ring sparkled on his pinky finger. His coat sleeve slipped down, exposing a gold Rolex Presidential perched on his wrist. "I'm buyin'."

"Thanks, Mike," Boggs said. When the waitress brought the drinks, he called for a toast. "Let's drink one to Carter—Richardson, too—and all the guys who didn't make it home."

"To all Rangers—past, present and future," Vasquez said, as glasses were raised. Then the conversation moved around the table, covering the highs and lows of decades of peace, prosperity and family lives.

"The Army was good to me," Johnson said, reflecting on his twenty-four years. His last tour was at Fort Benning, Georgia, where he retired as a sergeant major. He and his bride of thirty-eight years settled just off post in Columbus. He was working on a second federal retirement with the U.S. Veterans Administration. The job with the VA was not as exciting as the army, but it kept him in touch with the military. It also gave him time for his wife and two grown daughters. Both were college graduates and career women. There was also a five-year-old grandson.

"I love that little boy," he said, flashing a big smile. "'Course I can pick up and go home when he starts raising too much hell. One of the benefits of being a grandpa."

"I don't miss the army one damn bit." Michael Ray Calloway's story was something else. Discharged in 1971, he put the military behind him for good. His homecoming to the tiny town of Branchville, South Carolina, was little more than a stopover. "I was small-town, still am, for that matter," Calloway explained. "But I wasn't gonna live in one. So, I moved to Atlanta, met a beautiful girl, and got married. Bought a house on the north side. Not so many minorities, and all—sorry Johnson, nothing personal. That's just the way it was."

"Some things don't change." Johnson sighed, shook his head and sipped his beer.

Boggs sat quietly, wondering what Calloway would say next.

"Anyway, things were going good." Calloway continued. "My wife worked in a law office, so she was up on the legal stuff. She jumped right in the middle of women's rights and all. Went to meetings. Her women friends were in and out of the house. Hell, I didn't think much about it. I was selling the hell out of cars at a Lincoln-Mercury store. Thought I was the cat's ass, too. Had four pairs of alligator shoes—black, brown, cordovan and light fuckin' gray. Two hundred pounds of bullshit in a tailored suit. That's what I really was." He paused, took a deep breath, let it out and gulped a big swig from the longneck Budweiser. "I just wasn't paying any attention. That's when it happened."

"*Well?*" Johnson asked.

"She hit me with it in March of 1978. Said she loved me and all, but she thought she might be a lesbian. Wanted to separate—you know—so she could make sure and all."

"You're kidding." Boggs had been sipping a bourbon and water, listening casually. He straightened up and looked Calloway in the eye. Johnson and Vasquez leaned forward.

"Y'all know a Southern boy wouldn't joke about this. Hell, for a while I couldn't even talk about it. She just liked girls better than boys. Instead of me getting wild and crazy, I was kind of in shock. Besides, it wasn't exactly like she was sleeping with guys. Funny thing, too. She loved me to death—even when she thought she was gay."

"Hey man, how long did you stay with her?" Vasquez waded into the conversation.

"Not long." Calloway leaned forward, tapping his fingers softly on the table. "I was doing good 'til she brought a couple of her new gal pals over—hardcore dikes. They were going to the beach. That's when I decided enough was enough. We split when she got back.

"She never asked for any money, not one fuckin' dime. But I gave her the house. The only thing she asked me to do was meet her one year after we split—to make sure she was right. Sounded wacky, but I said okay. I mean, what the hell? The girl didn't try to break my ass. Besides, I still loved her. She was going through all that sensitivity crap, getting in touch with her inner self. Besides, I didn't think she'd meet me a year later anyway."

"Sounds like bullshit to me." Johnson shook his head.

"All true, I swear." Calloway raised his hand as if he were on the witness stand. "We met a year to the day after we separated. It was at a motel outside Atlanta. We hugged and kissed, and the next thing I know, we're going at it full bore. That was some of—no, it was—the best sex of my life. Afterwards we just lay there for a long time. Didn't say nothing, but I was thinking. Then I told her. Wonderful as it was, there wasn't nothing there but the sex, and this was *adios*."

Johnson was still shaking his head. "How'd she take *that*?"

"Just fine, actually. Said she loved me—loved being with me. Said she understood and wished me a nice life."

"And that was it, just like that?" Vasquez looked puzzled.

"Almost." Calloway whined. "We had such a great time, we decided to meet again the next year—just to be sure."

"You're full of shit, Calloway." Johnson leaned back in the bar chair.

"It's the truth, Robert. And we met the next year, too. Actually, we did it for the next three years. She didn't show up for number five. She'd got off the lesbian thing and was seeing a psychiatrist over in Atlanta."

"He was treating her?" Boggs fought back a smile, bringing the bourbon to his lips for another sip.

"Whatever he was doing, he did it good." Calloway reached inside his coat for a pack of Winstons then produced an old Zippo and shook his head. "Carried this lighter all through the war. Anyway, she and the shrink got married—still are. But I gotta tell you; I miss those little get-togethers. Every year on the anniversary date I just close my eyes in quiet meditation, remembering how great it was."

"You're too much, man," Vasquez said. "Sounds like Hollywood, and I live close enough to that screwed up place to know what I'm talking about."

"What happened was painful," Calloway said, "but it was a blessing in the long run. I was moping around the dealership after she left when a wholesaler gave me some advice. He said if I really wanted to make it in the car business, I'd start up a 'tote the note' operation. There's lots of them now—dealers doing their own financing. He said my hometown was virgin territory. He sketched it out for me on the back of a paper napkin. Buy old cars; mark them up a couple of grand. The customer's down payment covers the cost of the car. You charge him thirty percent interest on the balance and off you go."

"That's what you do for a living?" Vasquez asked.

"Did for a living," Calloway said. "For fifteen years back home in Orangeburg County. Turned it over to my nephew after the first few million. He's done a great job ever since." Calloway gulped the last swallow of beer and flagged the barmaid again. "I invested in timber land, too, but the stock market's my baby—good times and bad.

"I give scholarships to Carolina and Clemson every year. Give *three* over at S.C. State in Orangeburg. Blacks folks around there are my best customers." Calloway leaned forward, lowering his voice to a whisper. "Hell, ain't been that long since blacks could get good bank financing. Anyway, I talk too much. What's been going on with you, Mr. Boggs?"

Boggs was not ready to tell the post-war story of his life, but he hit the high spots. There had been a failed marriage. The best part, he said, was the daughter it produced. She was a practicing attorney.

"Got it together just like her daddy?" Calloway winked at Boggs.

"Beautiful and brilliant." Boggs beamed proudly, loosened his tie and sank back in the soft leather chair. He was getting comfortable with these old warriors of the past. He told them how he and his wife divorced when their daughter was five years old. "She's definitely her mother's girl," he said, "But she's the love of my life. I'd give her the world if I could."

Most of his time now was spent in Blowing Rock, North Carolina handling what he called "a few family business interests." There were more than a few holdings—scattered across the country and around the world—but he was careful not to elaborate.

"Bobby?" Boggs was eager to turn the conversation in a different direction. "How are things with you?"

"Oh, I'm okay, I guess," Vasquez said. "The artificial arm works fine. The bad leg's as good as it's going to get. The arthritis in the good one's the problem. We're not getting any younger, Barry."

"Amen to that." Boggs smiled, nursing the drink Callaway bought him. "How's your family and the business?"

"The wife and kids are fine. One grown daughter, another in community college. Roberto Jr. is a Special Forces officer."

"Outstanding!" That was the most enthusiasm Johnson had shown since the four men sat down. "I know you're proud of him."

"I am," Vasquez said, "but I worry more now than when he ran the streets in high school."

"Think he'll make a career of it?" Johnson asked.

"Looks like it. At least the country feels better about soldiers than when we were in."

"They're still not treated good enough," Calloway said.

"How's business, Bobby?" Boggs asked.

"Good," Vasquez said. "We cater to hunters and outdoorsmen—a lot of women, too. The San Bernardino Mountains are nearby, so we sell camping gear, fishing supplies—things like that. Plus, we've gotten into mountain bikes. Our firearms business is strong, too. We thought the discount stores would hurt us, but they haven't. We specialize in personal service. We've got a great repair shop."

"Well, gentlemen." Johnson pulled his chair up to the table. "I didn't know what to expect when we got together. But you guys haven't changed much. Vazquez is still quiet, Calloway's still loud and Boggs is still kind of reserved."

"Why, Johnson." Boggs sat up, pretending to be shocked. "You're more observant than I remember. What happened to that shy country boy from 1970?"

"He's educated and well traveled—a content and confident African-American," Johnson said as he broke into a wide, toothy grin.

"Well," Calloway said as a big smile spread across his face. "I'm glad you folks finally settled on what you want to be called. I swear to God. That's the biggest problem with this race business. Folks trying to figure out who they want to be. Hell, they're Americans. I just wish they'd let themselves be Americans."

"What about our black heritage, Mike? Doesn't that count for something?"

"Come on, Robert," Calloway whined. "We're all sitting here from different backgrounds, different national origins. Why are we really sitting here? Because we're Americans, damn it. Americans."

"Uh-huh." Johnson spoke slowly, with a hint of alcohol in his voice. "With your redneck background, what makes you an authority on race relations?

"Listen, my friend of color." Calloway's tone was sarcastic. "I met this African-American woman with a doctorate in history. She's been a close personal friend for some time."

Things got quiet—real quiet. Boggs, Johnson and Vasquez looked at each other—blank stares all around.

Johnson recovered first. "Bullshit! You? Involved with a black woman?"

"I believe its African-American now," Calloway said. "And I didn't say involved. But were close friends for quite a while."

"Bet that stirred things up at your mama's house." Johnson raised his hand and nodded at the barmaid for another beer. He had no intention of leaving this reunion early.

"Could've been a problem," Calloway admitted. "But my old man died in '88. He would've had a shit fit. If Mama knew about it, somebody else told her. We never talked about it.

"Besides, it's her mama that was the problem." Calloway's eyes widened as he sat back in the tufted bar chair and sighed. "It wasn't just a matter of color with her. She's a real Yankee from upstate New York. She wouldn't have been happy with me if I was blacker than you, Johnson. *All* of us down here are cotton pickers as far as she's concerned."

"Man, oh man." Johnson sighed. "I can see you two wheeling up in a big Lincoln at the country club. That would be something to behold."

"You'd never see us there. We go places like New York and Las Vegas. I even took her to Europe once. My little place at Hilton Head is nice and quiet, too. Y'all are welcome to use it, by the way. Matter of fact, Carter's been there a couple of times."

"Have you been in touch with any of the other guys?" Boggs was anxious to get off the subject of race.

"A few," Johnson said. "A couple stayed in the service. Others just went home and I never heard from them again. Martin was killed in Panama. Damn fine soldier. I haven't heard from anybody else in a long time."

"I heard from Carter—and you, Barry—that's about it." Vasquez said. "I think most of you guys live on the East Coast.

"I saw Carter every now and again," Calloway said. "They have those Ranger get-togethers down at Benning. To tell the truth, I've kind of put that stuff behind me. Don't get me wrong, now. We got a special bond, and all. It was just a long time ago.

"I did see a guy who was the intelligence officer with the Brigade when we were in Nam. Two years ago, I guess. I own a wood chip mill over near Ridgeland. He came with my timber broker. He'd met the guy over at Hilton Head. They got to talking about investments in timber and acreage. Sid Lacey—that's my broker—hunts with us sometimes, too. He brought the guy over to my mill. It's state of the art and all. Y'all might remember him. He was with the Brigade when our patrols got shot up. Captain Cain."

Boggs had been thinking of a way to excuse himself when he almost choked on his bourbon and water. "Haven't heard that name since the war," he said, showing little interest. "Miss, another bourbon, please?"

"Well, sir, you ain't missed much," Calloway said, continuing his story. "Like I said, he came to the mill with my broker. They walked up to where I was serving lunch. I cook for our crew every month or so. My guys were lining up to eat, and Sid walks up with Cain. Hell, I recognized him right off. Stuck out my hand and said, 'Captain Cain, you were the Brigade intelligence officer when I was a Ranger in Vietnam. How you doin'?'

"'It's Colonel Cain, retired,' he says to me. 'And what unit was that, again?' What an asshole." Calloway smiled, motioning for the barmaid to bring another Bud. "He just mumbled something about it being a long time ago. Damn, man! How do you forget that? He was standing right there when they brought us in from those patrols. How could he forget that bloodbath?

"Sid pulled Cain aside—told him I owned the mill, then Cain tried to be nice, and I let him. But I wouldn't give you two shits for that son of a bitch. Sid said he owns some big worldwide company. He and some South Vietnamese colonel—that's his partner—have a big place at Hilton Head."

"Small world," Boggs said under his breath.

"What'd you say, Sarge?" Johnson asked.

"Oh, nothing, just time to go, guys." Boggs's mind was spinning, and not because of the bourbon. "Got to get some sleep. Got an early flight. I need a phone number for you, Johnson. Calloway, too. I've got yours, Bobby."

Boggs said his good-byes, leaving the aging ex-warriors waiting for another round. He found a quiet spot in the hotel lobby where he made three cell phone calls. The first was to a general aviation airport in Columbia. He would land there the next morning and go to the bank Monday. The second call was to an old college friend he hoped would see him after he emptied Carter's safe deposit box. The third was to Dr. Terrell Raines of Camden. It was short notice, but Boggs knew his mentor and business partner would be glad to see him.

CHAPTER SIX:
A COMPANY MAN

PROFESSOR GRAYDON LYLE LIVED IN A cottage in Wales Garden, a short walk up the hill from Columbia's Five Points section, and an easy bike ride from his office at the University of South Carolina. Five Points was not only convenient for the International Studies professor, it was a welcomed relief from the stodginess of the state capital and the sameness of its suburbs. It was sprinkled with restaurants, bars and shops where young and old coexisted peacefully for the most part. Halter-topped coeds sipped beer under the hormonal gaze of boys longing to be Carolina men. At the same time, the girls collected drive-by stares from older guys who wished they were in school again. There were the ring-nosed, black-clad freaks and the buttoned-down, Greek-lettered khaki kids, and, of course, those who were not sure what they wanted to be. Genteel older ladies smiled politely, shuffling between shops along Harden Street and Saluda Avenue. Bikers, joggers, and a smattering of rednecks rounded out this human collection that flowed freely through their eclectic neighborhood.

"It ain't Greenwich Village," the professor liked to say in exaggerated fashion, acknowledging Five Point's limitations, "but it doesn't have to be, and thank God for that!"

In the old days, Lyle's cottage had been the garage and servant quarters for a stately, two-story stucco. He became the first and only paying tenant after its 1985 renovation. Though unintended, Lyle endeared himself to the widow who owned the property. On late spring afternoons, when the too sweet scent of cream-colored gardenias filled the yard, they would sit in the old green glider on her wide front porch. He would read her poetry, and she would tell him stories of her past. He was a pleasant diversion for her loneliness, and she was his living history lesson.

The widow died in 1995, and to Lyle's great surprise, she left him the cottage. As her lawyer predicted, the woman's son flew into a rage over the bequest. When he calmed down, he directed the attorney to offer Lyle $100,000 to vacate the premises, but he refused. He had long ago labeled the son "an arrogant prick who rarely visited his mama. He got his just desserts."

Now, on this beautiful spring day, Boggs stood on the steps of the ivy-clad cottage. The front door was open, the screen unlatched. The stereo purred softly with late-sixties stuff—something smooth, rich and melancholy by *The Ice Man,* Jerry Butler. It was from a vast collection of records, tapes and CDs. Lyle once proclaimed: "Choosing between women and music would be the most difficult choice of my life—really."

"Anybody home?" Boggs leaned against the screen door, cupping his hands around his face to block the glare from the sun. A shadowy shape emerged from the dark hallway. When his eyes adjusted to the light, Boggs recognized the lanky figure with a towel wrapped around his waist and another draped over his head.

"Come on in, BB." The raspy voice called Boggs by his college nickname. "Been in the shower. You're early."

"Sorry, Graydon," Boggs said as he stepped inside. "Hope I didn't interrupt anything."

"No, no." He flashed a quick smile. "But thirty minutes ago it would 've been coitus interruptus."

"Who's out there, Graydon?" A soft, sweet voice drifted out from the back of the cottage.

"My ex-wife! Run for your life! She's got a gun!" Lyle choked, smothering laughter in the towel he had been wearing like a hood.

"Graydon! *Please.*" It was the sweet voice again. There was a pause. "Isn't your ex-wife dead?"

"One of them is… I think." He was still snickering.

Boggs grinned and shook hands with his old fraternity brother—his best friend in college. Decades later, this friend-turned-professor was still the class clown, and anything less would have been a disappointment.

Lyle just stood there, dripping water on an antique Persian rug. His long arms were spread wide and his hands open like the Lord Jesus himself. Pungent, just-applied cologne filled the room, and a huge smile was plastered across his face. It was the same disarming one that had conquered young girls, grown women and God knows who else.

"How old's this one, Graydon? Twenty-one? Twenty-five?"

"*Easy*, brother. She's a practicing attorney. Old enough to be—well— my younger sister's daughter."

They both laughed.

"She's got a plane to catch. She'll be gone in a little bit. Get two Buds from the fridge. I'll join you shortly out on the side porch."

Lyle was about to dispatch his lady friend, but not before Boggs got a good look. He took cover behind a giant philodendron on the screened-in porch, hiding like a proud peeping tom with great anticipation and absolutely no remorse. Boggs had to know; did his old friend still have the gift?

The spring hinge on the front screen door creaked as she pushed it open.

Boggs parted the plant's big green leaves as she skipped down the front steps. She was tall with corn silk hair that fell straight over the shoulders of a tangerine-colored suit. He stared as she glided across the thick centipede lawn with the gait of a thoroughbred and looks to match. Not one of Graydon's grad school babies, Boggs thought. Not this time. This one was full-grown.

"Call me when you get to Atlanta," Lyle whimpered, trailing her down the walkway like a sad puppy whose mistress was leaving him behind. He was anything but debonair in rumpled madras shorts, free tee shirt from his favorite music store and flip-flops.

"I'll call, Graydon. I promise." She blushed as she smiled. "You were good today, real good. Now you behave while I'm gone."

Boggs, the voyeur behind the houseplant, hung on each sweet word. His eyes followed every fluid twist and turn as she slipped into the white Jaguar convertible. He watched as she let Lyle lean in and kiss her on the cheek so as not to muss her makeup.

"Great legs." Boggs sighed. "Great everything."

"Bye, bye." Lyle waved as she backed the car down the driveway.

"Damn!" Boggs said, watching the shiny convertible zip down the tree-lined street and disappear into the afternoon. "The boy's still got it."

The Professor sucked in his sixty-five-year-old gut, strolled around to the side porch like a conquering king and opened the screen door. "Yeah, yeah," Lyle said before his old friend could say a word. "She really is something. Now, where's that beer?"

Boggs grinned, bowed respectfully, and handed his friend the brown longneck bottle.

The Professor toasted his visitor, took a big swallow and let out a slow, satisfying breath. "Okay. You never call unless you got a problem. So, what's up?"

"Got a new wrinkle on an old story. Some of my guys got killed for nothing, and somebody needs to pay for this." Boggs knew instantly those were Carter's words, not his, and he softened the statement. "I'm not sure what I really mean. I just need your help analyzing a difficult situation."

"Shit, son! I'm no shrink, and you know I ain't a priest." Lyle had a tendency to over-dramatize things, but he was intrigued by what Boggs had said. "Must be one hell of a story here, and I'm dying to hear it."

"One of my patrols in Vietnam was almost wiped out. You've heard the story, but there's new information." He told Lyle about the letter, showed him what he found at the bank and explained Carter's fixation on Cain and Ha.

Lyle sat in a big wooden rocker sipping beer and listening to his friend talk for fifteen minutes straight. Then the Professor stood up, stretched and paced silently along the side porch. "Well," Lyle said, pursing his lips and clasping his hands behind his back. "This Cain could be a real bad guy. Actually, I'm aware of M&H International—high tech import-export.

Military specialists. They cater to the third world along with drug cartels and such. Might even deserve killing or at least having the hell scared out of them. But now? For some Vietnam thing four decades ago? You're not caught up in some kind of post-traumatic bullshit, are you?"

"Not until last night."

Lyle walked to the screen door. He looked up and down his quiet, shady street, tapped his fingers against the doorsill then turned to face his friend. "You might be able to terminate those two." Lyle lowered his voice, and was blunt. "But you'll need some professionals—foreigners, preferably. You're no kid—not even middle-aged, for God's sake. And you'd be risking everything. Besides, you're not a murderer—at least not any more. I'd think long and hard before taking up Carter's sword.

"Of course, *I've* never been a part of anything like this." The professor chuckled and took another swallow of beer. "But there was the time we stole the mid-term exam. No fatalities, of course." Lyle sank back into the rocking chair, flashed a devilish grin and rubbed his thick, salt and pepper mustache. "The crowning moment in my clandestine career!"

"I'd almost forgotten about that," Boggs said. "I saw Guerry and Jeffries at a political rally in Camden—maybe five years ago. They were nice enough, but that exam heist sure as hell didn't come up. Guerry's a doctor and a state senator. Jeffries is a family court judge, if you can believe it. The other burglar was Jinks somebody—can't remember his last name."

"Hartley," Lyle said. "Jinks Hartley. Saw him here in Five Points a couple of years back. Had a cute young wife with him. A couple of half-grown kids, too. Shit, he recognized me right off. It was like old home week. We talked a while. Then he pulled me aside while his family walked on ahead. Thanked me for including him on the exam caper. That 'B' got him the grades to beat the draft. Said he'd kept our secret all those years."

"Imagine that." Boggs's tone was sarcastic. "It's not something you'd want on a resume. That professor knew something was wrong when he graded the papers. No way we could all make B's. He slipped around the room like the Gestapo, cutting his eyes, waiting for somebody to break. He never came right out and accused us, but I could feel the heat."

"Goddamn!" Lyle's dark eyes sparkled. "It was exciting!"

"Yes, it was," Boggs replied. "Not to mention breaking and entering."

"Strictly speaking, it was a crime." Lyle rubbed his chin. "But I've come to regard it as a form of student protest—civil disobedience, so to speak. The bastard never quizzed us on the course material. It was always weird questions he'd pull out of his ass. No way to get a decent grade straight up. Seemed he hated Americans, and really, really hated the South."

"He did have a problem with fraternity boys." Boggs sighed. "He was fresh from Eastern Europe. First Hitler, then the Russians, for God's sake. Then he sees Fraternity Row discriminating against Blacks and Jews. No wonder he didn't like us." Boggs paused. "You know, I still wonder why they let me in. No blue blood in these veins. Just genes from cotton mill lintheads and sharecroppers. Those great-great grandsons of the aristocracy couldn't care less about us. We were *all* cotton pickers to them. Some of us were white, that's all."

"Jesus, son." There was sadness in the professor's voice. "Surely we've made some progress since then?"

"I suppose."

"Different times, BB," Lyle said. "A lot's changed."

"Anyway." Lyle was anxious to get back to his story. "The exam heist was my most exciting night in college." He paused, raising his eyebrows. "Second place goes to those two sorority girls I hooked up with after The Supremes concert in '65, but that's another story. But I remember the heist like it was yesterday." He leaned forward in the rocker, lowering his voice to a dramatic whisper. "Guerry and me—inside the old War Memorial on Sumter Street copying the exam. You—standing watch in the bushes outside. Hartley—across the street at the drugstore watching Sumter Street. Jeffries—covering the Pendleton Street side from the Gulf station.

"I swear to God, man. I wish I'd been a fly on the wall when that old Romanian graded the exams."

"He was a Czech, actually."

"Whatever." Lyle was annoyed by the interruption. "It was third degree time. The old professor knew somebody shoved one right up his ass. He just couldn't unravel it. Thank God nobody wrote a perfect exam. Nobody cracked. Good spy stuff, BB. Get goose bumps thinking about it."

"Foolish," Boggs said. "But I have to admit I'm glad we got away with it."

"Yeah, but it was just a reprieve for me," Lyle said. "I was still short a few semester hours. I'll never forget standing in front of the dean. "Man, I was begging for anything—an independent study or something! He just said, 'You're going to be cannon fodder, son.' Didn't even look up from the crap on his desk. Took a call from the Senior Senator to get me back in. Then I go out to Fort Jackson and flunk the damn physical. Asthma. They said I was 4-F. Anyway, they didn't have to tell me but once. I was out of there. I stayed home playing professional student when you guys went to war. Guess I'm still doing it."

"And doing it quite well," Boggs said, being careful not to rush his old friend down memory lane. But Lyle had reached a stopping point and sat quietly sipping yet another beer. Beneath the surface was a brilliant mind that understood international affairs and covert operations. He was now a full professor in the very department he helped burglarize those many years ago, and he was connected. "What's your gut feeling on this Carter stuff?"

"Number one." Lyle put down the beer bottle and sat up in the rocker with his feet flat on the floor. "Can't snag these boys through normal channels. They're slippery, and they're hooked up politically. The Justice Department is out, and the Army's out, too—way out. They've had a time with My Lai and that kind of bullshit. And just when they think that crap has stopped, here comes Iraq and Afghanistan. Your little incident is ancient history, if you haven't noticed." He looked Boggs straight in the eyes. "But if you get caught sniffing around these billionaires, one morning you might wake up dead. Hell, we'd all be at risk. A car wreck—sudden, fatal illness. A random, drive-by shooting? These boys could arrange it." He sank back into the chair, gently rocking and looking out toward the street.

"That said, you'd have to catch 'em flat-footed, somewhere they'd least suspect it." The professor leaned forward in his chair and lowered his voice. "The U.S. is the place—right here at home—their guard would be down. But man, oh, man, you're talking big-time risky."

"Cain's got a place at Hilton Head." Boggs pulled a plat and floor plan from Carter's collection of papers. "Supposed to be there every October."

"Let's see." Lyle pulled a pair of battered reading glasses from his tee shirt pocket. "Quite a place. *Jesus*, more like a compound. Several acres. Damned secluded." He bit his lip nervously and tapped his finger on the plat. "Ease out of the backwater somewhere. Cross Calibogue Sound to that island creek. Slip across the golf course. Bingo! You're there. You'd be coming in from the rear. Light, or no security at all—totally unprotected, I'll bet." Lyle pushed his glasses up into his salt and pepper hair, rubbed his eyes then looked up at his old friend. It was a dead serious look. "I'd want to see up-to-date maps—see the place first-hand, too. But… this could be a cool place for an amphibious assault."

"Hold on, Graydon." Boggs held up his hand like a policeman stopping traffic. "You've got the cart before the horse. Just give me an accurate read on Carter's stuff. With your CIA background and God knows what else, you can sort it out."

"CIA? I'm not now, nor have I ever been, with the CIA."

"Oh? That wasn't you standing on top of the American Embassy in Saigon? That wasn't you shuffling people up to the choppers when the whole thing came unglued? Come on, Graydon. I've seen that film ten times. That's *you*."

"Listen, son, It was me. I was there, but not for The Company. The old senator who got me back in school needed some eyes on the ground over there. One of his guys had read a couple of papers I wrote on the war, and they asked me to go—said I owed the old man a favor. I just got caught over there on a gig for the senator. That's all. At that point, I was like everybody else, just trying to get my ass out in one piece."

"You won't 'fess up, even to me?"

"That's all I can say, Barry. Anyway, even if there had been something there, I'd never tell you. Have I said anything about the exam heist? *No*."

"Okay, Okay." Boggs smiled. "You kept our secret."

"You know, BB, a raid down there at the beach could work." Lyle got off the CIA and back to the business at hand. "Lots of backwater—easy access to the Intracoastal Waterway. Then there's that big old Atlantic out there. Hell, the drug boys—a few of our classmates, I might add—got rich sneaking weed through the marsh back in the day. You could slip a squad-size team in there and do the deed. They'd be out before anybody knew what happened."

"How do you know about all that stuff?" Boggs baited his old friend.

"I'm a fairly well-read son of a bitch. Just leave it at that." He flashed his famous smile and leaned back in the rocking chair. "Anyway, leave Carter's things with me. We'll talk again in a few of weeks."

"We both agree this could be tricky." The concern showed on Boggs's face. "You be careful."

"Shit, son. Your secret's safe with me. It might be time for a little excitement in my life, and this could be it." Lyle cleared his throat, shifting to a business tone of voice. "Am I correct in assuming we're working on a paid consulting basis?"

"I'm crushed, Graydon." Boggs struggled to keep a straight face. "You sound like a mercenary. What about our friendship?"

"It has its limits." Lyle was dead serious.

Boggs pulled a letter-size envelope from his coat pocket. "I understand perfectly. There's five grand in there. Analyze Carter's claims. If they're legitimate, we can talk about some kind of action."

Lyle took the envelope, peeked inside and gently thumbed the fifty crisp hundreds. "This is way past serious, ain't it boy?"

"Let's just say I'm very curious."

"Okay," Lyle said, "but we may need to talk, and… I may need more cash."

Boggs printed a number on the back of his business card. "Call this number and leave a message—say, 'It's Dr. Brown's office. Your tests are back.' I'll call you."

"I say, old chap, seems a tad early for the James Bond stuff." Lyle faked his best British accent.

"You said Cain could put us in the cemetery. Why take chances?"

Lyle shrugged. "Okay, okay."

Boggs called the general aviation airport where he had landed after the flight from Charleston. He told them to have his plane ready and arrange for the rental car to be picked up. He and Lyle said their good-byes. His next hop would be a short one—forty miles away in Camden. He would visit his mentor—the man who helped a troubled boy change his ways and chart a better course toward manhood.

CHAPTER SEVEN:
MAYWOOD

OCTOR TERRELL RAINES TURNED UP THE collar on his old hunting coat as the pinks and blues of an April sky faded into twilight. He had just sipped the last drop of bourbon from a plastic cup—a little insurance against the cool breeze slipping into Maywood with the darkness. He shifted on the oak bench outside the butcher house where the deer hunters always gathered and gazed down the long lane dividing four hundred acres of freshly plowed bottomland. The smell of rich, turned earth hung in the quiet country air. The old physician sighed as he scanned the hardwood tree line, hiding a swamp near the Wateree River. He owned everything he could see from his seat on the bench and much, much more. Maywood Plantation covered 4,500 acres of the best farmland and wildlife habitat anywhere in the Southeast, but his thoughts were on Boggs—coming on short notice and without a clue. "Should be here by now," he mumbled. "Something's got him out of sorts."

Now in his eighties, Raines coaxed his aging eyes to read the face of the old railroad watch his father had given him. It was 6:35 p.m. when he heard the rumbling Ford V-8 then looked up as the headlights broke clear of the shadowy tree line and stopped. Doctor Raines lifted the wool cap from his head, brushed back a shock of snow-white hair. The doctor knew Boggs would stop there, get out of the truck and walk just a few yards to the tiny family cemetery. His mother and father were buried there. Later there would be laughter, a little drinking and some talk about business. When things settled down, he would try to find out what brought Boggs home.

Freddie Jones, a short, muscular black man with graying hair, was behind the wheel of the Ford F-250. Born in a sharecropper's house at Maywood, he and Boggs grew up running wild through the woods and waters of the plantation. Like his father and grandfather before him, Jones had never lived anywhere else. After a brief stop at the cemetery, Jones steered the truck past the five-bedroom house everyone called "the cottage", turned sharply to the left and coasted down to the butcher house. By the time the truck stopped, the old man had filled his cup and was pouring bourbon for Boggs and Freddie.

"How are you, Doc?" Boggs smiled broadly as he slid out of the pickup and extended his hand. "And Miss Claire?"

"I'm fine. Claire's in Camden. Business over there tomorrow. She sends her love." The doctor shook Boggs's hand, smiled and pulled him close for a hug. "Good to see you, son. How was the flight?"

"Short. Columbia to Camden's barely a check out ride." He turned to his boyhood friend and slapped him on the back. "Smoother than Freddie's driving."

Although the night was cool, the three men sat on the bench talking about old times, warmed by the bourbon and years of friendship. As usual, the doctor would not let the conversation end without recalling a deer hunting incident decades earlier.

"It was about two hundred yards—straight over there." Raines pointed toward the tree line across the plowed field.

"I'll never live that down." Boggs shook his head in dismay.

"Tell it, Doc! I love them stories!" Freddie was in the mood. He had killed a few beers waiting for Boggs at the Camden Airport, and now the bourbon was taking hold.

"I was a younger man," Raines began. "Barry was a tough and troubled thirteen-year-old. His daddy had just died." The doctor went on to tell the story of Randall Boggs, Maywood's farm manager who had been killed in a freak accident near the duck pond. The elder Boggs carried a shotgun across his lap as he drove an old tractor along the shoreline. When the trailing bush hog hit a stump, it tilted the tractor; the shotgun slid from his lap, banged against the wheel well and fired. Boggs was struck in the thigh at point blank range.

"When you found your daddy slumped over the steering wheel, that's when your boyhood ended, but that deer hunt was important, too," the doctor said. "That showed me you had character—reckless as hell, but character."

"Yes sir," Freddie said. "I thought we were headed for the electric chair."

Barry and Freddie were running the hounds that day. They hollered and rang cowbells, warning the hunters as they trailed the dogs through the trees. The boys were following the hunt master's orders, which kept them a safe distance from any shooting. One hunter—a real estate man from Columbia—had left his stand, wandering to the edge of the tree line. A deer bounded into the cotton field with yelping hounds close behind. The deer saw the hunter and cut back into the trees, running straight for the dogs and the two boys. The hunter fired blindly into the trees. Rusty, a champion hound, caught a single buckshot pellet in the head, and was dead before he hit the ground.

"Rusty was your favorite, wasn't he, Freddie?"

"Yes sir, Dr. Terrell. I still miss him. When the weather cools off and we get ready to hunt, that's when I 'specially miss him."

Another pellet struck a pine tree and sent bark flying. A quarter-sized piece hit Freddie just above his left eyebrow and he was bleeding.

"Hold your fire!" Barry waved his hand in the hunter's direction and knelt down for a closer look at Freddie's face. "Hold your fire!"

The little boy cried as he rocked Rusty's lifeless body in his arms while Barry cut a piece of cotton flannel from his shirttail to dab his forehead.

"Y'all boys seen my deer?" The hunter slurred his words as he stumbled through the brush toward the youngsters. He stood silent for a moment, then looked down at Freddie and the lifeless hound. "Sorry. Y'all were in the wrong place. Now hop up from there. We gotta find my deer."

"You didn't kill no deer, mister," Barry said. "Just our best dog. Damn near killed us. Who the hell let you on this hunt?"

"Watch your mouth, boy," the hunter snapped. He was big—over six feet—and ready to teach a thirteen-year-old a painful lesson. "You don't know who you're talking to."

"Yes, I do." Barry was shaking. It was anger, not fear. "I'm talkin' to a stupid son of a bitch. You got no business out here with a gun."

This big man, with his fancy new hunting clothes, also had a silver liquor flask. He had been sipping steadily since the hunt master left him at the deer stand. He was half-loaded when he fired the Browning over and under. Now this angry drunk was closing in on the boy with the big mouth.

In an instinctive, fluid motion, Barry pulled back the slide on his battered old Mossberg pump, snapped it forward, chambering a shell. He brought it up to his shoulder and aimed at the man's chest.

The hunter stopped dead in his tracks. "Hold on, son," The big man's red face started to sweat. "It'd be awful if we shot each other out here today."

"Yes sir, it would." Barry had stopped shaking. His voice was calm. "But it ain't gonna happen. You fired that over and under twice and didn't reload. If anybody gets shot, mister, it'll be you."

It was Barry and the big salesman standing there in the trees. The boy's narrow, focused eyes assured the man he faced the biggest selling job of his life. And he started selling—hard. "Now I am sorry about the dog—the colored boy, too." There was newfound contrition in the hunter's voice. "I'll buy y'all another dog. Hell, I'll buy a pack of dogs. I'll just put my gun down, sit right here and have another drink. Okay?"

"Barry." Freddie's eyes were as big as saucers. "I'm gonna get Dr. Terrell."

"You okay, Freddie?"

"Yeah. I'm okay." There was a trickle of blood from his forehead, but Rusty's blood covered his plaid flannel shirt and faded jeans. "Just don't shoot. Please don't."

Freddie scampered across the field, but it was a short run. Dr. Raines was riding Jack, his sorrel quarter horse, through the cotton toward the standoff in the tree line. He pulled back on the reins as he met Freddie.

"Is that your blood?"

"Mostly Rusty's, Dr. Terrell. This is mine," Freddie said, touching the lump on his forehead with his right hand.

"What happened?"

"Barry's … gonna shoot … that man!" The little black boy with the swollen face was excited and out of breath. "He killed Rusty!"

"Good God. Jump up here." Raines reached down for Freddie's arm and swung the boy up behind him. "Hold on." He snapped the stirrups against the horse's flanks, and old Jack trotted toward the tree line. He could see Barry with his shotgun pointed at the unsteady Raymond Jackson who had taken several swigs of whiskey since the incident began. He was taking another as Raines rode up.

"Put the gun down, Barry," The doctor spoke in a soft, kind voice. "Nobody needs to get hurt."

Barry did not move, but he cut his eyes toward the doctor to let him know he was listening.

"Come on, son," the doctor said. "What would your daddy say?"

"Boy, do what Dr. Raines says." Jackson's slurring was worse. "Your daddy—"

"Quiet, Mr. Jackson." The doctor could smell the sour mash floating on the afternoon breeze. "You broke club rules—leaving your stand and drinking in the field. Fortunately, this boy, not his deceased daddy, has you in this position. His father would have thrashed you soundly."

Barry hung on Raines's every word. His father had respected this man—the authority figure in their lives. He missed his daddy and felt abandoned now. He knew he would go to the reform school for this.

"Barry?"

"Yes, sir."

"Put the shotgun down. You don't want to shoot Mr. Jackson, do you?"

"No, sir, but he shouldn't be here. He could have killed somebody. Killed Rusty as it is."

"I know," Dr. Raines said. "We'll sure miss him, but we've got to end this before something terrible happens."

The boy sighed, clicked on the safety and slowly lowered the shotgun.

"Good choice, boy," Jackson slurred. Like too many salesmen, the deal was closed, and he was still running his mouth. With his judgment and salesmanship impaired, Jackson was about to undo the doctor's effort to save his life.

"Mr. Jackson, I won't ask you again to be quiet." Raines's voice was stern. He was clearly disgusted with his guest. "Put the flask away. Hand me your shotgun and start walking toward the butcher house. And Mr. Jackson, this little unpleasantness never happened, if you know what I mean."

"Never happened?" The hunter's eyes widened and his jaw dropped. "I want— I demand—this boy be punished, sir." The booze had Jackson by the throat. His tone was angry. "It won't end here. I'm calling the sheriff!"

"I don't think so, Mr. Jackson."

"You don't?" Jackson wrinkled his forehead and frowned.

"I do not." The doctor's voice was calm, his tone polite. "When you sober up, you'll want to speak to Mr. Robert Davis, president of D & R Real Estate. He'll tell you I'm the majority stockholder in that fine firm."

Jackson may have been under the influence of alcohol, but his head was clearing fast with this revelation. He had been courting D & R Real Estate with a proposal vital to his company's growth. Jackson knew he was on dangerous ground. He would have to swallow his pride to save the deal. The old man held all the cards.

"Mr. Jackson?" Raines was pleasant, but impatient. "Do we have an understanding?"

"Yes sir, I think we do."

"We're beyond the thinking stage, Mr. Jackson. I want your word. This matter stays in this cotton field. Am I clear?"

Jackson, still reeling from the whiskey, looked at the old man and then at Barry. The boy held his breath.

Then Jackson nodded his head. "You have my word, sir. It stays here, in the field."

"Barry?" Raines turned his attention to the thirteen-year-old with the shotgun. "You share the blame for this, too. You'll leave this matter in the field as well. Pointing a shotgun at Mr. Jackson is serious business. We'll talk about punishment later."

"Yes sir." Barry knew he had dodged the biggest bullet of his young life. The doctor had saved his backside—for now.

"Thank you, Dr. Raines," Jackson said, turning toward the butcher house. "I appreciate the way you handled this."

"Mr. Jackson? There's one other thing," the doctor said. "You'll need to speak to Dr. Ingram, our veterinarian over in Camden. He knows the breeders whose bloodlines are acceptable at Maywood. Rusty will be hard to replace, but I'm sure a suitable puppy can be found."

"Uh … yes sir." Jackson felt the tug on his wallet. He was in for a financial spanking because of his poor judgment. Raines had nothing but champion hunting dogs. "I'm sure we'll find the right puppy." Then he continued his long walk across the cotton field. If he had had a tail, it would have been tucked between his rubbery legs.

Barry fought back a smile as Jackson stumbled away, but he knew the doctor was not finished with him either.

Raines never let Barry forget the cotton field incident. It became the spark for a new relationship between the two of them. The doctor had cared deeply for Barry's father, and from that day forward, he transferred those feelings to the younger Boggs. They spent time together in the fields, on the ponds and in Dr. Raines's study. They talked about everything— school, Raines's World War II service, his decision to study medicine and life in general. It began as the doctor's attempt to salvage a troubled youngster then Barry became the son the old man never had. He listened and caught on fast. His manners improved, and he began to read at the urging of his mentor. The boy's success became the old man's passion, culminating in graduation from Camden High School with honors. Dr. Raines had hoped he would select Washington and Lee University in Virginia—the doctor's alma mater. But it came as no surprise when Barry picked The University of South Carolina at Columbia. The boy wanted to stay close to home, and Carolina was barely an hour away.

—⚊⚊—

Darkness had overtaken Maywood by the time the trio finished their drinks and reminiscences. The doctor invited Boggs and Freddie into the cottage for a dinner that Lessie Mae Smalls had "just thrown together on the short notice you gentlemen kindly gave me." Having cooked for the Raines family for half a century, her culinary skills were a legend in the Rembert community, but she never, ever threw a meal together. It was a country feast of roast pork, wild rice; string beans with her own green tomato relish, homemade bread and sweet iced tea. Then Lessie Mae brought out the five-layer chocolate cake.

"Miss Lessie," Boggs smiled. "You're the best."

"You just patronizing me, Mr. Barry," she said sternly. "You been all over the world, and you know this ain't nothin' special."

Boggs smiled broadly. "I'd rather eat here than any place on earth."

Freddie excused himself. There was a big job near the river the next morning. He would need an early start. Boggs and the doctor walked from the dining room to a gentleman's den. Eighteenth century leather chairs rested on oriental rugs. Trophies from African safaris hung on all four walls. Boggs knew the story of each one. The most prominent was the head of a Cape buffalo hanging above the stone fireplace. The trophy evoked vivid memories for Boggs. He had been at Raines's side when he dropped the monster decades ago.

The doctor poured brandies then opened a mahogany humidor, inhaling the aromatic tobaccos of real Cuban cigars. An old friend kept it filled for him.

"Can't smoke the damned things anymore." He sighed, easing back in a tufted leather wingback. For a few silent moments, he studied Boggs as he watched the flames waltz through the oak in the fireplace.

"You've been quiet." Dr. Raines broke the silence. "That funeral troubling you?"

The protégé could not deny what the mentor saw in his eyes. "It was sad. Troubling, too. Buddy Carter still had a lot of life to live. Cancer. Had a wife and two beautiful daughters. He left me a letter about the war, and that's the troubling part. Felt guilty for not telling me what happened to one of my patrols. The letter kind of stirred things up again."

"You want to talk about it?"

"Not really, Doc." Boggs forced a smile and sipped the brandy.

"You learn to live with it—not forget it—but live with it." Disobeying his physician's orders, Dr. Raines dragged a wooden match across the cracked tile hearth then breathed life into one of his Cuban illegals. "It's been like that for me, too. How many years since D-Day? We took a direct hit going into Omaha Beach. The whole platoon killed—except Warren Corriher and me. We talked every June 6th after the war until he died in '93."

"It'll pass." Boggs had no intention of going deeper into the story and switched the conversation to business. "I'm sure you're keeping up with our interests here and abroad?"

"I am, indeed." The doctor puffed on his cigar. "You've done an excellent job this year."

"I can't take all the credit," Boggs said. "You set everything up right to begin with. You've made me a wealthy man." Then he smiled. "If I haven't thanked you lately, please accept my heartfelt thanks."

"You say that every time I see you." Raines paused for another puff. "And you don't need to keep working so hard. We could bring in a sharp young person—you know, to learn the business."

"Not yet," Boggs snapped. "I love what I'm doing."

"Then keep doing it, for God's sake." The doctor smiled and took a sip of brandy. Thus ended an impromptu meeting of the Maywood Corporation executive committee. Both officers said and heard what they wanted. Maywood, with its assets in the millions, was in good hands and purring along.

While the rest of Maywood slept through the night, Boggs was restless. Finally, with a wool blanket wrapped around his shoulders, he walked through the predawn silence to the butcher house and sat on the old oak bench. It was good to be back, if just for one night, and he smiled as he watched a shooting star streak across the dark sky. Like the boy who had roamed the fields of Maywood years ago, he made a wish, but Carter's revelation would not fade away.

CHAPTER EIGHT:
THE REV. MACDONALD

Boggs rarely went to Blowing Rock on weekends. He left it for the tourists. He, better than anyone, understood their flight from the lowlands to the beauty, peace and climate of the mountains. So, he willingly gave them a couple of days. It was more than a fair trade, he thought, but this Saturday morning in late April was different. The Rev. Roger MacDonald had invited him to town for coffee and conversation. Boggs had few close friends, but this rugged Scotsman was probably his best. It was a welcomed break for Boggs who was trying to manage Maywood's business interests while worrying about Professor Lyle's research. It was early, and the traffic was light when he turned off Hwy. 221 on to Main Street. He was happy to find a parking space in front of their favorite café. The clergyman was sitting on the patio, nursing a steaming cup of coffee in the cool morning air. He stood as Boggs walked up.

"Keep your seat, Padre," Boggs said, leaning down to shake hands with the Rev. MacDonald.

"Barry, my lad." Rev. MacDonald spoke with a rich Scottish accent. "You've been missed up here. Got your fill of the flat lands, did you?"

"It's not so bad, Padre." Boggs forced smile. "Anyway, it was hardly a pleasure trip—funeral for a Vietnam vet. Got to see guys I haven't seen since the war. What's new here?"

"The usual." The minister sighed. "Some of the early birds will be arriving soon. There's the quibbling to look forward to—how to run the church for the season. Some things never change."

"By the way." The Padre cocked his head to one side and grinned. "Ann Johnson phoned. She'll be up from Florida soon. She always asks about you, laddie."

"Come on, Padre," Boggs said, "That blind date was a favor to you—she's not my type."

"Not your type, lad?" the minister asked. "What is your type? She's rich, beautiful—blond, lovely figure—everything a virile man could desire."

"Too many virile men already. Three trips to the altar, I believe. Not to mention her twin boys—teenage hellions. I'm way past raising kids. No, Padre, I'm out."

"Now laddie, you've hurt my feelings. The minister struggled to keep a straight face. "I'd envisioned you and that lass with—let's say a little something going on by the Fourth of July."

"I'm sure you mean well. And she's gorgeous—I'll give you that—but no more match-making," Boggs said. Then he smiled. "You're not that old, Padre. Give her a call. Spice up you life. Surely, there's a little something left from your days with The Regiment."

"No, laddie, not me. Way too young for me and certainly not with a parishioner." Then the minister spoke in a softer tone. "Wouldn't feel right with any woman—not yet. Probably never. I don't think I could find someone to take the place of my dear, dear Evelyn."

"How long's it been, Padre?"

"Four years next September 23rd." The Scotsman paused, gazing down Main Street where couples and families were moving about, enjoying the clear, cool morning. "Worst day of my life. We were planning a trip to Scotland. She needed something from a store over in Boone. Shouldn't have let her go. Should've gone myself. It's me that truck should've hit."

"Padre." Boggs patted his friend on the arm. "She must have been a wonderful lady, but you've got a lot of life ahead of you. Besides, I don't want to go hauling you and that damned old MG out of a ditch again."

"Aye, Barry, I was a damned mess back then," the minister said. His eyes sparkled and a sheepish grin slipped from behind a silver-gray beard. He looked around to see if his four-letter utterance had offended anyone within earshot. "Excuse the language, my boy, but it's a perfect description of me at that particular time. Without your help, I'd be defrocked or dead down the side of a mountain."

"Lucky it was me and not a deputy who found you," Boggs said, recalling the first time he me Rev. MacDonald. "You'd have wound up in the pokey."

"Pokey, indeed." The minister chuckled.

Boggs remembered their first meeting as if it were yesterday. The good reverend was drinking heavily in the days and months after his wife's death. Boggs was returning from Blowing Rock one afternoon when he spotted Rev. MacDonald perched on the crumpled right front fender of an oft wounded, red MGB-GT. It was hopelessly wedged in a ditch. His white clerical collar was unbuttoned and flapping in the breeze. His red face rivaled the label on the fifth of Johnny Walker dangling from his right hand. He had just finished a stirring rendition of the first verse of *Onward Christian Soldiers*, and was breaking into the chorus. He had perfect pitch.

"Sir?" Boggs said. "Are you okay?"

"In a manner of speaking, laddie." The minister's speech was slurred. "Are you the Good Samaritan? Perhaps... you are a...member of The Regiment who'd not leave a mate behind."

"Actually, I'm a back-sliding Sagitarian. I live just down the road," Boggs tried not to laugh.

"I-I'm not familiar with that denomination."

"What happened here, Padre?"

"A slight, unfortunate mishap," the minister said. "Had a feeling that curve would get me sooner or later. Appears it was sooner. Had hoped to reach the home of Mr. Melvin Green."

"You're friends with Mr. Green?"

"In-indeed," the reverend said. "More than friends. I am his minister. Don't look the part, not in this pitiful circumstance, but it's the sad truth. I am the Rev. Roger MacDonald, associate minister at Scot's Creek Presbyterian Church near Grandfather Mountain. And please, laddie, accept my deepest apology. I am a bit lacking… in-in the reverential department… at this particular time."

"Well, Padre." Boggs shook his head as he glanced at the MG wedged in the ditch. "I'll give you a ride to my place. It's just up the road. We'll call a wrecker. Excuse my manners, Padre, I'm Boggs—Barry Boggs."

"Bless you, lad," the minister said. "You'll be sparing Mr. Green the discomfort of seeing me pissed—second time in a month, I believe. I'm indebted to you."

"Think nothing of it," Boggs said. "By the way, that regiment you mentioned. Was it the British Special Air Service?"

"It was a long time ago, before I heeded Christ's call. Long before I met my beloved and recently departed Evelyn. Northern Ireland, the Middle East. There was honor, a lot of sadness, and death. It was another life, another time, laddie. In some ways, best forgotten."

From that chance meeting on a mountain road, Boggs and the Rev. MacDonald began an acquaintance that grew into a close friendship. The minister listened to his friend's war stories and recollections of a painful personal life. Boggs was there when the broken-hearted minister grieved for his beloved Evelyn. The two men provided therapy for each other, and Boggs efforts to help the Rev. MacDonald dry out probably saved his ministry. The Padre would never get over his loss, but at least the drinking had stopped.

Now, on this beautiful April morning, Boggs was prepared to retell his worst war story with the new twist. He was not looking for advice; he just felt compelled to share the revelation with his closest friend—a man who could understand it all.

Boggs had been staring at nothing in particular, as if in a daydream, and his friend sensed it. "Well, now, you've been a wee bit quiet. Bad trip down the mountain, was it?"

"Sorry, Padre," Boggs said. "It was sad from the start and got worse. An old Ranger named Carter died of cancer." As he spoke, he reached inside his jacket pocket and produced Carter's letter. "This is the worst of it. Carter left it for me. It raises serious questions—points fingers. I'd like you to read it, but I'll understand if you don't want to."

"It's your call, laddie." The minister sipped his coffee. "The café's filling up. Maybe we'd better move along."

"Let's walk to the park," Boggs said. "I don't want to keep looking over my shoulder." The two men said nothing as they strolled past the shops, and a stand for the horse-drawn carriages. They climbed the steps to the tree-shaded park where Boggs stopped to glance at the stone and bronze monument listing the town's war dead.

"Let's walk out to the back corner. At least I can light my pipe out there." The minister made himself comfortable on the smooth slats of a wooden bench, recently painted in anticipation of the coming summer season.

"No smoke police out here," Boggs said.

"Thank God. I'd be the last to want to harm a soul, but this correctness business has gone a bit too far. So, you want to tell me about it?"

Boggs opened the letter and looked around, making sure they were alone and began to read.

The Rev. MacDonald sat expressionless as he listened, drawing gently on the old carved pipe to keep the tobacco burning.

"Carter left more documents in a safe deposit box in Columbia," Boggs said. "What's your take on this, Padre?"

"Sad, sad story," he replied. "Damned sickening, really. I don't fault the lad for keeping the secret. Little chance commanders would believe his story over that of some officer. Then there was that Vietnamese—corrupt bugger."

"Carter lived with it for a long time," Boggs said. "Then they dedicated 'The Wall' in Washington. When he saw Mrs. Richardson drag Danny's fingers across the names, I guess it set him off. He became a man with a mission—an obsession, really. I truly believe he was going to kill Cain and Ha if he had lived."

The Rev. MacDonald sat quietly with the old pipe clinched between his teeth, watching the children on the merry-go-round and swings. He even kicked an errant soccer ball back to a youngster who had let it get away.

"Not planning to take up that lad's sword, are you?"

"Don't mince words, do you Padre?"

"Come on, Barry. We've both been there—fighting to keep our mates and ourselves alive. We know what it means to lose men—even lose them because of someone's stupidity. But this is different. You lads were sacrificed to save some smuggler's drug deal. Now, I won't talk to you like a schoolboy. God knows we're both way past that. I know it hurts, but don't do anything rash, laddie. He smiled and put his hand on Boggs's shoulder. "My admonitions are blatantly selfish. You're my best friend, and I'd hate to lose you. I'll sure pray for you, if you don't mind."

"I don't mind, Padre," Boggs said. I'll take any help I can get."

"You're sure about Ann. Johnson?" The minister's eyes sparkled as he changed the subject. "You don't want another shot at the lovely Miss Ann? She's a fine looking lass, smart, too. And did I mention that she is loaded?" The Padre struggled to keep a straight face as he stood and stretched. "By the by, did I also mention her twin boys are staying with their dad this year?"

"She's all yours." Boggs smiled for the first time since they sat down. Then he stood, and the two men walked slowly toward the stone steps and Main Street where the tourists were enjoying the day.

"I'm always here for you, Barry," the Padre said. "And, of course, I'd be available for a mission—if you know what I mean."

"Come on, Padre." Boggs chuckled. "Old farts like us?"

"Now, aren't you the one who just said I should have a go at Ann Johnson? If I'm not too old for that, then I'm not too old for a job."

"That's different," Boggs said, "and there's no job. Besides, you put that stuff behind you years ago."

"So I did, laddie. Just remember I'm here, if you need me."

"Thanks," Boggs said.

The minister nodded. "Now, could I talk you into buying an old Scotsman lunch?"

CHAPTER NINE:
UNEXPECTED GUEST

B OGGS TOSSED ASIDE WEDNESDAY'S NEWSPAPER AND pushed the reading glasses back in his graying brown hair. "For God's sake, Graydon. It's the end of May." One-sided conversations had become a weekly ritual since visiting Lyle in Columbia, and once again, there was nothing from the professor. He knew Lyle's work would take time, but he had expected something by now. He leaned against the deck rail outside the kitchen, brooding as he gazed out across his long-range view. Was Carter right? Was Lyle dragging his feet? Equally important, was Boggs prepared to take the next step—risking everything for his long lost Rangers?

This setting was his favorite spot for sorting things out, and while he did not always succeed, there was consolation in the view. The placement of his house was no accident—a panoramic scene with Grandfather Mountain sitting off in the distance. "As close to God as I'll ever get," Boggs whispered, looking across the peaceful hills to the valley below and inhaling the aroma from the coffee he had just poured. The cotton sweater he had pulled on at the last minute felt good as the morning sun began to warm his shoulders. He was enjoying the beauty of the morning when he heard footsteps on the stairs.

"Beautiful place you've got. Too damn many steps, though." It was Lyle, trudging up the stairs toward his wide-eyed friend. "And it's awfully cold for May, for God's sake."

"So much for security." Boggs's tone was sarcastic. "You must've come up dry."

"Quite the contrary, my boy," Lyle said, out of breath when he reached the deck. "Any of that coffee left?"

"Inside. Cups are above the sink." Boggs frowned, shaking his head in disgust. "I didn't expect this—not a personal visit—but get your coffee then tell me what's going on."

"Sorry, Barry." Lyle wore a sheepish grin when he stepped back out on the deck. "Had to do this in person. Man! This is one fine place. Timber frame. Stone. Cedar. Eighteenth century mixed with mountain stuff. Cool, really cool."

"Glad you approve." Boggs was still smarting from the professor's surprise appearance. "I suppose you'll need a place to stay."

"Rented a cabin back toward Blowing Rock. All the comforts of home. Plus, my lawyer-friend's with me. She's at some fancy spa getting all rubbed up. We can cover your options while she's occupied." Then he lowered his voice. "Who's here?"

"Just us," Boggs said. "What options?"

"Mr. Carter's got me excited." Lyle said. "That boy was dead on the money. No pun intended, of course. Cain and Ha are something else. Mostly legal now, but the seed money came the dirty way." Lyle shuddered as a chill rode in on the mountain breeze. He sipped the coffee, then continued his analysis. "Most of their edgy shit's too old to prosecute in a real court—at least what you're concerned with, but I doubt you'll go that route. Now, they're also in deep in the Middle East and North Africa with their computers and probably arms but that's another story."

Absorbed in his old friend's work, Boggs had forgotten about the security breach. "How strong's the evidence?"

"The dead man's testimony's the strongest." Lyle was matter-of-fact. "But Carter's story tracks with everything that happened—times, dates, who was where and when. We were able to corroborate some of the black market stuff Cain and Ha were involved in Vietnam, but nobody will talk publicly about it. No doubt they were asshole buddies in Vietnam, even tighter now with much, much higher stakes.

"Carter got some good information from the Justice Department. Got it on the sly, courtesy of dead Ranger Sciavo's baby brother. He was a young lawyer at Justice when Cain was on a short list for a diplomatic post. They're supposed to check you from stem to stern, and young Sciavo was doing some of the grunt work. When something didn't smell right, Sciavo wanted to dig deeper. That's when somebody put the quietus on the probe. Still, the dustup killed Cain's nomination, but without embarrassing repercussions for M&H."

"Kind of fishy."

"More than that." Lyle set his coffee cup on the deck rail. "Sciavo could've lost his job…or worse. Those boys have hurt some folks, long after they sent y'all into the shit. But the rough stuff is more discreet now. Hell, when you've got their dough, you don't need to run around wackin' people. Just smother 'em with money." He smiled and winked at Boggs. "Don't sell these rascals short. They've got influence all over the place—Congress, foreign governments—you name it. They throw cash in all directions.

"In Vietnam they linked stolen military equipment with the drug trade. It was a black market bonanza," Lyle said. "Sad part is they weren't unique. A lot of that went on—a lot of looking the other way, too. And just like at home, the little guys paid the price."

"Let's hear the options." Boggs spoke without emotion.

"You got three, as I see it." The professor dragged a rocking chair out near the deck rail. "The first one's easy—just forget it. Do nothing. It was a long, long time ago. I'm dead serious, now. Put this Carter stuff behind you. Get hypnotized or something.

"Plan two," Lyle said, holding up two fingers in a wiggling peace sign as he spoke. Then he balled his hand into a fist and slammed it on the deck rail. "Shoot these bastards dead. Avenge your Rangers. Maybe then, you'll get some peace. Then, again, you may just get a trip to the shrink. The electric chair is also a distinct possibility. This ain't like shootin' some jerk sergeant or lieutenant in the back during a firefight. Present company excluded, of course."

There was a long pause as the old friends sat in silence; rocking and watching cotton-ball clouds cast shadows across the ridges and into the valley below.

Boggs broke the silence. "Can't wait to hear plan three."

"Number three—my personal favorite." There was a devilish sparkle in Lyle's eyes. "We'll let those two crooks live to a ripe old age—minus twenty million or so of their ill-gotten gain."

"Extortion?" Boggs furrowed his brow and sank back in the slatted wooden rocker. "I had something a little more painful in mind." He pursed his lips, stood and slung the now cold coffee over the rail into the feathery hemlocks below.

"Your choice, BB." Lyle leaned forward, bringing the rocking chair to a sudden stop. "Ain't much difference in plan two or three—logistically speaking. Risks are about the same, too. At least with plan three, we're not setting out to kill anybody."

"But people could get hurt," Boggs said

"Absolutely." Lyle's response was quick and serious. "We've got huge risks with an operation like this. Once we get rolling, something could go wrong. I don't want it to happen, but somebody could get killed. I'd bet on it, actually." They sat quietly for a few moments before the professor spoke again. "But think about it. How many old vets could you help with that kind of cash? Sad part is it won't bankrupt M&H—not even close." Then he smiled. "But those two would never get over losing that much dough. Never. Not to mention we'll scare the living shit out of them."

"When do we—when do I—have to make a decision?"

"Tomorrow." Lyle's tone was businesslike. "I'll be back in the morning. Oh…with plans two and three, you could be out a couple of hundred grand. You'll get it back if plan three works. You lose it all if we just kill 'em. And, by the way, I'd be the one running the extortion plan, as you've dubbed it. But let's call it what it is—a major league kidnapping."

"You? Lead a kidnapping?"

"Me," Lyle said, "unless you've got somebody better. If it works, you get seventeen point five million for your vets. We'll hide it in a trust nobody will ever find. The cash can't be traced. The rest—the two point five million—is for my associates and me. Plus, I'll repay your initial investment."

Boggs folded his arms across his chest and frowned. "You make it sound like a simple business deal."

"I'm partial to the kidnapping," the professor said, ignoring Boggs comment as he promoted his plan of choice. "And it's got to be next October. Cain and Ha go to the beach for several weeks every fall—haven't missed in years. Of course, we'll need an experienced combat team.

"I may have somebody in mind," Boggs said, "if we go with this kidnap thing."

"I'm sure you do." Lyle's tone was arrogant. "Karl Schiller, possibly?"

Boggs was stunned. He had never mentioned the name in Lyle's presence.

"What do you know about Schiller?"

"I've done my homework. It's all right here." Lyle unfolded a copy of the local newspaper, exposing a brown legal binder. "I kept it tight, but complete—fifty pages. Damn fine work, even if I say so myself." Then he leaned back in the rocking chair. "I know all about the two patrols affected by Cain's redirecting the Ranger teams. Know about their families. I know damn near everything.

"If you go with plan three, we can offer Schiller up to a half a million. I'll pay him out of my two point five. The ransom deal has to fly, of course. If it's a bust, our mercenary boys will be lucky to get home—wherever that is for guys like that. If he takes the job, Schiller picks his team, but with my blessing. I'll handle everything on this end. It'll take some worldwide razzle-dazzle to protect the loot, but I'll have that covered, too.

"Now." Lyle's tone was serious. "We've got one tough security problem. It's the M & H agent-in-charge. Got to deal with him separately. He's too damn good for our boys in the field. But I've got a plan."

"What do you mean, Graydon?"

"It's covered briefly in my report—page twenty-seven, I believe. But don't worry. It ain't murder."

Boggs sighed. "That's a relief."

"According to my research, your buddy Callaway's got a hunting camp in the backwater near Hilton Head. This little soiree will be a lot easier if he'll let us use it. And I'll bet he'll play this game. He's one of the good ol' boys at heart. Bet there was a time when he'd pay money to get into a good fight. Plus, he's a rich small-town white boy with a black lady friend. Jesus, Lord! He's crazy or the most courageous SOB around. Stir in all that old Ranger stuff, and I'll bet he jumps in."

"What don't you know about us, Graydon?"

"Very little, Barry, very little." Lyle spoke with confidence. "I'm a fucking fiend when it comes to research, and you wouldn't want it any other way. You've gotten more than your five grand worth. Besides, I'm damned excited about this little deal. Damned excited! Read my little analysis. It's excellent."

Lyle stood, stretching his long arms skyward as he gazed down the mountain and into the valley below. "Enough for now. I need a break. Got to meet my lawyer. Speaking of women, you ever hear from Katherine Rutledge? Never knew her married name."

Boggs recoiled from yet another lightning bolt hurled by his old college friend. He had goose bumps, and they did not come from the cool mountain air. He shrugged, trying to hide his uneasiness. "What made you think of her?"

"Hell," Lyle whined. "I don't know. Thought you two would have been together for life. Just wondered if you ever heard from her, that's all."

"Not a word." Boggs stared out across his long-range view. "We spent a weekend together before I went to Vietnam. Never saw her again after that. She wrote me four or five times. I never wrote back. Big mistake, I guess."

"Listen, BB." The professor leaned against the deck rail next to Boggs. "Maybe you ought to look her up. See how she's doin'. Sounds like there's still a little something there."

"The only thing there is a memory, even if it's a pleasant one. We were just kids—a lifetime ago. Just leave it at that."

"I see." Lyle paused, almost wishing he had kept his mouth shut. "Anyway, just read my report," he said, changing the subject. "Then sleep on it."

"What?" Boggs eyes were on the mountains, his mind somewhere else.

"The plans, the options. Mull 'em over then burn that stuff when you're finished." Then the professor strolled toward the stairs. "I'll be back in the morning—ten o'clock sharp."

"Yeah." Boggs shook his head.

"You'll make the right decision." Lyle turned and waved before disappearing down the steps. "Till tomorrow. Ten sharp."

Boggs eased back into the rocking chair, trying to gather his thoughts before digging into the report. Lyle had replaced it in the folded newspaper and left it sitting precariously on the deck rail. Boggs rocked the chair gently for a few minutes, watching the breeze lift the edge of the newspaper, exposing the brown legal binder. Then he reached for it before the wind could toss it down the mountainside. He thumbed through the pages, stopping cold on the last section divider, a plain white page with five words typed in the center. Chills raced up his spine as he read the single line typed in bold, black letters. "Plan Three: Mr. Carter's Sword."

CHAPTER TEN:
PLAN THREE

"DAMN YOU, GRAYDON."

It was three a.m., and Boggs sat on the edge of the bed, cursing Lyle as if he were there in the room. He blamed Lyle for triggering a dream—a nightmare, really—with Katherine Rutledge at the center. He rubbed sleep from his eyes, fumbling in the dark for the Winstons in the nightstand drawer. He had quit smoking, but still kept a pack around for times like these. He fired one up and took a couple of deep drags, coughing as the smoke reached his lungs. It did nothing, save remind him the decision to quit had been the right one.

Carter's story was troubling enough. Now, the appearance of Boggs's first love—as a middle-aged woman conjured up in a dream—made it a banner day for emotions. It would have helped had this Katherine-in-the-dream not pushed him away when he tried to hold her. "Why didn't you answer my letters?" When he tried to explain, she laughed him off. "You never really loved me." Then she taunted him. "You can't be thinking of me now. It's too late, Barry. I have my life. You've earned the right to grow old—alone."

Boggs knew the Katherine of decades ago would have run away with him, defying the wishes of her wealthy parents. "A nice boy," her mother had said countless times, "but no money and certainly no family name." Boggs jokingly referred to it as his socio-economic shortcomings. Then there was the Army and Vietnam. He could imagine getting a *Dear John* from Katherine, dictated by the old society bitch, herself. For whatever reasons—fear or selfishness—he had refused to carry such personal baggage into combat. Years later, when he was financially secure and self-confident, he brooded about his behavior toward Katherine and what might have been. He was surprised at how little it took to open that scrapbook—a familiar place, a song, a whiff of perfume, or a young woman's brown hair falling gently over the collar of a cotton-print dress. Although his memories were passionate at times, he would always convince himself she never gave him a thought. He would simply rationalize each melancholy trip as an old fool's flashback to a time forever lost then laugh at himself, but there was no laughing tonight. This dream was neither wistful nor pleasant. It was a sound scolding from the woman—more precisely, an unkind vision of that woman—he had left behind.

Boggs was still awake when the gentle rain drifted into the mountains before dawn. Amazing, he thought, still puzzled by Katherine's appearance in the dream. He had spent the previous day pouring over Lyle's analysis and weighing the options before making a decision. That night he had dropped off into a peaceful sleep—no wartime nightmares, no tossing, and no turning. He had not slept so soundly since Carter's funeral. Then the aberration of the girl whose kiss marked his heart forever paid the surprise visit, tormenting him in the darkness. Having recovered from the nightmare, he slipped under the covers for what he hoped would be a few hours of peaceful sleep.

When Boggs opened his eyes again it was nine fifteen. He had just enough time to shave and shower before the professor returned. He looked out the bathroom window, pleased that a gentle breeze had blown the clouds away, leaving a clear blue sky. Lower temperatures had ridden in with the overnight frontal passage, insuring a cool morning, and he chuckled, remembering Lyle's aversion to mountain weather. "Serves the bastard right," he said, "dredging up this Katherine stuff."

Boggs expected his old friend to whine about the cool morning, but it would be brief. He would be pleased with Boggs's decision. He had come to the conclusion he would rather be a covert, philanthropic kidnapper than a revenge-crazed killer. He could live with the idea of taking millions from M&H International to help needy veterans. So what, he thought, if it sounded like something out of Sherwood Forest. At least he could claim a little patch of moral high ground, even if it were supported by loose stone and sand. Forgetting what happened to his Rangers had never been a consideration.

"Great God," Boggs whispered as he walked out on the deck. "I'm as bad as Graydon, rationalizing this thing." He checked his watch. It was ten o'clock sharp, and there were footsteps on the stairs.

"Coffee, my boy. Coffee! I'm freezing my ass off." Lyle wore a new suede jacket, obviously purchased from an outdoor shop in nearby Boone. The tag was still attached to the sleeve.

"Good morning, Professor. You know where the cups are," Boggs said. "That should warm you up. And speaking of warmth, how can a man with a lawyer like yours complain about a little chill?"

"She was especially warm." Lyle raised his eyebrows. "But that was last night. As you can see, all I got wrapped around me now is this dinky-ass jacket. She bought it for me, so I had to wear it."

"She has excellent taste," Boggs said. "If this deal goes down right, you can buy all the expensive clothes you want."

"Plan three?"

"Damn risky," Boggs said, "but it just might work."

"Yeah," Lyle said, rubbing the sleeve of his new coat. "If it doesn't, she can give this to her next boyfriend. We'll get those crappy uniforms in the federal pen. Don't you hate that cheap shit?"

"Come on in. I built a fire. Get your coffee. We need to talk about this… plan three." Boggs was ready for business. "I guess that's enough punishment for Cain and Ha. Plus, there could be some money for needy old vets. Of course, saying we'll do it is one thing. Doing it's something else."

"True, Barry, but it can be done—with excellent planning and a little luck. Man, that fire and the coffee took the edge off. It's a little tricky, but my plan is sound. Slipping a team through the backwater in October is our best opportunity."

"You're sure? We haven't even been down there."

"You haven't," Lyle said, "but I have. I'm on the payroll, remember? That villa is accessible by water. Our boys can be in and out in a few hours, but we've got to get Calloway on board. His hunting camp is critical."

"October's deer season. How can he keep hunters out?" Boggs asked.

"He owns the damn place—three thousand acres—lock, stock and barrel. He can do any thing he wants. Say he's going to have special hunts only. He'll think of some damn lie. He's a used car salesman, for god's sake. Bottom line is his redneck buddies won't be out there getting in the way.

"You'll have to go to Orangeburg. Read Carter's letter to Calloway, but go easy on details. No names. Just tell him the deal is together. It's payback time for one of his favorite assholes. If he's scared—and I can understand that—he can leave the country in October. If not, he can stick around for the fun. God forbid, he says no."

Boggs raised his eyebrows. "I thought you said we were too old for this stuff?"

"We are—for the raid," Lyle said. "We'll pay some tough, young hard asses to take that risk. But I thought you old boys would like to be there when we scare Cain and Ha and take their money."

"With what it's costing me, I should have a front row seat." Boggs smiled broadly for the first time since the professor showed up.

"Don't worry, son. You'll get your money's worth. Right now, you've got to contact your boy Schiller in South Africa. Tell him there's a special job. Tease him with the personal angle, but no details. We'll send him a plane ticket—first class. Fly him here for a little set-to about the project. If he jumps in, we'll get crackin'. But you need to sell Calloway on the idea before Schiller gets here."

"And where will you be?"

"My associates and I will be running around like our asses are on fire. And, of course, we'll be spending your money."

"A comforting thought," Boggs said. "Who are your associates, any-way?"

"You don't know them, and they don't know you." He spoke in a con-descending professorial tone. "It's got to be this way. Need to know, man."

"Fair enough." Boggs nodded. "But you've got the lives of good people in your hands. Just show me some serious command control. Keep the circle tight. You violated security when you showed up yesterday unannounced. No more of that crap, okay?"

"Roger that, sir," Lyle said, mocking the military jargon. Boggs face was flushed. The professor was on dangerous ground and quickly changed his tone. "I'm real sorry, Barry. From now on, I promise to keep the bullshit to a minimum. I know this is life and death stuff, but we can't lose our sense of humor, can we?"

"Apology accepted," Boggs said. "I do have one other question. Any alternatives to the target date?"

Lyle walked over to the full-length windows and gazed at Grandfather Mountain in the distance. "It's a one shot deal, Barry. M&H plans to merge with two competitors early next year. Their cash position has to be at its apex for the deal to go down. If my research is right, we could clip 'em for a hundred million—maybe three times that. What we're taking will be a pittance."

Boggs rested his elbow on the stained oak mantle piece above the field stone hearth. "It's October or not at all."

"You got it. The stars, the moon and the money have to be in place. Then there's another reason—kind of personal. "I've envisioned this huge Christmas party with gourmet food and fabulous gifts for everybody." Lyle said. "Man, I'd be real disappointed if we don't pull this off."

"Maybe you could invite Cain and Ha," Boggs said, succumbing to his friend's levity.

Lyle took another slow sip of coffee. "Extraordinary thought, BB, but even I'm not totally insane."

CHAPTER ELEVEN:
CAPE TOWN

THE SLIM FIGURE CLAD ONLY IN khaki shorts stood with arms folded, tapping the telephone receiver against a tanned left biceps. He gently bit his lip then returned the phone to its cradle. He pushed back his streaked blond hair and walked out on the balcony of his Cape Town apartment, unfazed by the cool air. His blue eyes climbed towering Table Mountain, squinting as he gazed into the clear June sky. The terrain surrounding the South African seaport was stunning, but Karl Schiller had something else on his mind—the peculiar conversation just concluded with Boggs.

Schiller was puzzled; why would Boggs fly him to the states to discuss business? He had worked for the American before, and each time, the details had been routinely settled by telephone. But this time, Boggs had been vague, alluding to a personal angle.

"You'll find it fascinating," Boggs had said on the telephone. "You're my only choice, and confidentiality is critical."

The secretive tone fueled Schiller's curiosity. He would fly to America to hear Boggs out. At the very least, it was a matter of courtesy. His father, Walter Sigwald, was killed in Vietnam while serving with Boggs. Boggs had even offered to pay Schiller's college expenses in America, had he been interested. When he decided to join the West German Army after university studies, Boggs encouraged him and even traveled to Germany when the young officer was commissioned. They stayed in touch after Schiller left the German Army to market his talents in the Third World. Their friendship had produced lucrative security contracts for Schiller—one in Europe, another in Central America. He knew little of Boggs business interests, but payment had always been prompt, and the amounts generous. Fortunately, the work had not been dangerous—a damned sight easier than his work on the Dark Continent.

"Yes," Schiller said, turning his back on the landscape and stepping inside. "I will fly to America."

"Did you say something, darling?"

"Oh…no, *liebschen*." He looked up to see a statuesque redhead wearing nothing but emerald lace bikini pants. "I have an unexpected consulting opportunity. Actually, I must leave tomorrow for Europe."

She pouted as she leaned against the doorsill, but made sure Schiller got an eyeful of her flawless figure. "Can we make this trip…together?"

"No, Sylvie—not this time. I must travel on business for at least one week—possibly two. It is at the request of an old family friend. For now, we have today and tonight together. So, let's not waste a moment. It would be sinful to waste such time. Do you not agree?"

"Would it matter if I disagree?" The tall beauty stood in the center of the doorway. Her outstretched hands now grasped the sills on each side.

"Probably not," Schiller said, making no attempt to hide a sheepish grin. Then his eyes wandered up from her toes to the tips of her beautifully manicured fingernails.

"Well, we mustn't waste time if you're leaving tomorrow." She frowned and turned around slowly, stepped inside the bedroom and slipped out of the silk panties. Then she looked over her shoulder. "Perhaps I can give you something to remember me by. Now, come to me…you sinful man."

Schiller, the soldier, knew when to follow orders. He gave her a snappy salute and goose-stepped toward the bedroom, anxiously anticipating his remembrance.

"And what is the reason for that?" She stood, hands on hips, with a puzzled look on her face. "You are an instructor at university, not a *Nazi*,"

"Oh," Schiller said, shifting his mind into damage control. "Only a joke, Sylvie, my darling—following your orders, you know, to join you for romance."

"You know such military things make me nervous, Karl." Then she sighed. "But, I know you didn't mean to upset me, so…come to me—now."

Incredible, he thought, as he took her in his arms. She knew every inch of his body, and a comical gesture was as close as he had ever come to being found out.

———✗✗✗———

While he spent the previous day and memorable night with Sylvie, Schiller arrived on time at Cape Town International Airport where a first class ticket awaited him. What a pleasant surprise, he thought. Boggs had begun his sales pitch at the ticket counter. There were times when Schiller had worked for much less than the price of a first class airline ticket. Many of his business trips began in the noisy cargo hold of an ancient DC-3 or something worse. Now, he was in first class, being pampered and relishing the free ride.

Sitting comfortably in his window seat, Schiller watched the South African coast fade into a distant haze. Then he gently bobbed the ice cubes in a glass of Chivas Regal with a swizzle stick, smiling as the pretty brunette flight attendant glided by. Looking out at the vast Atlantic, his mind could not help but drift to the business at hand. Why had Boggs been so secretive? Then there was the yet to be disclosed personal angle. Schiller made a mental note to be especially careful in analyzing that aspect of the job, but he was confident about one thing: whatever his old friend had planned sounded different this time. It would not be what the Americans liked to call a walk in the park, but he smiled as a tiny chill crept up his spine and danced across his shoulders. As pragmatic as he was, a little excitement had worked its way into the equation.

"Maybe the job of a lifetime," he whispered.

"Another Scotch?" The pretty flight attendant touched his arm softly as she spoke.

"No." He smiled politely. "No thank you. This is enough for now."

Schiller was getting high on something else.

K E N   W E B B

CHAPTER TWELVE:
RECRUITING CALLOWAY

Mike Calloway stood on his dealership showroom, staring at his Rolex Presidential. The old building on Highway 21 near Orangeburg, South Carolina had housed a tractor company until he gave it a facelift, but he kept it simple, vowing never to change the familiar red brick façade. Employees, on the other hand, did change, and there was a personnel matter to handle while waiting for Boggs. He could understand—this time—why Rich Calloway, his nephew and general manager, had deferred to the owner.

"Elloree." Calloway called to a leathery-skinned old man who was leaning against a sleek black Jaguar in the center of the showroom.

"Yes sir, Boss." The old man straightened the full-Windsor knot in his silk tie and walked over. He hitched up his sharply creased trousers then tugged on the lapels of a red and black plaid sport jacket. He would have been dapper, indeed, if the clock could have been turned back a few decades. He snapped his fingers, pointing his forefinger at Calloway. "Got somebody you want me to work, Boss?"

"Not right now." Calloway turned to the blond behind a u-shaped desk against the showroom wall. "Celia? Ask Robert to bring up the car, would you, please? And, uh, hold my calls. Let's walk the lot, Elloree."

Moments later they had crossed the smooth black asphalt to the front line of detailed used cars. Calloway never liked parting company, but he had come up with a plan to let Will "Elloree" Fogler down easy.

"You know, Elloree." Calloway folded his arms across his chest. "We talked about retirement last year. You're seventy-three and need to enjoy life."

"I'm enjoying it just fine," Fogler said. "I'll quit next year."

"Nope," Calloway said. "That's what we agreed on last year. Time to get off the sales floor and get on the golf course."

"Come on, Mikey," Fogler whined. No one else called Calloway "Mikey" and got away with it. Only the dealer's father—who had been Fogler's close friend—had called him Mikey, and Fogler never invoked the elder Calloway's memory unless he was in trouble. "What'd I do wrong?"

"What you've been doing all your life," Calloway said, getting to the crux of the matter. "You're stuck in the old days. Times have changed. You haven't. We can't talk to people like we used to—the blacks, the gays, women. You've heard of political correctness?"

"I got plenty of black customers—women, too. Get along good with 'em."

"But you hurt their feelings sometimes, even when you don't mean to. We can't afford that today. I don't need problems like some of these restaurants or big corporations have. There's a bunch of sue-happy sons of bitches out there—blacks, whites, gays, lesbians, even Presbyterians. Everybody's waitin' for a business to slip up. Next thing you know, I'll get sued and have to send all y'all to charm school. It'd break my ass."

"Sorry I let you down." Fogler leaned against a highly polished Grand Prix, head bowed and both hands fumbling with the loose change in his pants pockets. "Your daddy and me—we were like brothers. Sure glad he ain't here to see this."

Calloway put his arm around Fogler's shoulder. "You haven't let me down. You helped build this business. Anyway, it's semi-retirement. You can do dealer trades, and I'll pay you birddog fees on your old customers."

"Under the table?"

"Hell no," Calloway snapped. "Let me finish. It's just time to let the younger kids work the lot. You need to have some fun."

"Well," Fogler sighed, looking over his reading glasses. "Can I drive a demo till I find something?"

"You won't need it." Calloway spoke matter-of-factly. "See that Cadillac Robert just brought up? It's yours."

"I don't know what to say, Mike." Fogler broke into a wide smile. "I always told your daddy you'd be somebody special—first class." Fogler hugged his boss, pulled a white monogrammed handkerchief from his coat pocket and wiped his tears.

"Hot-a-mighty damn!" Elloree danced and strutted his way toward the Cadillac. The girls from the business office and the sales force were waiting with a golf shirt and a new putter for the new semi-retiree.

"This is great, Uncle Mike." Rich walked up with a camera. "You got class."

"And you better damn well pay attention." Calloway whispered the warning through a toothy grin, watching the hugs and backslapping around Fogler and his Cadillac. "This is the last time I'll handle something like this. I pay you big money to be the general manager."

"No problem, Uncle Mike. I get the message."

"And Rich, I want a picture—a little write up, too. Put it in the county paper. I want his friends and his enemies to see it."

"Yes sir." Rich headed toward the celebration with his marching orders. "Y'all get in around Elloree. Smile big, now. We're gonna put this in the paper."

Calloway was happy for Fogler, but even prouder of himself for eliminating a potential problem with the African American community. The leaders had been grumbling about Fogler's treatment of some black customers. Two black salesmen had also complained to Rich about Elloree's showroom behavior. His retirement should satisfy them all. Conversely, Calloway protected his position in the white community by giving Fogler a sendoff in a shiny Cadillac. He chuckled, thinking about how the tax-conscious old salesman would react when he got the 1099 for the car. Still basking in his public relations coup, Calloway failed to notice Boggs step from a car at the lot's lower entrance.

"If every customer gets that kind of treatment, I'll buy today," Boggs said as he walked up behind Calloway.

"Thought you'd call when you got to town." Calloway extended his hand to his old team leader.

"Caught a ride with a manager from that plant down the road," Boggs said. "His company plane landed a few minutes after I did."

"Perfect timing—lunch," Calloway said. There's a little restaurant over near the lake. Takes about fifteen minutes. We can talk and ride. Ain't gonna be lookin' at charts and pro formas and shit, are we?"

"Not today." Boggs chuckled and followed Calloway to a jet black BMW Seven Series. Boggs eyed the car like it was the new girl in town wearing a tight sweater and short skirt, and Calloway caught him.

"Used," the dealer said proudly. "Only got thirty-five thousand miles. Too goddamn expensive new. Get in."

"Who's the old guy by the Cadillac?" Boggs asked.

"A salesman," Calloway said. "Retired him today. One step ahead of the NAACP."

"What?"

"Heard some grumbling about the way he treated a couple of minorities. He's just old school. Wasn't calling folks the N-word, thank God. He just talked down to some of them. At least they took it that way. He never hurt anybody, except with that big mouth.

"Then—this was about a month ago—he insults this gay professor from one of the colleges. The guy wanted to look under the hood of a car on the showroom floor. Elloree says, 'What are you, professor? A mechanic? All you need to know is where to stick the key and where the gas goes in.' Elloree thought it was funny. There was some snickering on the showroom, too. Now, guess who got the call from the head of the college?

"You gotta understand. I ain't out to change hearts and minds. The only man who could do that they hung on a cross. But like the Sunday school song says, 'Red and yellow, black and white, they are precious in his sight', and they're all precious in my dealership. Can't let nothin' get in the way of them drivin' Calloway cars."

"Just business," Boggs said.

"Precisely, Mr. Boggs. Now, what brings you down off your mountain? What are you selling today?"

Boggs stared out the window of the big BMW, looking across the fields of cotton, corn and soybeans thriving along Highway 301. It reminded him of Kershaw County where he grew up. For a moment, his life passed in front of his eyes but it was back to reality when Buddy Carter's revelation crashed into his memories of home.

"Must be serious," Calloway said.

"What?"

"What you came down here for."

"Oh, yeah. Sorry. You're right, Mike. Life and death serious."

"For God's sake." Calloway frowned. "What is it?"

"Carter left a death bed letter. He blamed Captain Cain and Captain Ha for what happened to our patrols in Vietnam. They changed our orders to keep us away from a smuggling deal. They were afraid we'd stumble on it and mess it up. So, we went into the Catcher's Mitt, and the rest is history."

Calloway made eye contact with Boggs, then pulled off on the shoulder. He looked straight ahead for a few moments. Then he turned to Boggs. "Would you run that by me again?"

"Sounds far-fetched, but I've had someone good looking into this. The circumstantial evidence and Carter's death-bed declaration, make a strong case."

"How long you known about it?" Calloway asked.

"Since the funeral. Carter's preacher gave me a box with the letter in it."

"You had it when we got together?"

"I couldn't tell you, Mike," Boggs said. "Couldn't tell anybody. I had to get it checked out. Besides, I hadn't seen you guys in years—except for Bobby Vasquez."

"Can anything be done—legal, I mean?"

"It's too late," Boggs said. "At least that's what my guy tells me. The charges are old. The Army wouldn't want it. Politics, too. Cain's a big political contributor here and abroad, not to mention M&H International is huge."

"Something ought to be done. Goddamn, I'd like to personally kick their asses."

"That's why I'm here," Boggs said. "If you're interested, I'll go on. If not, just forget we ever talked. We could wind up in jail if it fails. Not to mention the danger involved."

"What's the plan?"

"Something's in the works, and you'd play a big part," Boggs said. "Shall I continue?"

"I'm listening," Calloway put the big German car in gear and pulled out on the highway. "That little restaurant in Santee's a few minutes away. Don't make big decisions on an empty stomach."

Boggs continued, describing the M&H villa at Hilton Head, why Calloway's hunt club was important, along with the critical October time frame. Boggs steered clear of a hard sell. The car dealer would see right through it.

Calloway pulled into a parking space outside Henry's Restaurant just off I-95. "Serious jail time if we get caught?" he asked.

"Maybe. Worse if somebody gets killed." Boggs tried to smile. "Probably go to hell no matter what happens."

"Whew," Calloway said. "I've prepared myself for the hell part. I'm mostly there already. Don't think I'd like the jail thing. Gives me the creeps thinking about some big convict givin' it to me in the, uh…well…you know what I mean."

"Don't flatter yourself, Mike. They like the young boys." Both men laughed.

—⚙—

"I'll be ready for a new car in the fall." The hostess grinned, welcoming the two men to the restaurant. She reminded Calloway all her cars had come from his lot. "I'm expecting a special deal," she said, hugging him like he was her daddy—well, maybe more like an uncle by marriage.

"Don't worry, honey," Calloway said. "I always look out for you. Now, how's about a quiet corner. Got a little business to discuss." The usually talkative car dealer said little as they ate, but he hung on Boggs's every word.

"Well, Mr. Boggs, the catfish was excellent. This thing you've cooked up sounds damned good, too."

Boggs listened, and, characteristically, showed little emotion. He waited patiently for Calloway to jump in, out, or put him off.

"Need any cash?"

"Not a penny, Mike, but thanks." Boggs sensed Calloway was in.

"And we won't be keeping any of the money—personally, I mean?"

"Not a cent," Boggs said, "except for expenses and financing the team. And I'm prepared to lose that."

"This is crazy—old farts like us doing this—but that scum needs to be punished. They fuckin' betrayed us. If we get killed, well, God can have us. If we get caught, we'll be damn good company in the big house over in Atlanta." Calloway waved the waitress over to the table. "Charlene, honey, bring me a big slice of that coconut custard pie. How 'bout you, Mr. Boggs?"

Boggs raised his hand in protest and shook his head.

"Can we bring Johnson in on the deal?" Calloway asked.

It was a reasonable question, but Boggs was not ready for it. The bigger the circle, the bigger the risks, he thought. A failed mission could add new tragedies to those old ones they hoped to avenge. "Tell you the truth, I haven't thought about Johnson." Boggs chose his words carefully. "You want him in?"

"Just thinking out loud. That's all. Don't know if you remember, but he and Brown were real close in Vietnam. He took it real hard when that boy got killed. We even talked about it at Carter's funeral. He still sends roses to Brown's mama on Memorial Day. She told him she got flowers from Carter, too. Kind of tells you something, don't it?"

"Things are coming together," Boggs said. "But… I'm wondering; could Johnson be more loyal to the government than to us? He was a career soldier and still works for the VA. Plus, he talked like he's living the good life—grandchildren and all."

"Ain't nothing to do with him being black, is it?"

"No," Boggs said softly. "Hell no,"

"I really want to talk to him, Barry. I'll drive over to Columbus—take his temperature—if it's okay."

Boggs weighed the issue in his mind. He needed Calloway for a lot of reasons, but a wider circle scared him. Boggs's problem was simple. Where would Johnson's loyalties lie? Would it be the government that provided paychecks and two careers or the Rangers from the past?

"Wouldn't feel right without him." Calloway broke the silence. "Besides, he'd make a great cellmate if we get caught."

"Okay Mike," Boggs said, "but that's as wide as it gets. And if he gives you the slightest bit of resistance, no hard sell."

"Who else is in?"

"That you know? Bobby Vasquez, maybe. Travel distance? His health? I just don't know yet. He deserves to be in."

"He'd probably want to shoot both those bastards," Calloway said.

"Probably, but they're no good to us dead. I'm sure he'll see the logic in the plan."

"Excellent pie, Charlene. Excellent." Calloway grinned as the ever-attentive waitress topped off their glasses of sweet iced tea then scooted back beyond earshot of their conversation.

"Got a leader for this thing?"

"A fine one." Boggs spoke with confidence. "He's young, smart and experienced. He'll bring his own team—all from outside the country."

"Jesus, man! I'm gettin' chills."

"The leader's got a personal stake in this as well," Boggs said. You'll get to meet him and the professor."

"The professor?" Calloway furrowed his brow. "Who's he?"

"You'll meet him soon enough. He's handling intelligence and logistics." Boggs grinned. "He's crazier than you are, Mike."

"If that's true," Calloway said, "count me in. It'll be worth it just to meet the man."

CHAPTER THIRTEEN:
LEADERSHIP
CONFERENCE

"YOU DO KNOW WHAT THIS BOY looks like?"

"It's been a few years, but I'll recognize him." Boggs looked out across the runway at Columbia Metropolitan Airport, then turned back to Lyle. "You've seen his picture. Pick him out of the crowd, and I'll pay for dinner."

"Hope he's not wearing some 'Jungle Jim' outfit—bush jacket, snake boots—shit like that. This is Columbia, South Carolina, not LAX. Weirdos still get strange looks in this town. And, uh, you're buying dinner anyway." Lyle waved the barmaid over for another Budweiser. "You write this off, don't you?"

"Yeah, like the drug dealers filing with the IRS."

"Right." Lyle chuckled. Nothing serious had been said for several minutes, nor was it taken that way. "Plane's coming in." He pointed to a jet taxiing toward the terminal, obeying hand signals from a ground crewman in the heat and humidity of the June afternoon. "Hope our boy's on it. Another beer and I'll have to paddle out of here."

"That's the Atlanta flight," Boggs said.

"Shit, son." The professor leaned over, looking his friend in the eye. "Most all of 'em are Atlanta flights before they get here."

"I told him to meet us in the lounge," Boggs said.

Ten minutes later, passengers walked briskly from the gate to the center of the terminal. A handsome couple, more interested in each other than rushing to the baggage claim, brought up the rear. She was a brunette, slim and stunning in a black silk dress. Her diamonds flashed points of light in every direction. Her companion wore a three-piece tropical wool suit in classic tan custom-tailored in London and a blue shirt of Egyptian cotton. His raw silk tie in red, blue, and gold fell from a perfect Windsor knot nestled in a spread collar. Each strand of blond hair was in its place, and his steel blue eyes sparkled behind round horn-rimmed glasses.

Several women passengers nearly stumbled, trying to catch over-the-shoulder glimpses of the tall, tanned fellow, whose every step was a confident one. Even Lyle was impressed as this duo-from-GQ glided effortlessly along, engrossed in smiles and private conversation, oblivious to the people around them.

"Wonder how that SOB keeps a high-maintenance lady like that?"

Boggs rocked back in his chair and grinned. "By working for you, I believe."

"You…are…kidding," Lyle said. That's Schiller?"

"In the flesh." Boggs was amused that the professor failed to pick their man from the stream of passengers. "I thought you had a picture, since you know so damned much."

"He had a beard in that photo. Looked heavier, too," Lyle mumbled, watching Schiller bow slightly and kiss the hand of the beautiful woman in black.

"*Au revoir, Madame,*" he said as her hand drifted slowly, almost reluctantly, from his gentle grasp. "*C'etait un plaisir. Je vous souhaite une bonne vacance avec votre famille.*"

"My, my," Lyle whispered. "If he's half as good in the field as he is with the ladies, I expect an extraordinary mission."

"We'll see." Boggs watched Schiller's eyes follow the lady into the stream of passengers flowing toward the baggage claim. Boggs stood, but said nothing, allowing his friend to savor his farewell to the lady in black.

"Good afternoon, Dr. Schiller," Boggs said, startling the man from South Africa.

Only then did Schiller realize he was standing at the entrance to the airport lounge. "It's been a long time, Barry." Schiller extended his hand.

"And it's not Doctor—not yet. Consulting is hampering my doctoral studies."

"Quite a lady, Mr. Schiller." Lyle did not wait to be introduced. "I'm Graydon Lyle—an old friend of Mr. Boggs. He's told me a lot about you. Left out the part about your exquisite taste in women."

"She is quite lovely." Schiller sighed. "But, alas, quite married. He's a Frenchman with business interests in the Carolinas. She's meeting him here for vacation."

Lyle rubbed his chin. "Well, son, You're a smooth operator, real smooth. I admire that in a gentleman. Yes, I do."

"*Merci, monsieur.*" Schiller grinned, blushing in the face of the compliment.

"You'll have to forgive Graydon," Boggs said. "He fancies himself as a rather smooth operator. He also has the utmost respect for others skilled in that fine art. And he's partial to the French countryside. You two have a lot in common."

"Too bad we couldn't have met in France," Schiller said.

"Indeed." Lyle nodded in agreement. "Join our little venture, and you'll have money for lots of vacations *en Provence.*"

"I'm intrigued," Schiller said. "I flew a long way to discuss it."

"We'll get to that soon enough," Boggs said. "We'll lay it out when we get to Graydon's house."

—☩—

Forty-five minutes later, the three men were sitting on the screened porch at Lyle's Wales Garden home. Schiller sat quietly, listening to Boggs's story about the December patrol and the new information about Cain and Ha. Then Lyle outlined the plan to kidnap the two executives.

"I have a personal interest in this matter because of my father," Schiller said. "But, in truth, I did not know him. My mother was pregnant with me when he was killed. It was your war—your men, Barry, but I could have an interest in your project. It is all about risks versus rewards."

"We won't ask you to work cheap," Boggs said. "But I'd hoped the family ties would mean something."

"They do, Barry," Schiller said, "but it's still a business decision."

"We're talking six figures," Lyle chimed in. "A healthy cut for your team as well. You interested?"

"Possibly," Schiller said without the slightest hint of emotion. "But I'll need to think about it. The jet lag is catching up with me. An hour's rest, then a discussion over dinner, perhaps?"

"Certainly. I'll show you to the guest bedroom," Lyle said. The three men stood and stretched. They had talked for two hours straight.

Schiller followed Lyle inside, leaving Boggs on the porch. When they reached the bedroom, Schiller thanked him for his hospitality.

"You're welcome," Lyle said. "And, by the way, Barry's a little uneasy discussing money, but I'm not. Play your cards right, and you could become a millionaire."

"Really?" For the first time, Schiller allowed the tiniest hint of emotion to creep into his voice.

"Really," Lyle said, detecting his guest's curious reaction to the seven-figure remark. "The money's there, son, and you're the man—the only man Barry wants for this job. It's all honor and revenge with him." Then he set the hook a little deeper. "But I'm more like you—pragmatic and business-like. You just go along with what ever final figure Barry throws out."

"And who, Dr. Lyle, is running this mission? You or Barry?"

"I'm running it—on Barry's behalf, of course. And we will accomplish the goals he's set forth. It's an extraordinary opportunity for you, but not a word about this in front of Barry." The professor leaned against the door-sill, lowering his voice to a whisper. "Chisel this in stone: I will deliver the money. Lots more than you're even thinking about. Pleasant dreams." Without saying another word, the professor turned on his heels and strolled down the hall and out to the porch.

Boggs was pacing nervously. "Well?" the wide-eyed Boggs asked. "What do you think?"

"He's one pragmatic guy. All business. And he'll give it careful consideration—maybe even ferret out some stuff we've missed. But I flipped the bait ever so gently under his nose. I've given him all the damned line he wants. I'm sure he'll swallow the bait whole."

"Meaning?"

"Meaning we won't even have to reel him in. He'll be jumping in the boat with us by dinner tonight."

CHAPTER FOURTEEN:
JOHNSON'S DOUBTS

T HEY STREAKED PAST IN PICKUPS, SUV's and on motorcycles their mothers had begged them not to ride. Windshields were emblazoned with all too familiar decals—Infantry, Airborne, Ranger—and Calloway had to chuckle at their bravado. He knew these young warriors sailing down I-185 South toward Fort Benning, Ga., were blinded by a belief in their immortality. Calloway had suffered from the affliction decades ago.

In the heat of this July afternoon, Calloway was returning to Fort Benning for the first time in years. His life was far different now, as was his reason for going, but still related to the war that never quite went away. And there was a lump in his throat, just like the one decades ago. His stomach churned as if he were a young recruit bound for jump school. He even changed his driving style, slowing to the speed limit—a subconscious act, to delay his arrival at Robert Johnson's house.

"What if Johnson thinks we're nuts? What if he calls the cops?" Calloway talked to himself. That paranoia so familiar to so many salesmen was working its mischief on the car dealer. He had even considered a retreat until the moment he pulled into Johnson's driveway.

"That your car, mister?"

"Yep," Calloway said, sliding out of the leather seat of the black BMW. Once out, he stretched, wincing at the bursitis in his right shoulder. Then he knelt slowly, getting eye-to-eye with the little boy who greeted him. He was dressed in red shorts and a blue Atlanta Braves T-shirt. "Your granddaddy Robert Johnson?"

"Yes, sir. He's up there." The boy pointed to the man on the porch. "My name's Robert, too."

"My name's Mike." Calloway grinned. "Me and your granddaddy were in the army together."

"You a paratrooper?"

"Only when I had to be, son," Calloway said. "Only when I had to be." Then he looked at Johnson, patiently watching the cross-generation exchange from the porch. "He's a fine looking boy, Granddaddy."

"Thanks," Johnson said. "Got his mama's looks, thank God. Come on in. Meet the wife."

After a brief exchange of pleasantries, Mrs. Johnson excused herself and walked outside to keep an eye on her busy grandson. She left the two men sitting quietly, if not uncomfortably, in the family room. Johnson's Army medals, memorabilia and a photo history of his family covered an entire wall.

"Robert." Calloway broke the silence. "What say we ride out to the post?"

"Thought you hated that place," Johnson said.

"Wouldn't mind seeing it now—you know, after all these years. Besides, we need to talk. Private-like."

"You here to recruit me for Amway or something?"

"Hell no," Calloway said with a sigh. "Nothing that easy."

Johnson was puzzled. He had never seen Calloway's serious side—except in combat. That was reason enough to ride with him to Fort Benning.

"I'll tell the wife we're going out for a while," Johnson said. "You'll stay for dinner, okay?"

"Thanks, Robert. Another time. Gotta get back after we talk."

Johnson's house in a Columbus suburb was about fifteen minutes from Fort Benning. Little was said during the ride, other than small talk about how the years had changed the place.

"Jones is buried over there." Johnson pointed to the post's main cemetery at the corner of Benning Drive and Custer Road. "Remember him?"

"Kind of," Calloway said. "Real skinny kid from Memphis. Hung around with you and Washington."

"Nothing wrong with your memory."

"Hadn't forgot he whipped my ass outside that bar in Saigon, either." They both laughed. "I had it comin.'"

"That was a long time ago." Johnson sighed. "And it didn't keep y'all from fighting side by side. Damn, I wish those guys were riding with us right now. Miss 'em a lot. Where to?"

"The towers. Maybe they'll be training out there today."

"The towers?" Johnson raised his eybrows. "Little trip down memory lane, huh?"

"Sort of," Calloway said, turning in the direction of the airborne school where young soldiers learn to jump from perfectly good airplanes. From a distance, the towers looked less like training aids and more like giant red and white carnival rides. Soldiers dressed in camouflage stood in line, each waiting for a ride to the top. When a fully deployed parachute was released, the student floated two hundred and fifty feet to the ground.

"It gives them a taste of it," Johnson said, "but it ain't jumping from a plane."

"I wouldn't know," Calloway replied, watching a soldier drift gently to the ground. "The wind was blowing too hard when we were supposed to train on the towers. My only jumping was from planes. Actually, I jumped out of the first airplane I ever flew in. Ain't interested in doin' that again."

"Look, man." Johnson pursed his lips and looked Calloway in the eyes. "This nostalgia stuff is nice, but why'd you haul me out here? Not to watch training, I'm sure."

"You're right. It's more than that. But first you've got to swear—I mean really swear—not to tell a soul what I'm about to tell you."

"Jesus, man. What's the big secret?"

"Come on, Robert." Calloway sighed. "This ain't no joke. Do you swear?"

"Oh hell yes." Then he paused. "I swear—unless it's murder or a matter of national security."

"It ain't national security," Calloway said. "It's about Carter. It's about a letter he wrote before he died. He kept a secret about the patrols—Boggs's and Fort's."

"What could he have known? He was wounded and had to stay back."

"That's the point, sort of. He knew why we were dumped in the middle of the shit."

"What?"

"That's right. Two officers were in cahoots and got our orders changed. It was Cain and Ha, that ARVN captain. They wanted to keep us away from their smuggling deal. Our first orders would have put us too close. That little switcheroo put us in on top of NVA regulars."

"How'd Carter know?"

"Heard 'em talking after it was all over. He'd been drinking and was sleeping it off, hiding behind a filing cabinet in headquarters. It was the middle of the night when they came in and woke him up. He wasn't supposed to be there, so he just stayed put. The letter said they were bragging about how well it worked."

Johnson said nothing as he leaned against Calloway's car and stared at the sprawling fields around the towers. He looked up at a droning C-130 heading for the drop zone near the Chattahoochee River.

"Washington and I made our first jumps down there," Johnson said. "Same plane, sitting right next to each other. I was scared shitless. He was the coolest guy on the aircraft. Saw him damn near every day after that, until they brought him back in a body bag."

"I'm sorry, Robert—springing it on you like this," Johnson said. "But I couldn't write you a letter. We owed it to you to tell you in person."

"Who is 'we'?"

"Boggs and me. Carter left this stuff with his preacher. The preacher gave it to Boggs. Carter had been after Cain and Ha for years. Sounded like he planned to kill 'em both, but he got sick."

"Are you serious?"

"As a heart attack, and I already had one of those nasty things."

"So," Johnson said, "what can be done now? It's been years."

"That's why I'm here. There's a plan, and I'll tell you about it. But first I got to know if you're on board. If not, this little chat never happened. I'll go home. No hard feelings what-so-ever."

"Is this something stupid and dangerous?"

"Double-fucking dangerous," Calloway said. "Illegal, too. But we won't be doing any shooting."

"Y'all planning to kill these guys?"

"Nope. Just ask them to make a big donation to some needy Vietnam vets."

"They're going to donate money—just like that? Right, uh huh."

"Actually, it's a damn bold plan—kidnap Cain and Ha and hold them for ransom. They're still business partners, billionaires, too. They'll pay millions to get loose."

"You know how crazy this sounds?"

"Yep."

"You know all the details?"

"Only what I need to."

"Well, let's have it."

"You in?"

Johnson sat for a minute, looking across the training fields at the soldiers moving about. He looked down at the deep scars on his wrists—a lifetime reminder of a brief, but harrowing, experience as a prisoner of war.

"I'm almost in. I guess," Johnson said with a sigh. "But there's lot I'd like to know before I commit a hundred percent."

"Sorry, Robert. Said too much already. You'd have to be available on a moment's notice—late summer or early fall. You wouldn't have to travel far. Besides, we'll be observers, mostly. There's a team of young guys. They'll make the grab."

"I guess I'm giving you a strong 'maybe'," Johnson said. "Lots to think about—family, job, spending my retirement years in jail. Minor stuff like that. Know what I mean?

"Look, man, I understand. You had a great military career. The medals, the benefits and all. That job at the VA—around all those bureaucrats. Real exciting—"

"Come on, Calloway. I know where you're going with this. I care about those boys who died. Think about them almost every day. But, it was a lifetime ago. I've got a good life now—finally enjoying my family. I've got to think about it. That's all. This Carter stuff is a lot to take in at one time."

"No doubt," Calloway said. "And this won't be an ol' boy get together for a few beers at the Holiday Inn. It's damned serious, but I've made up my mind. I'm gonna be there."

"Let's get back to the house," Johnson said, looking at his watch and changing the subject. "I want to see little Robert before my daughter picks him up."

—w—

Johnson's grandson was playing on the front lawn under the watchful eye of his grandmother when Calloway and Johnson arrived.

"Little Robert!" Mrs. Johnson frowned as she looked over her reading glasses. "Don't run up to that car. You wait here for Granddaddy."

"I thought this stuff was behind me," Johnson said, opening the car door. "I love my family. They mean everything to me. But I'm not taking this lightly, Mike. I'll think on it hard—real hard. Pray about it, too."

"I know you will. You'll do what's right for you."

"Damn nice car." Johnson grinned as he eased out. "Maybe I'll get me one when I grow up. Oh, my regards to your African-American lady friend. Still can't get over that. I'll call you soon."

"Thanks, Robert. It'll be an honor to have you with us."

"I haven't signed up yet, Calloway. Like I said, I've got some thinking to do." Johnson closed the car door and began walking up the driveway. Then he stopped, turned around and motioned for Calloway to wait.

Calloway lowered the window as Johnson walked to the driver's side.

"Mike? When's this war gonna be over for us?"

"Not yet, Robert." Calloway put the car in reverse, looked up at Johnson and forced a little smile. "Call me—soon."

Johnson was left standing in the driveway, a kind of no man's land between everything he cherished and painful news from a time in his life he longed to forget. He turned and walked slowly toward his grandson who was kicking a soccer ball on the manicured centipede lawn. He had some thinking to do.

CHAPTER FIFTEEN:
WEDDING PLANS

"GIVING YOU AWAY WOULD'VE BEEN NICE." Boggs's tone was pleasant, but without emotion.

"Dad." The young woman sitting next to him on the leather sofa sighed softly. Her lip began to quiver, and tears welled in her eyes. "I'm so sorry about all this. Mom's obsessed about you and the wedding—completely unreasonable. But you'll always be my daddy."

"Biologically, at least," Boggs said, smiling as he took her hand, lifted it to his lips and placed a gentle kiss behind the sparkling diamond engagement ring. "Of course, this is about what I expected from your mother. Time hasn't healed much. Except for you, that marriage was just a short stretch of rocky road—my fault, mostly.

"But," he said, "I've got no hard feelings for Martin. He's always treated you like his own. More of a father than I ever was. I guess it's right that he walks you down the aisle."

"You'll still come, won't you?"

Boggs leaned forward, resting his elbows on his knees and lacing his fingers in a prayerful fashion. "I've blocked out the time in December. Now I'll have to juggle things around."

"Everybody will." She sank back in the leather sofa. "Like I said on the phone, Rob has to be in Richmond on the new job by mid-November. The third Saturday in October is the only day we can get the church."

"I've got critical business the end of October." Boggs breathed slowly and shook his head, thinking of the telephone conversation earlier in the day.

The professor had called before his daughter arrived, leaving a message on the answering machine. "Our huntin' trip's on for late October—either the third weekend or Halloween weekend. I'll mail an itinerary and follow up by phone." Lyle's words had seemed innocent enough, but the coded message was clear: Plan Three was coming together.

"There's a lot at stake, Lauren." Boggs blended truth and falsehood as he spoke. "I may have to travel overseas on a moment's notice." Then he put his arm around her shoulder. "Who knows? I might even need a good lawyer like you. But, I think I can make the wedding on the twenty-third."

"By the way." Boggs shifted the conversation. "How are things, financially, I mean?"

"Fine, Dad. Just fine. Martin offered to pay for everything, but Rob and I didn't feel right about it. We saved some money, so we're paying part."

"Listen, Lauren, I don't want to step on anybody's toes." Boggs's thin smile turned to a smirk. "Particularly, your mother's. But I'd love to write a check for everything, and I do mean everything."

"That would be wonderful, Dad." She put her head on her father's shoulder, then she looked up. "But Mom would go ballistic. I was supposed to call you with all these changes. She doesn't know I'm up here, much less telling you everything."

"Writing that check might be worth it," he said, rubbing his chin. "Haven't seen her fired up in a long time." They both laughed. Boggs stretched as he stood then walked to the windows. He stared into the mist shrouding the mountains, shoved his hands in the hip pockets of his faded jeans and leaned against the windowsill. Then he turned to his daughter. "I wouldn't do that to you. I've created enough confusion in this family already, but I'll never stop being your daddy. And just because you're getting married doesn't mean you can't come to me for help. I'm dead serious. I'm just a phone call away."

Lauren stood up, wiping tears from her cheeks as she walked toward Boggs with open arms. "I know you love me. I just hope you'll come to the wedding. Mom will behave. I promise. "I'm so sorry about the way you've been treated, but please, please come. Do it for Rob and me."

"I'll put on an old brown suit and my best humble estranged father face."

"Oh, stop it, Dad! You'll be the best-dressed man there," she said with a smile. "Besides, you don't do humble that well." She walked toward the French doors leading to the deck. "Got to get back to Charlotte."

"You didn't have to come all the way up here," Boggs said, "but I really appreciate it. Now, be careful driving down the mountain in that fog."

"I will, Daddy. I promise." She was still looking at her father as she opened the door, pushing it into a gray-bearded man dressed in a dark suit and clerical collar.

"Oh!" she said, startled by the man standing in the threshold. "I'm sorry."

"Don't be, lass." The Padre tipped his cap and bowed slightly. "I'm the Reverend Roger MacDonald—Padre. That's what my dear friend, Barry, calls me."

"I'm, uh, Lauren Boggs," she said, recovering from the surprise and extending her hand. "I'm his daughter, from Charlotte."

"By way of law school at Chapel Hill, a recent graduate, I believe? Your dad tells me everything. Getting married at Christmas, correct?"

"Closer to Halloween, actually."

"Saints preserve us." The minister chuckled.

"I truly hope so," she replied. "Dad does tell everything, doesn't he?"

"Indeed. He's proud, child. You're the light of his life."

"Okay, Padre." Boggs blushed. "Step aside. She needs to get out of these mountains before dark."

"Drive safely, lass," the Padre said.

"Second fatherly warning in five minutes." She smiled, hugged her father again and stepped outside. "Nice meeting you, Reverend. Look after Dad's spiritual well being, won't you? He needs it."

"I will, lass. I truly will. I'll put in a good word for you, too—precautionary, of course."

She laughed as she disappeared down the stairs.

"A lovely young woman," the minister said. "I see the resemblance and why you're so proud."

"She's a great kid," Boggs said. "Come on in. Something to drink?"

"A soft drink, if it's handy."

"What brings you to my neighborhood?"

"A pastoral call. Mr. Green's been a bit under the weather. A little sur-gery, but he's on the mend. I was this close to you and thought I'd stop." He looked over his glasses and lowered his voice to a whisper. "And you-know-who continues to inquire."

"'You-know-who?'"

"The lovely Ms. Johnson, of course. She's still got you in her sights."

"Come on, Padre. You're not encouraging her?"

"I am not. Told her you're in a serious relationship, someone from South Carolina. Guess I lied a little. Didn't I?"

"For a good cause." Boggs chuckled as he reached into the refrigerator for two Diet Cokes. "Your boss will forgive you."

"I've already asked him, and as you well know, laddie, I'm no virgin in that department." The Padre pursed his lips and sighed. "I'm sure my transgressions are piled as high as old Grandfather Mountain over there.

"Anyway." MacDonald lowered his voice. "What's new with your war story? Will you lads confront those officers?"

The questions caught Boggs off guard, and he paused before answering. "Little chance. My guy—the investigator—says there's nothing legal we can do. The charges are too old. Besides, those two are big shots with mil-lions and political clout. Doesn't leave us much to work with."

"I see." The Padre appeared disinterested as he sipped the soft drink, but suspected Boggs was doing a little lying. The Reverend had been standing outside the open windows longer than Boggs or his daughter had realized. With his eavesdropping, he had got an interesting bit of information—Boggs's mention of critical business in late October. The nosey Padre had made a mental note.

"Thanks for the soda." The Reverend broke the silence. "Time to go."

"No need to hurry, Padre."

"Have to, Barry. It's been a busy day. A busy July as well. And it's hot-ter than usual up here." He pulled a handkerchief from his pocket and mopped his brow. "I'm looking forward to some cooler weather—October, maybe."

"Surely before then. This hot spell's unusual," Boggs said, offering the Padre little else to fuel his suspicions.

"I'm off, Barry. God bless you." Rev. MacDonald grinned as he stepped across the threshold and walked toward the stairs. "Dear God," he whispered under his breath as he trudged down the steps. "The lad's up to something. I can feel it."

CHAPTER SIXTEEN:
THE ITINERARY

A ROAD WEARY BOGGS CLOSED HIS eyes and sank back into the driver's seat of his Range Rover, waiting for the garage door to open. In the two hectic weeks since his daughter's visit, he had been mired in corporate negotiations and travel, and the calendar had flipped from July to August. If he had ever thought Terrell Raines's making him a partner was a gift, trips like the one just completed dispelled that notion.

The first leg took him to New York for three days of meetings with Maywood's asset managers. Next, it was on to London for five days and the yearly review of the corporation's European interests. Then it was back to Atlanta to negotiate timber contracts for the Maywood holdings in the Carolinas and Georgia.

The overhead door groaned open, and Boggs sat up, rubbed his eyes and eased the Rover into the garage. It was good to be back in the mountains. It was as if his body and spirit said thank you for bringing them home. He always looked forward to his homecoming ritual—standing in silence on his deck, inhaling the cool, clean air, and gazing at the ridges and peaks surrounding him. But the ritual had to wait. He had checked his messages earlier in the day between flights at Hartsfield International in Atlanta. The professor had called.

"It's me. Sorry I missed ya," Lyle's message began. "Everybody's on board for our little soiree. Halloween's the only time all the guys can make it. Mark your calendar. I'll send the details."

Once inside the house, Boggs dropped his luggage on the thick oriental runner in the foyer. He walked straight to a marble-topped chest where his housekeeper always left his mail. He ignored the newspapers, unceremoniously pitching the offers of gold and platinum credit cards. He rifled the rest, anxious for something from Lyle when a picture postcard caught his eye. Printed under the caricature of a white-bearded old soldier was the simple inscription: "Forget Hell!" Dressed in Confederate gray, the geezer in the cartoon was draped in the red, white and blue battle flag of The South's lost cause.

There was a hand-written note on the reverse side of the card. "They're still printing this stuff after all these years. Losers, nor their progeny, never forget. It doesn't mean they're right. It just means they can't forget. By the way, I'm sending you a CD of some old Civil War songs done by re-enactors. There's even a stirring rendition of 'Dixie'. I doubt you've heard it played like this."

Boggs furrowed his brow, anxious for Lyle to get on with it. "Where the hell's he heading this time?" He knew the professor's affinity for pranks and riddles.

"Play this stuff on your computer in absolute privacy. Some of it's a bit raucous." Then Lyle's note concluded: "Can't wait for your reaction." He had scrawled "GL" at the bottom.

Boggs was trying to unravel the significance of the card when the door bell chime broke his concentration. He dropped the card on the chest, walked to the front door and smiled at the familiar face on the other side of the leaded glass.

"Afternoon, Mr. Boggs." The deliveryman was dressed in the company's blue knit shirt and shorts. "Package for you, sir."

"Thanks," he said as he signed the handheld computer and handed it back to the courier.

"It's been a while since I've had a delivery up here." With Maywood business, several packages a week were common, and the courier had become friendly with Boggs. "Been traveling, I guess."

"A little." Boggs tone was friendly, but he kept his eyes on the overnight letter, scanning the sender's block on the air bill. It was from Columbia and not Maywood business. Usually happy to talk with the young man,

Boggs was preoccupied with the professor's games and skipped the chit-chat. "I'm really busy—got to handle something right now." He reached in the pants pocket of his custom tailored suit, produced a gold money clip and stripped off a twenty.

"You don't have to do that, Mr. Boggs. We're not supposed to take tips."

"Bullshit. Buy your girl a few drinks." Boggs raised his eyebrows and grinned at the young courier. "Thanks for bringing this out. See you next time."

"Thank you, sir." The young courier turned to leave, then stopped and smiled. "You're the coolest guy on my route, Mr. Boggs."

The front door had barely closed when Boggs pulled the tab on the express envelope. Inside was a compact disk sealed in shrink-wrap. "The South's Greatest Hits" proclaimed the title. A handwritten note was printed on a yellow sticky pad sheet pressed on the CD. "Remember, play 'Dixie' first."

"The South's Greatest Hits, my ass." Boggs smirked, shaking his head as he walked past the three huge windows. Any other time and he would have stood before the expanse of glass to gaze at the mountains. This time he barely looked, heading straight for his office and opening the CD along the way. He sat down at his desk, powered up the computer and slipped the disk into the CD slot. In a matter of seconds he was listening to a stirring rendition of "Dixie". The professor was right. Boggs had not heard it played in years. In his high school and college days, the spirited anthem of the old South had fired up the fans at sporting events, drawing standing ovations. Some would shout a blood-curdling rebel yell or, more appropriately, what they thought was the legendary battle cry of Confederate troops. There was no one left who really knew what a rebel yell sounded like. Long since taboo at respectable public events—a concession to racial sensitivities and changing times—the song seldom got a public hearing anymore. Rousing as "Dixie" might have been in his youth, it failed to stir Boggs now. Times have changed, he thought.

"Welcome, y'all!" The voice came from the computer speakers, abruptly ending his moments of Southern nostalgia. "Please enter the inscription from the post card and your Social Security number to continue this program." The voice was pleasant, almost cheery in an electronic kind of way.

"Graydon, you're one crazy son of a bitch."

"You have twenty seconds to make your entries," the computer voice said. "You may try only once."

"Boggs sat up straight in his chair, carefully typed what the voice had requested and hit enter on the computer keyboard. In a matter of seconds, an aerial photo of Hilton Head Island, Calibogue Sound and the adjacent South Carolina mainland, appeared.

"The base camp is here." The friendly voice spoke again, accompanied by a cursor moving up the May River and marking the camp's location with a red star. "That's the staging area. All activities, following acquisition of the principals, will also be conducted at the camp."

The cursor moved again, back down the May River, across the sound and into a creek penetrating Hilton Head Island, leaving a broken blue line in its wake. "This is the route the team will follow," the voice continued. "The landing is here. They will move on foot to the high ground, cross the golf course, complete their tasks and return to the base camp."

"Extraordinary." Boggs was stunned by the quality of the Lyle's work. Weather, travel, law enforcement, contingency plans and, of course, the money were all covered. The quarter of a million dollars was needed now, the voice said, then detailed how Boggs was to make the funds transfer— from various off-shore accounts via a circuitous computer route that no law enforcement agency nor anyone else could decipher.

Boggs pursed his lips, folded his arms and sighed. Things had moved from abstract, belated feelings of bitterness to a very real and daring plan for punishment and revenge. Early in his conversations with Lyle, Boggs had believed he was strong enough to pull the plug on any plan. Now there was a strange old feeling—first as a tingle, then a full-blown chill. He had not felt this way in years. In his heart Boggs knew there was no turning back. Plan Three had taken on a strange and dangerous life of its own.

"Heady shit, ain't it?" It was as if the electronic voice, seemingly created in the professor's own image, had read Boggs's mind.

"Heady shit, indeed," Boggs said, nodding in agreement with the computer's voice and knowing he had chosen the right man.

Boggs flinched when the doorbell rang; it was as if his secret had been uncovered and that they—whoever they were—had come for him. He hurriedly shut down the computer then took a deep breath and walked from his study, closing the door behind him. When he stepped into the foyer, a woman dressed in a fur coat was peeking through the front door sidelight.

"Good God." he whispered through a forced smile then opened the door.

Ann Johnson, the Floridian who summered near Grandfather Mountain and had an eye for Boggs, cuddled the collar of the full-length mink around her neck and stepped inside. A diamond ankle bracelet and open-toed alligator spiked heels—all courtesy of her most recent ex-husband's alimony agreement—completed her ensemble. The beautiful tanned body beneath the coat was mostly a gift from a generous God, but there were a few well-placed nips and tucks by Boca Raton's best plastic surgeon.

"Sorry Boggs," she giggled as she swished past him and out to the kitchen. "Should've called. The Reverend MacDonald thought you'd appreciate some company up here in this big lonely place."

"Who else is here?" she asked without looking back.

"Uh...nobody," Boggs said, struggling to maintain his composure as her perfume and champagne-laced breath wafted by. "Just-just me."

"Perfect," she said as she twirled to face him. "You won't come to my mountain, Mr. Boggs," she said. Then she pouted as she looked down at her chest. "So, I've brought my...little twin peaks to you." Her sultry words slipped through a sheepish grin, and, without the hint of a blush, she let the mink fall from her bare shoulders and down past her elbows. There was not a swimsuit tan line to be found.

She was not new to this kind of stunt, Boggs surmised, but he just shook his head and smiled. "Looking for a roll in the hay, are you?"

"You won't get me in some hillbilly barn," she said with a wink. "That leather sofa by the fireplace," she said, pointing to Boggs's favorite piece of furniture in the house, "that'll do, but there must be a wonderful king-size in the master suite."

"Your choice Madame," Boggs said, warming to the spirit of her little game. "How 'bout a drink first?"

"It would be my third since lunch," she said, "and I've got to drive my new SL back to Grandfather Mountain."

"Think you can handle those curves?" Boggs asked.

"Not the question at hand," she said, turning toward the sofa and letting the mink drop to the hardwood floor. "Question is: Can you handle these?"

Boggs sighed. "Think I'll have that drink."

—m—

Thousands of miles away, Karl Schiller sipped coffee in his Cape Town apartment, admiring a beautiful leather-bound journal. The professor's gift had just arrived from the United States. There was a nice thank you note inside, recounting the pleasantries of their recent meeting in South Carolina. It had been at that meeting that Lyle had told Schiller to expect the leather journal and what to do with it.

"Karl, you agreed to return to Columbia in October to lecture my doctoral students," Lyle wrote. "The arrangements are made, and I'm holding you to it."

"I like this crazy guy." Schiller smiled, inhaling the rich leather scent of the new journal and dragging his strong fingers across the textured burgundy grain. "One of the great bullshitters of the western world."

In one smooth motion, Schiller pulled a slim knife from his pocket, pressed a button in the ivory handle and a razor-sharp blade snapped forward. He took a moment to admire the weapon's craftsmanship; after all, it was much more than a souvenir. He had used it to slit the throat of an uncooperative Army officer in the Darfur section of Sudan. That was in 2004, but in his mind's eye, it was yesterday, and he had no regrets. Now he carefully slipped the stainless steel blade into the edge of the journal cover, sliding it along as if he were opening a business envelope. When he turned the journal on its side, a compact disk dropped out.

"Ah-h-h." Schiller held the disk between his thumb and middle index finger, admiring the flat piece of highly polished plastic. He was sure it contained his marching orders, and this once-in-a-lifetime opportunity, not the orders, was on his mind. He rocked back in the swivel chair in front of his computer, watching the disk reflect the afternoon sunlight around the apartment ceiling. He snapped the chair into an upright position and inserted the disk into the CD drive. "Now." He spoke almost reverently. "Let's have a look. I will wager that you are my little passport to paradise."

CHAPTER SEVENTEEN:
VENISON STEW

"RISK? AIN'T NO RISK, BOYS." THE wiry little man perched on the running board of a big Ford cab spoke with conviction. "We'll shoot a couple of does—field dress 'em right there. Won't be no noise with my crossbow, either." He tugged on a well-oiled cap he had picked up at the NAPA parts store then smiled at his audience of two. His camouflage shirt was frayed and faded, his blue jeans soiled. The ancient jungle boots on his tired feet should have been tossed years ago. An unfiltered Camel, burning between fingers yellowed by a forty-year habit drooped an inch of ash. Even the blue-green airborne tattoo on his right forearm was fuzzy and fading. The only thing about Vernon Lee "Dinky" Betts that had not aged was his affinity for trouble. "Nobody'll hunt there till the frost," he said. "Maybe not then. Talk's all over the chip mill. You heard it, Hazel."

"Yeah, Uncle Dinky, I heard." Hazel Knight showed little interest, as he bit a peanut butter cracker in half and chased it with orange soda. "Calloway's not opening the hunt club till Thanksgiving. But that don't mean the game wardens won't be pokin' around. The wildlife boys got the same computers the cops got. You get caught, and it's a free ride north. Know what I mean?"

Betts knew what his nephew meant. There was an outstanding warrant waiting for him in Anson County, North Carolina. The charge was assault and battery with the intent to kill. Dinky had come home sick from work one day to find his girlfriend in bed with another man. According to the sheriff's report, "the naked male subject was shot in the legs, left buttock, and scrotum area as he fled the premises of the mobile home." Fortunately, the .20 gauge was loaded with birdshot or the charge might have been murder.

"If I'd wanted to kill him," Dinky had explained to Hazel, "I'd of shot right when they was on the bed. But I got to laughing—even before I picked up my gun. You see, I was watchin' from the hallway. Now, Irene's a big girl—real big. But Neil, the shift foreman over at the mill, he's a little biddy guy. He looked like a monkey trying to fuck a propane tank—I swear! He was all over her, a gruntin' and a groanin', and couldn't get nothing done. I was laughin' so hard I had to duck in the kitchen so's not to let 'em see me. I finally got myself composed, brought that old Winchester to my shoulder and shouted: 'Neil! You rotten little mother!' Man! He hopped off that heifer like she was a hot wood stove. His eyes was big as pie plates. He bounced off that bed like one of them Olympic gymnastic boys. Then he done a summersault right past me in that little hallway. He was a runnin' wide-ass open when he hit the trailer door." Uncle Dinky grinned. "And I do mean wide-ass open.

"So, out of respect for Neil—makin' me laugh and all—I gave him from the trailer steps out to the mailbox before I cut down on him. That—that right there—proves they weren't no intent to kill on my part."

Uncle Dinky's humor was lost on the Anson Country Sheriff's Department, not to mention poor Neil. Dinky got the bad news when he phoned Irene's neighbor the day after the incident. According to the neighbor, the victim spent several painful hours in the hospital while they picked birdshot out of his legs, backside and private parts.

Uncle Dinky was a pretty fair student of jailhouse law, and he understood another conviction would put him in the three-strike category. It could mean a life sentence, and at sixty-three years of age, he had no intention of spending his golden years in a North Carolina prison. So, he fled the Tar Heel State and the assault warrant. He headed west, across the mountains to Tennessee, where he dumped Irene's Buick Regal, then hitchhiked down to Atlanta. He stopped there just long enough to call his nephew over in South Carolina. Hazel not only promised him a hiding place; he wired him cash at Western Union. In a matter of hours, Betts was on a bus heading east to Hazel's place near Cottageville in the South Carolina Low Country.

Hazel was Dinky's sister's boy by her first marriage. He rarely spoke to his mother who was struggling with husband number three, but it had been Uncle Dinky's fishing trips and war stories that bonded the two. He would not turn his uncle away. Hazel owned a logging truck and was under contract to Calloway's wood chip mill near Ridgeland. So, Hazel bought another chain saw and put Betts to work in the logging business. He paid his uncle cash under the table and struggled to keep the rambunctious fugitive under wraps. It was a challenge, even in a rough, rural subculture where probing personal questions were unwelcome and rarely asked.

—⚏—

"Look," Dinky said. "I ain't done nothing but cut trees and ride to the chip mill since I got here. It's time for a little fun. You know how we used to love to hunt and fish together when you was a little boy. This'll be like that."

"Y'all count me in, if you do it," said Earl Mallard, who sat on the ground, resting his back against the left front tire of the mud-splattered truck. His right cheek was filled with a wad of Red Man. He pursed his lips, leaned forward and spat a stream of brown, smelly liquid in the dusty roadbed in front of him. "I can cook venison stew with the best of 'em. It'll taste even better knowing it came from Mr. 'Big Shot' Mike Calloway's place. That SOB repo'd my truck when the chip mill shut down that time."

"See, Hazel! See! Earl ain't scared of Calloway. We could slip in there one night and shoot a couple of deer before dawn. Nobody'd hear us. Shit, we could do it even if somebody was down at the hunt club. Kind of reminds me of my days in the Highlands with the Montangnards."

"Number one," Hazel said, "I don't want to hear that Vietnam shit this early in the mornin'. Number two—a great big goddamn number two—our income depends on the chip mill contract. No work, no money. Understand?"

"Come on, Hazel." Earl, Uncle Dinky's cheerleader in the debate, chimed in. Like Dinky, Earl was no stranger to the state penal system. He had done his time, but, unlike Dinky, Earl was not a candidate for a return trip any time soon. "Just give it some thought. We ain't done nothing like this in a long time. Besides, I'm suspended from that club up at Four Holes Swamp. Can't go back till Thanksgiving Day."

"Break's over," Hazel snapped. "Let's haul wood. Stop talkin' this deer poaching bullshit."

"Poachin' is a mighty strong word, Hazel." Dinky stood up and rolled the bill on his raggedy cap. "We just want to have a little fun, that's all."

"I know you get bored at my place," Hazel said. "But you're puttin' a little money aside. Better than that, you're staying out of jail. Don't mess up a good thing. If it's venison you want, I'll get y'all a hind quarter—maybe even a loin—and you can cook up a big stew."

"It ain't got the excitement of killin' it yourself," Dinky said, folding his arms across his chest and frowning at his nephew. "But I guess you're right, Hazel." He turned toward Earl and winked. "Probably is a bad idea."

"Yeah, Hazel." Earl wrinkled his forehead and jumped in, though uncertain where Dinky was headed. "You're probably right. A bad idea. We could have bad luck and get in a mess of trouble out there."

"Glad y'all are comin' around, showing a little common sense," Hazel said.

Dinky and Earl smiled, nodding their heads in agreement. When Dinky was sure Hazel was not looking, he winked at Earl again. Earl winked back.

Hazel grabbed the driver's door handle and swung up into the cab of the big Ford stake body. "Break's over. Let's haul some wood."

Dinky and Earl shuffled around to the passenger side. Dinky raised his leathery right hand, covering his mouth.

"Halloween weekend." The rumble of the big Ford diesel cranking up drowned out his whisper, but Earl got the message and gave Dinky a thumb's up. "Don't say nothin' to nobody, Earl."

CHAPTER EIGHTEEN:
THE PADRE'S FAREWELL

T HE REV. ROGER MacDONALD STOOD SILENTLY at Scot's Cemetery gate, staring at Grandfather Mountain and the clear blue North Carolina sky beyond. While autumn leaves bathed the peaks and valleys in tribute to a bountiful summer past, there was also a dire warning in this glorious display of seasonal color. Cold and dangerous days lay ahead, and nature's double meaning was not lost on this Presbyterian minister. Finally, his eyes drifted down the slopes and along the ridges, coming to rest on an old maple at the far corner of the graveyard. It was there that his beloved Evelyn had been laid to rest four years earlier. The tree was ablaze in its crimson fall finery, and the reverend was regaled in his best ceremonial garb, that of a Scottish highlander. It was his heritage, to be sure, but he reserved the plaid for special occasions. It had hung in a dark closet since her death, but he wore it today for Evelyn. She had dearly loved things Scottish—the kilt, the leather sporran, and the tiny razor-sharp knife tucked in the top of an argyle stocking. A bagpipe was draped over his left arm. How she had loved the pipes. In his right hand, he clutched chrysanthemums in bronze, burgundy and gold.

The minister had visited Evelyn's grave many times, sharing thoughts and even venting his frustrations. Above all, he would come to restate his undying love. She had been his reason for living. Slowly, reverently, he stepped on the first of seventy-three fieldstones leading out to the grave. It was never an easy walk, and especially difficult today.

Reverend MacDonald's feelings were driven, in part, by a physician's warning. Even more worrisome was the risky venture he believed his best friend, Barry Boggs, had planned, but the minister had made his decision. He would join Boggs's mission with or without an invitation. So, in his highland best, he had come to this peaceful Blue Ridge mountainside to explain himself to Evelyn, and say what could be his last goodbye.

"Dearest Evelyn," he whispered as he knelt before the gleaming white headstone. Then he paused, gently placing the flowers beneath her name. "I am here again, and I am well—except for the doctor's news. It's my heart, lass. It may take surgery to set things right, but that must wait. My dear friend Boggs has cooked up a little job—at least I'm convinced he has—and I'm obliged to go. Boggs saved me after I lost you, Evelyn. He helped me put the whiskey away. We were warriors in our younger days—different armies, different lands—but warriors and brothers all the same. Now that you are gone, he's my best friend on this earth. He doesn't know it, but if he goes on this…this mission, I'm going too. And I must be honest, my love. It's as much for me as it 'tis for him. It's rare, indeed, when an old man gets to act like a crazy lad again and—just maybe—make a difference. And I'm sure it's my last chance.

"You know I miss you, Dearest. Thought I'd never get past those first painful days. I even cursed the Almighty in my grief. Now, at least, I can thank Him for the joy we shared. They were the very best years of my life.

"Maybe I'll visit again. Maybe, I'll join you soon." He looked away from the grave, staring silently into the mountains and smiled. "Surely our Heavenly Father has saved a wee bit of forgiveness for me.

"Evelyn," he said, running his fingers across her name etched in stone. "May the Lord hold you in his loving arms, and may He allow us to meet again in Paradise." The reverend rose to his feet, wincing a little at the arthritis in his left knee, then filled the bagpipe with air. With tears streaming down his face, he sent the prayerful strains of "Abide with Me" flowing down the hillside into the peaceful valley below. It had been her favorite hymn.

"Farewell, my love," he said, making no attempt to wipe away his tears, then he turned and retraced his steps along the fieldstone path, never once looking back.

As he reached the cemetery gate, Mr. MacDonald's thoughts had shifted to the mission he believed Boggs had planned—avenging four U.S. Army Rangers slain decades ago and thousands of miles away. He had never met them, but in that strange camaraderie of combat, he felt he knew them. He had lived that life long before heeding the Lord's call, and it would always occupy a corner of his psyche. Now, if his instincts were right, the next few days could be like old times—exciting and very dangerous. He had prepared himself, at least as well as a seventy-year-old man could, but he had no delusions. These could well be the last days of his life.

CHAPTER NINETEEN:
CLIMB ABOARD

ON THE LAST FRIDAY IN OCTOBER, two days before Halloween, Boggs sat in the predawn silence of his mountain home—the only place he had ever found peace. He was face to face with a personal D-Day for which he bore total responsibility. He brooded; he anguished. For the first time in years, he bowed his head in silent prayer. If God really was out there, Boggs dare not speak to Him aloud, given his history of indifference toward a higher being. When he opened his eyes, he found no relief in the autumn darkness and certainly no reason to turn back. In a matter of hours, this millionaire with everything to lose and decades removed from his warrior days would take up a dead man's sword.

Boggs sat on a stool next to a granite-topped island in the kitchen, his hands wrapped around a steaming coffee cup. It warmed him against the early morning chill, but was no match for the eerie cold slipping in from the past.

As a young sergeant in Vietnam, Boggs had sat at a wooden table in a mess tent, struggling with a letter he hoped would never be delivered. Had he been killed in combat, it would have gone to his mother's little frame house at Maywood. Along with some GI insurance and personal affects, the letter would have been the last contact with her son.

Boggs had composed two letters before midnight, one to his daughter Lauren and the other to the Rev. MacDonald. He hoped they, too, would never be opened. Now he stared at buff-colored envelopes propped against a brass teapot. On one he had penned, "My Dearest Lauren." The other simply said, "Padre." Unlike the one composed in Vietnam, both had been written by an older man, painfully acknowledging risks a young soldier might have ignored.

"You're the light of my life," he wrote to Lauren. "I'm so proud of you and your new husband. What a beautiful bride you were! I just hate I missed so much of your childhood. The guilt will follow me forever." He went on to describe the general terms of his will. There would be a generous bequest to his sister in South Carolina. The mountain house and a half-million dollars would go to the Padre. The balance, about fourteen million, would go to Lauren. He named the lawyer handling his affairs, adding that the attorney had a letter for Dr. Raines as well.

In writing to the Padre, Boggs called the Scotsman his best friend—a comrade in spirit—thanking him for the times shared and prayers offered. "Say one more for me, Padre, then sprinkle my ashes down that hillside where you buried Evelyn. You'll be there someday, too. I'll be in better company than I deserve."

With the grim correspondence behind him, Boggs put the coffee mug in the dishwasher, wiped the countertop and pulled on a dark green cotton sweater and an old leather flight jacket. Then he stepped outside on the deck for a look at his mountains, their huge silhouette barely visible against the predawn sky. He leaned against the black locust rail, breathed in the cold, clean air and swore to God he would be back.

—∾∾—

First light was still hiding behind the mountains to the east when Boggs arrived at the small airfield near Boone. He spotted the familiar shape of his twin-engine Cessna parked near the flight office. The ground crew had followed his instructions to have the plane ready at first light. Two shadowy figures caught his eye as he eased the SUV into a parking space near the office. Boggs recognized the first man—flight line worker Gary Morgan—when he walked under a security light.

Morgan glanced up at the Rover's headlights and waved in their direction.

Boggs pulled a shoulder bag from the back seat, locked the SUV and walked toward his airplane. The second person, hidden by the darkness and light fog, was still a mystery, and Boggs watched the stranger as he drew closer. Seconds later the figure emerged from the fog—ramrod straight, dressed in faded camouflage, a faded tan beret and jungle boots. A time warp, Boggs thought. It could have been someone out of an Errol Flynn movie, but who? "Sir, can I help you with—" Stunned, Boggs stopped in mid-sentence. "Good God, Padre!" MacDonald looked twenty pounds lighter with close-cropped hair and a clean-shaven face except for a neatly trimmed mustache. "What's going on here?"

"A little trickery. I'll admit it, Laddie, but I've got damned good intelligence."

"Meaning?"

"I'm not here to see you off, Barry. I'm going. This is it. The mission. Payback for those lost boys." He stepped closer to a speechless and wide-eyed Boggs. The Padre bent his six-foot-three frame over, whispering in his best friend's ear. "I owe it to you, and God knows I'm doing it for the souls of those lads. We're warriors and brothers—all of us. We're pledged to take care of our own."

"Padre." Boggs shook his head, turning his back to the minister then looking at his watch. First light was breaking over the mountains. "I love you like the father I hardly knew—the brother I never had—but have you lost your mind? Please, please go home. Don't do this. It's not your fight."

The minister put his hand on Boggs's shoulder and sighed. "Tis my fight, Laddie," he whispered with a smile. "I refer you to a place you seldom go—my Boss's handbook. You've heard the words. Saint John, the fifteenth chapter, thirteenth verse: 'Greater love hath no man than this; that a man lay down his life for his friends.'"

Boggs said nothing as he stared into the darkness across the airfield. Tears welled in his eyes, and his lip quivered. He knew the words, their beauty and the pain. He had heard them on dusty landing zones, in the muddy rice paddies and under the dark green cover of jungle canopies. When he regained his composure, he turned to his friend. "Padre, it would kill me to hear those words read over your body. This isn't a golf weekend. Do you understand me?"

"Perfectly," the Padre said. "We've both made trips like this in our time."

"That's what worries me. Our time's passed for things like this." Boggs checked his watch again, glancing at the sun's thin edge creeping above the mountains. There was a schedule to keep. The professor would be waiting at a small airfield near Camden, South Carolina. He looked poker-faced at the Padre and sighed. There was no other solution. "Climb aboard."

—⁂—

Lyle looked more like a cartoon character than a professor, leaning against a fence post outside the airfield office. He was dressed in beige chinos, sky-blue sweater and a bright red polo shirt. He wore a golf cap he had picked up at The Masters three years ago and tortoise shell sunglasses. The ever-present Budweiser was chilling in a bright Koozie dangling from his right hand.

"Look at that bugger." The Padre smirked, nodding toward the professor as Boggs taxied the Cessna to the small terminal. "How'd you like to have that going with us on a job?"

Boggs fought back a smile, his first of the day. "Let's offer him a ride. There's plenty of room."

"Bloody right," Padre said. "We'd be landing every ten minutes for him to make a pee."

Boggs chuckled as he hit the brakes, bringing the Cessna to a stop. "Got to find our passenger, Padre. Stretch your legs. Hit the head. Get something to drink, and don't wear that beret. And, Padre, if anyone asks you, you're on a hunting trip."

"Aye, Laddie—varmint-hunting." MacDonald winked, then climbed out of the plane and walked toward the airfield office.

Boggs headed straight for the professor, grinning at the golf attire. "What's with the clothes?"

"Tourist camouflage, son." The two men shook hands, but Lyle held on, pulling Boggs closer. "Didn't know you'd signed on Field Marshal Montgomery."

"It's a long story," Boggs said.

"Can't wait to hear it," Lyle said.

"He's former SAS. Got more combat ribbons than my team put together."

The professor frowned. "And he's ninety fuckin' years old."

"In his seventies, actually. The short version is he's my closest friend from the mountains. Says commandos are all brothers. My fight's his fight—all that stuff. Besides, once he figured I was up to something, I couldn't leave him behind. He won't get in the way. I promise."

The professor pushed the Master's cap back on his head and furrowed his brow. "It's your money, honey, but if something happens to that old fart…Goddamn, son. Who's gonna explain it?"

"He's a widower, Graydon. No children. Just his church near Grandfather Mountain. They think he's on a birding trip."

"*Birding*?" Lyle raised his eyebrows.

"Yeah. You know, bird-watching."

Lyle shook his head. "Great damn cover story. Who wouldn't believe that?"

—⁂—

About thirty minutes into the flight, Lyle leaned around from the copilot's seat and looked at MacDonald. "Reverend?" Lyle asked. "Haven't heard much from you back there."

The Padre had been quiet since the trio left Camden. "Nothing much to say, Professor." MacDonald, who had been dozing behind dark aviator glasses, pulled himself up in the seat and stretched. "Just enjoying the peace and quiet—catching a few winks on the way to wherever it is we're going."

"I understand you've got quite a military record."

"I put in my time."

"I'm sure you know this trip could be a difficult one."

"Won't be the first." The Padre leaned forward. "By the way, Professor, Barry tells me you've got quiet a record in the spy business."

"Mostly teaching," the Professor replied.

"Indeed," the Padre said. "My work's been mostly preaching."

Boggs kept his eyes trained on the flight instruments, doing his best to suppress a grin as he listened to the sparring between his passengers.

"What do you know about the place we're going to land?" Boggs took the conversation back to business.

"The airstrip belongs to a crop duster," Lyle replied. "Good record with the FAA. Excellent reputation in the area. Flew choppers in the Army. I'm paying him handsomely to use his airstrip, and he's tickled shitless. Said he even cut the grass. The airstrip is plenty long enough for this plane. It's halfway between Walterboro and the hunting camp. There's a Jeep waiting for us, too. We're just in the Low Country for some golf. Some birding, too, I guess…thanks to the Reverend. You know, getting away from the wives for a few days."

"I'm a widower," the Padre said matter-of-factly.

"Just fake it, Reverend." The professor smirked. "Just fake it."

"There is one other surprise," Boggs said, turning to the professor.

"And what the hell could that be?" Lyle snapped.

Boggs sat quietly for a moment, looking out at the blue sky in front of him. Then he turned to Lyle. "Calloway and I will be going in with the team at Hilton Head."

The professor said nothing at first then took off his Master's golf cap and placed it carefully on his knee. He creased the crown just above the yellow map of the United States embroidered on the hat. He shook his head slowly from side to side as a painful grimace stretched across his face.

"Mother of God," the minister whispered as he sat back in his seat making a compact version of the sign of the cross.

The professor gently lifted the cap from his knee, and, without warning, slapped it against the passenger window—once, twice and a third time—before carefully placing it back on his head. "Why?" he whined. "Why, goddammit? Why? With all this work—meticulous planning to keep you safe and get this job done—you want to be John fuckin' Wayne. We're already taking Friar Tuck along for the ride.

"Can't I talk you out of this?"

"No way," Boggs said.

"Well," the professor said, "it is your money."

"Yes, it is." Boggs replied.

"Well, then," the professor whispered as he pulled his Master's cap down over his eyes. "I think I'll take a nap now. Oh, and Padre?"

"Yes, Professor Lyle?"

"Would you dust off your very best prayer for the lost and feeble-minded and fire it off with us in mind?"

"Actually," the minister said, "I prayed it several times since you slapped the window with your cap."

CHAPTER TWENTY:
SIDETRACKING SECURITY

"For God's sake, Michel! Take the weekend off." Cain was annoyed with his security chief, Michel Regout. "Philippe can handle it. Mr. Ha has his own people. "Just be back Sunday evening."

"Only if you're absolutely sure, sir," Regout said. The exaggerated concern oozed out with his French accent. He knew Cain would give him the time off. He had already rented a car and planned to rendezvous with his pretty new friend near Charleston. He had spent the lunch hour in one of Harbour Town's finest haberdasheries, outfitting himself with crisp cruise wear. He purchased tropical wool trousers, a silk jacket, and two striped cotton shirts—end-of-the-season stuff on sale. He had whined until the shop's tailor agreed to rush the alterations and deliver the clothes to the villa two hours later.

"Go, before I change my mind," Cain said. "There's no security risk here. Couldn't be safer. This is Hilton Head."

"Thank you, Colonel," Regout said. "It is so very kind of you."

Listening to the conversation, Philippe Marceau immediately saw through Regout's ingratiating antics. Marceau rolled his eyes skyward—behind the colonel's back, of course—then stuck his forefinger in his mouth as if to gag himself. Marceau was not happy that the security chief was leaving his ass-kissing duties behind for Marceau to handle. Regout was pushing it, but not to the point the old man would change his mind.

"Michel?" Cain called to Regout as he left the villa and walked toward the garage.

"I've seen your…southern belle twice." Cain lowered his voice to a whisper. His face was stern. "She seems to be a nice girl with a family here on the island. So, you damned well better behave yourself. Any misconduct could reflect on my excellent reputation, and I won't tolerate it. Do you understand?"

"Completely, Colonel."

Cain alluded to an incident five years earlier; Regout had been accused of abusing a young woman on the French Riviera. Because he was a valued employee, and more importantly, to protect his own reputation, Cain had put cash in the right hands, not only keeping Regout out of jail, but preventing a scandal. The colonel also made it clear the chief's indiscretion was his first and only one.

—⁓—

Charleston was two hours up the coast by Interstate 95 and U.S. Highway 17. The Isle of Palms was just a short drive across the Cooper River. Regout had double-checked the directions the girl had given him, and they were accurate. With a fresh haircut at a salon near Hilton Head's second traffic circle, he was dressed and coifed to conquer the southern belle he had met ten days earlier.

From that moment at sunrise when Caroline Deschamps was jogging on the beach and stumbled into his arms, the two had been inseparable. There were early morning runs, lunches when Regout could get away, and frequent phone calls. He had even invited her to the M&H villa on two occasions. Both times she appeared in the skimpiest of bikinis, sunning herself beside the pool under the Indian summer sun. Regout interpreted it all as sexual advances, although she refused his requests to go out with him at night. She said she was visiting her parents at their island cottage with her brand new divorce papers in hand. It had been a stressful time, she said.

"I must spend time with mother and daddy while I'm here." Her explanation traveled on a smooth, syrupy southern accent. "My seeing another man so soon would surely upset them. Come up to Charleston," she had begged. "I have a cottage at the Isle of Palms. We can have some privacy, and it won't worry my parents."

Regout embraced her logic. He ate it up, by God. He was mesmerized—sun-streaked blond curls, green eyes catching the October sunshine, a stunning figure and prospects for a romantic getaway. After all, he had seen *Gone with the Wind* and other films portraying the American South with its genteel women and chivalrous men. He had lapped up the sweetness of the waitresses, the shop girls and the polite older ladies he had encountered on the island and in nearby Savannah. That barrage of Southern hospitality contributed to the ease with which he had dropped his guard.

Far from the Old South of Rhett Butler and Scarlet O'Hara, Hilton Head was a place apart from the rest of South Carolina. Once an island refuge for the wealthiest hunters and outdoorsmen, its Southern orientation was now more geographical than social. Today's Hilton Head bustled with well-heeled northerners, some Carolinians and others from all points on the compass. The water separating this island playground for the rich from the mostly rural mainland was far wider than it looked.

Regout drove the 108 miles to Charleston in about two hours. Once he crossed the Ashley River Bridge, he was in what some affectionately—others mockingly—called The Independent Principality of Charleston. Miss Deschamps's directions included a side trip through the historic downtown section. Regout was surprised by the city. It was not old by European standards, but it had Old World charm. He drove past the beautiful homes on the harbor. He saw The Battery, Rainbow Row and the old, narrow market off East Bay Street. Today's shoppers found persons of all ethnic hues hawking everything from cheap trinkets to the most expensive Low Country gifts and wares. Tourism, not human oppression of the past, was the main concession of the day.

Regout was happy to get away from the stiff and arrogant Cain. He considered Ha an irritant as well, nicknaming him "the little weasel". He smiled as he looked at the incredible view of Charleston Harbor, the USS Yorktown and Fort Sumter off in the distance. Thank God, Regout thought, he was away from his bosses for the weekend.

The side trip had been nice, but Regout was bored with the cultural detour. He was ready for the weekend ahead and getting naked with Miss Deschamps was at the top of his very short list. Cain's admonition not withstanding, Regout fully intended to enjoy himself.

It was on the bridge that his cell phone jolted him back to reality. Caroline had his private number, but he did not expect her to call. He had also given the number to Marceau in case of an emergency. He tensed, letting it ring a second, third and fourth time. Finally, he answered. "Regout."

"It's Caroline, Michel." She poured on a gracious a helping of southern syrup. "Havin' a nice ride, darlin'?"

"*Tres bien*—very good, Caroline," he said. "I am looking forward with great anticipation to our weekend."

"Me too, Sweetie. But there's been a change of plans."

Regout's heart nearly skipped a beat. "Is something wrong, my dear?"

"Not at all! Things are wonderful! I have a surprise for you. Forget the Isle of Palms for now," she said. "Have you crossed the big bridge yet?"

"I am on it, actually," Regout said.

"Good. Follow the same directions I gave you. Stay on Highway 703. Just look for Bright's Cove. Takes about ten minutes. Turn right and follow the street to the docks. I'll be waiting in front of the most beautiful boat. We're going on a little cruise—just the two of us. It's my surprise!"

"How wonderful, my darling. I will see you very soon." Regout was back on top of the world. His fears Cain would call him or Caroline would cancel had drifted away on the gentle salt breeze. Now they would have a romantic evening on a private yacht. "Tremendous!" he said as he squeezed the steering wheel of the rented Chevy.

Regout was at Bright's Cove in a matter of minutes and found the docks without any trouble. She was waiting, smiling and waving at her date who seemed overcome by it all. Maybe it was the anticipation, but she was more beautiful than ever, dressed in a white cotton fisherman's sweater with matching jeans and her blond curls flowing in the breeze. She ran up and hugged him when he got out of the car.

"This is fantastic," Regout said. "Is this your boat?"

"Don't I wish. It belongs to some business friends. Let's get on board. We'll take the Intracoastal Waterway out to the harbor then have drinks and a lovely dinner. You'll see the city and the islands from the water. I'm so glad you came."

The boat was a bright white Bertram 54 sport fisherman with the latest navigation equipment and amenities. With its size and power, it was perfect for a late afternoon cruise. The crew of two included a young, muscular captain with close-cropped hair. His tan was dark and rich even though summer was over. A second young man, equally fit, served as the steward.

"Would the lady and gentleman like a cocktail?" the steward asked as the captain eased the boat into the waterway.

"Isn't it just beautiful out here today—nice and cool," she said. "I'd love a bourbon and water."

"A Scotch on the rocks, please," Regout said, polite as ever.

The boat had been the *Sure Thing* just a few weeks ago, but her new owners renamed her the *Million Dollar Baby*. All her records were current. All safety equipment was in perfect order, meeting or surpassing U.S. Coast Guard standards. The crew's qualifications were impeccable.

Regout was well into his first Scotch as the boat entered the harbor, when his eyes felt tired. Maybe it was the drive from Hilton Head. He had never been prone to seasickness, but he felt a little unsteady.

"This is wonderful, Michel." Miss Deschamps put her arm around his waist, giving him a gentle squeeze. "Hope you're not too tired, driving up here and all."

"I am quite well, *merci*, Caroline," he said, though he was beginning to feel dizzy. "Some water, please," he said.

The steward smiled, handing Regout bottled water. He took a few sips, but he was in trouble and he knew it.

"Sweetheart, let's go below where it's private. Hope I'm not being too forward." Poor Regout heard every word the lovely Miss Deschamps said, but any thoughts of drawing her close and taking her in his arms were dashed. He was sinking fast.

"My hands," Regout said as the water bottle slipped from his grasp and bounced on the carpeted deck. "They're numb." He was frightened and it showed. "My vision is blurred. Help me, please!"

"You'll be okay, Michel. You're not going to die. At least not today." Those reassuring words were the last Regout heard from Caroline Deschamps or anyone else in American waters.

—⚏—

"Appears to be down for the count, Captain." Regout's southern belle spoke in a crisp, clear British accent. Gone were the sweet Southern syrup and magnolia blossoms. The Belgian had missed something important, linguistically speaking. Caroline Deschamps, his beautiful belle of Charleston, was only sort of southern—if one stretches the region to include the south of London. She was, in fact, Jane Bennett, a princess of dialects and, until recently, a resident of Great Britain. Without letting this poor, swooning bastard touch her beyond holding hands or putting his arm around her shoulders, she had him precisely where she wanted him. He was head over heels in heat and had left Hilton Head, convinced a generous helping of Southern-style sex—what ever that was—awaited him at The Isle of Palms. Ironically, this girl from England had lured the Belgian with the same ante bellum silliness that had worked for decades. Local boys, Yankees and fellows from around the world had fallen for it—still do, for that matter. Regout had bought the performance hook, line and sinker, as they say down South.

"How's the weather?" she asked.

"Fine, ma'am," the captain said as he turned the boat toward the open sea.

"How long to the rendezvous point?"

"Fifty-five minutes, ma'am."

"Thank you," Bennett said. "Now let's get the cuffs on *Monsieur* Regout. If he were to wake up, we'd have a very dangerous fellow on our hands." The steward cuffed Regout, checked his vital signs and made sure he was resting on his side. The last thing Bennett needed was for him to vomit and choke to death.

"Captain," Bennett said when she returned to the bridge. "Would you please send a message exactly as I dictate it?"

"Yes, ma'am."

"The message is: 'The gang's all here. We're on time.'"

The captain followed the script perfectly, and moments later the reply came back over the radio loud and clear: "Wonderful news. We'll be waiting."

"Perfect." She smiled for the first time since Regout went down. "Will this thing go any faster?"

"Yes, ma'am." The captain grinned, nudging the throttles as Bennett stood beside him on the bridge. He could tell she was enjoying the ride. He had been told—warned, actually—that she was beautiful but all business. They were right on both counts.

The ride to the rendezvous point passed quickly. The steward kept an eye on Regout, but nothing changed. He was dead to the world. Bennett went below several times to see for herself. There were two fishing boats off in the distance, a freighter and an orange-striped U.S. Coast Guard boat, but there was nothing else in sight as the sport fisherman closed on the rendezvous point. The captain checked his global positioning system periodically, but he remained on course. It was hard not to be with a satellite guiding the way.

"We're within two miles, ma'am," the captain said, pulling back on the throttles. "There's a small boat—right there. Looks like he's heading toward us."

Bennett brought the Navy binoculars to her eyes in time to see a light signal from the smaller craft. At her direction, the captain signaled him back. The two boats closed on each other.

"She nodded to the steward. "Let's bring our passenger up on deck, shall we? They'll want to finger print him to verify his identity."

"I thought he might be fish food, ma'am," the captain said. It was the first time he had offered an opinion about anything since the excursion began.

"Not this lad, Captain." Bennett smiled. "He's going to a land far, far away. No more Southern girls for him.

"Oh, Captain," she said, getting back to business. "I don't expect trouble, but please keep your weapons at the ready during the exchange. You lads do know how to use those things?"

"Yes, ma'am. We were both Rangers—First of the Seventy-Fifth. Tours in Iraq and Afghanistan." He nodded toward the steward. "We've both got Glock 40 cals and he's got an M-16. Some heavier stuff down below, too. We're ready," he said as the smaller craft pulled alongside the *Million Dollar Baby*.

A short, gray-haired man, speaking with a French accent, looked up from the smaller boat. "I believe we have packages to exchange."

"We do, indeed," Bennett said. "Would you like to come aboard?"

"Thank you *mademoiselle*," the little man said, trying to keep his balance as the smaller craft bobbed up and down. Once aboard, he pulled a photograph from a small black briefcase. It was old, but it appeared to be Regout. The little man looked at the unconscious form and back at the picture again. "*Bon*," he said. His associate fingerprinted Regout and compared the new prints with the set pulled from the briefcase.

"*Oui, monsieur*," the associate said. *C'est lui*,"

"Now," the short man said. "I must look at his back. There should be a scar—about four centimeters." He rolled Regout over and unceremoniously jerked the new cotton shirt out of his trousers. "And it is there. *Tres bien*."

"You may now inspect this package, *mademoiselle*." The older man handed Bennett a black canvas bag.

"Thank you, *monsieur*," she said. "Please excuse me for a few moments."

Jane Bennett could feel the excitement, but dare not let it show. She had rehearsed this moment so many times she did it without thinking. She took the bag and walked slowly, but deliberately, down below. She put the bag on the table in the small galley and checked for anything unusual—including booby traps—then opened the latch.

"Thank you, Heavenly Father," she said softly. Inside were rows of neatly banded hundred-dollar bills. She inspected the money exactly as Professor Lyle had trained her to do. No counterfeit problems that she could see. The $2 million was all there.

"*Merci, monsieur*," she said as she came back on deck.

"*Merci, mademoiselle. Merci beaucoup*," he said, bowing slightly. "It is pleasure to deal with such a professional and, may I say, most beautiful woman."

"You are most kind, *monsieur*."

The old man's associate summoned a third man from their boat. He was a tall, heavy-set black man who dragged Regout from the Bertram to the smaller craft.

Bennett's captain and steward were discreet, but their automatic pistols were cocked and ready inside their jacket pockets, and the exchange concluded without a hitch.

"*Bonne chance*—good luck—as you say in the English." The old man waved his soft wool cap as his boat eased away.

"The same to you, *monsieur*," Bennett said then turned to her captain. "Let's get out of here the second they're clear," she whispered. "By the way, how long will it take to get to Hilton Head?"

"Not too long, ma'am," her captain said with a smile. "We should have you there in time for a late dinner."

"Thank you, Captain," Bennett said, smiling as she looked into the wind and reflected on her first day at work on a new and very different job. The assignment had been far, far easier than she could have imagined.

CHAPTER TWENTY-ONE:
THE DEADLY DOGLEG

O N A LATE OCTOBER NIGHT, WHEN the dog days of summer were faint, humid memories, two small boats drifted silently where the May River flows into Calibogue Sound. Karl Schiller, his stern face distorted by black and green camouflage, crouched in the bow of the lead boat watching his GPS system. While it functioned perfectly, Schiller liked to check landmarks and range markers for himself and lifted the night vision binoculars to his eyes and panned around the sound to the South Carolina mainland and back.

A West German by birth, Schiller was a soldier of the world by choice. In his early forties, he was tanned and tempered by dangerous work in Africa and the Middle East. He was addicted to adventure and got high on its cash rewards. While comfortable with this assignment, the location was worrisome. Then there was that personal angle—the hook Boggs had used to draw him into the mission, but, as always, it was risks versus rewards for the pragmatic Schiller. The professor had dangled seven figures, and Schiller had taken the bait.

Boggs sat in the bow of the second boat, rubbing a smooth leather holster that held the Colt .45 he hoped never to fire. He looked over his shoulder at Calloway, giving him a quick smirk from behind swirls of camouflage.

"Good to go, Barry?" Calloway whispered into the breeze as he tapped Boggs on the shoulder.

"Yeah." Boggs half-chuckled. "If Carter had left his letter unwritten, we could be home planning our retirement."

Both men smiled as they stared off in the darkness.

Even with his misgivings, Boggs was committed, but unlike Schiller, the money was less important. It was more about retribution and revenge. Boggs believed closure was little more than a psychological catchword for whiners, and it had barely crossed his mind. The possibility of losing everything—fortune, reputation and even his life—was very real, but nothing could distract Boggs now. A decades-old feeling of excitement, anger, and fear had swaggered out of a distant Vietnamese jungle and chased the "what ifs" away.

"Just our little boats out here," Schiller said in a whisper that rode the salt breeze like a lonely surfer then disappeared. Confident his GPS squared with his visual sightings, he raised his hand and the outboards fired in unison, pushing toward the barrier island between the sound and the open sea. His eyes darted between the green glow of the GPS and the big island, watching its shadowy silhouette play hide and seek in the patchy fog. "Danke," he whispered. He was truly grateful for the good weather. Except for the Atlantic's notorious autumnal mood swings, little had been left to chance.

The trip through the backwater had been uneventful, though crossing the Calibogue in small boats had worried Schiller. But to his surprise, the purring outboards had easily pushed the Zodiacs over the gentle swells in the sound.

Good fortune continued as the boats entered a tidal creek that pierced the big island in a ragged, twisting fashion. Two kilometers into the little waterway, Schiller spotted the marker left by earlier reconnaissance and gave the signal to kill the engines. Their beachhead—in this case, a simple, weathered dock—was a hundred meters away. His boats had not been seen, and his thoughts skipped ahead to the return trip. It would be challenging, but his head cleared quickly. "First things first," he muttered. The hard work ahead must go without a hitch. Still, he was buoyed by the silence—broken only by a gentle salt breeze and unconcerned mullet skipping across the creek. The island waited quietly, save a chorus of crickets singing joyfully in an unknown key and the solitary hoot from an owl further inland.

The first boat hit the dock with a muffled thud. The second was close behind. Within seconds seven shadowy figures disembarked, towing the rubber boats alongside the dock and into the marsh grass.

It had been a textbook start—hiding the boats and moving inland—and all went well until one of the seven startled a whitetail doe hiding along the trail. The doe bolted from its bed. The man raised his shotgun, and, for a split second, seven months of elaborate planning rested on the tip of a tense trigger finger.

"Bullshit!" Ernst Krueger cursed in a whisper he fought to restrain.

The others, with weapons at the ready, breathed a collective sigh. Two of them smiled.

"Good English, Krueger," Schiller whispered, injecting humor into a situation where tension was already building. "Language class goes well, yes?"

"Ya, ya, Herr Oberst." Krueger snarled in his native tongue.

The leader's smile faded, he raised his hand, and the team came to silent order as if the deer incident had never happened.

Each man wore faded tiger stripes—jagged black and green camou-flage favored by special operators in Vietnam—and soft boonie caps in the same pattern. Schiller had argued military clothing was melodramatic at best and downright risky at worst, but his suggestion of jeans and sweat-shirts had fallen on deaf ears. Professor Lyle had insisted the uniforms set the tone for the message being delivered, even if it was decades late.

Krueger carried a Mossberg pump—short barrel with an extended magazine—perfectly legal in gun shops across America. A Colt .45 was holstered on a web belt circling his thick waist. The pistol could have been legal, but the silencer was not. The burly thirty-two-year-old was Schiller's point man, and contrary to the leader's remark, his English was excellent.

Schiller cradled his Heckler & Koch machine gun like a newborn. A Colt was tucked in a shoulder holster under his left arm. The professor had selected the .45 as the handgun of choice. It was readily available, it standardized ammunition, and Lyle had guaranteed these weapons could not be traced.

John Withers, the little Englishman, was the radio telephone operator who shadowed Schiller. He carried two cellular telephones in his shirt pockets—one a prepaid burn phone, the other a satellite phone. A laptop computer was packed in a black nylon case and strapped under his left arm. For contact within the team, each man would switch on a radio headset closer to the target. Withers' other pocket bulged with an M60 hand grenade which he carried each time he took the field. When asked why, he would just smile. "Tradition, lads—comforting in a tight spot."

'Doc' Vervoort, the Belgian, was next. A skilled medic, he had performed surgical procedures on previous missions. Along with first aid supplies, nylon cord, heavy tape, and plastic zip ties were stored in his assault pack. Then there was the black cotton robe, a white muslin sheet, and two Halloween masks—a craggy witch's face and a ghoulish gray skull with open mouth and sagging, hollow eyes. Like the rest, Vervoort carried a Colt. After all, he was a warrior first; he had taken more lives than he had saved over the years.

Ex-Legionnaire Jean Dessart was the last of Schiller's handpicked men. His mother was Dutch, his father Belgian, but he never said where home was. It had been years since he had one. Dessart carried a soft, waterproof rifle case with a tranquilizer gun inside. The case also held a straw kitchen broom and a striped golf umbrella.

Krueger moved out on the leader's hand signal, and the others slipped into place without hesitation. Schiller was next, with Withers and Boggs in tow. Vervoort and Calloway followed with Dessart covering the rear. Slowly, cautiously, they slogged their way in from the creek. The footing improved as they moved toward higher ground, and it was there that they stepped into the gun sights of the first sniper.

Barely breathing, the sniper watched Krueger though a night scope mounted on an M-16. It would be simple; after an easy head shot on Krueger, he could drop the second man before the first hit the ground. When Krueger stepped within ten meters, the sniper gently pressed a World War II-style clicker.

Krueger froze.

"My God." Bobby Spencer shook his head as he slipped the clicker back in his pants pocket. "I'm nuts for joining this party." A thirty-year-old Australian, Spencer had been hiding in the brush for hours before the boats had landed. He and Jackie Cao, a second sniper positioned further inland, had been dropped off together. Their ghillie suits, decorated with native foliage, were invisible in the dense cover.

Schiller knelt beside Spencer. "How are things, Bobby?"

"Very well, sir," Spencer said, "but bloody boring."

"Anything from Cao?"

"Nothing, sir." Spencer's whisper was raspy and low. Then he smiled. "Some rather robust farting from Jackie's position four hours ago. To be fair, it might have been wild boars—swamp gas, possibly."

Schiller smiled. If there was a team member who felt obliged to find humor in a tense situation, Spencer was the man.

"Seriously, sir." Spencer tried to control the sheepish grin behind the camouflage. "Just one little moment around 4 p.m. Two white-haired blokes walked through the brush—came within ten meters. They cursed a lot but didn't see me." The sniper handed Schiller a golf ball with a slice that seemed to smile back. "Looking for this, no doubt. How 'bout a round after work?"

"Not this time," Schiller said.

Spencer adjusted his position after the team arrived, still covering Schiller's back but he moved toward the creek to watch the Zodiacs. The boats were out of sight, but a motion detector would beep in Spencer's headset if anyone got too close.

On the move again, the team snaked its way along a narrow footpath bordered by longleaf pines, wax myrtles, bays and live oaks. Autumn was slow to reach the coast where hardwood leaves clung to branches for dear life while blessing this odd collection of travelers with dark, dense cover. Evergreen needles provided a soft pathway on the forest floor, and the cat-quiet column cautiously picked up the pace. Within minutes they were close to the end of the woodland head that jutted up from the creek like a long triangle.

Kreuger stepped carefully to within a few yards of where the woods stopped. Cao was hiding to his right, waiting and watching as Spencer had. Krueger flinched when he heard the clicker and muttered under his breath. "I hate those little fuckers."

Schiller raised his hand, bringing his team to a halt. He lifted the binoculars to his eyes, searching for anything his sniper might have missed.

Cao, who had been watching the target constantly, motioned the leader to move closer.

"What have you got, Jackie?"

Cao frowned. "Two very big Rotweillers, sir. Unless they're penned up, we'll have to put them down."

"Two?" Schiller asked.

"Yes, sir. Our spy missed the second one."

Schiller had his own feelings about the spy, but it was pointless to discuss it now. The dog was the leader's first surprise, but experience had taught him to expect others.

Schiller motioned to Withers for the cell phone. He flipped it open and dialed a stored number.

"Yes?" The answer came on the fourth ring from twelve miles inland.

"Gang's all here, sir. Lovely evening." Schiller raised his eyebrows.

A few seconds passed, and the response came wrapped in a soft, southern drawl. "Y'all be careful and take care of my 'ol boys."

Schiller recognized Professor Lyle's voice and smiled, but it vanished as an old, haunting chill raced up his spine, drawing his shoulder blades in. Goose bumps appeared on his arms and his legs tingled. It always happened when the shooting was about to start. No matter how many times he had been here, and there had been many, nothing in his psyche could match that feeling of anticipation and fear. He had tried drugs, but they paled when compared to a sprint along the treacherous wall of combat. One slight slip, one misstep, and the game could be over—forever.

Once again, the leader turned his night vision glasses toward the end of the woodland head; it was there the forest ended abruptly, and lush, green Bermuda turf began. The twelfth green was barely visible, one hundred-twenty yards to Schiller's left at the eight o'clock position. Its white sand bunkers coaxed what light they could from the night sky. The twelfth tee box was two hundred yards to his right at five o'clock. Simply put, his team was hiding in the bend of the dogleg. It was not a perfect place for a crossing, but it was the only place for this one. He focused on the target—a stone and cypress villa forty yards across the fairway. Night-lights glowed softly at the corners of the lavish hideaway, and a clear blue pool, sheltered decks, and winding pathways confirmed its coveted privacy.

Schiller sighed at the wealth spread before him then a thin smile crossed his lips. "Hilton Head," he whispered, "where we take up Carter's sword and I become very, very rich." A stoic expression replaced the smile as he nodded to Boggs and Calloway then glanced at his men—the ones he counted on most. They pledged allegiance to no country, but to a man, would risk death for Schiller—if the price were right. And this time it was.

Once again, Schiller gazed across the fairway toward the objective. He breathed in the rich salt air then let it out slowly as he rubbed the face of an old green Army watch his father had worn in Vietnam. At this moment, a mission conceived in Boggs's loyalty and fueled by others' greed, had found a life of its own. Schiller was poised to lead his first raid on American soil.

CHAPTER TWENTY-TWO:
THE ASSAULT

S CHILLER FOUGHT BACK A SMILE, PLEASED with his decision to cross the fairway. He knew Lyle would call it poor management—selfish and foolhardy—but the second guard dog had forced a change in plans. Another man would be needed at the rear of the villa, and he would be that man. Schiller could feel the rush, and in return, he would gladly take the professor's heat. Still fighting off the smile, he signaled his men to move closer.

"Krueger, your task is unchanged." Schiller spoke in a whisper. "If there is a dog outside, Cao takes the shot from that large tree." He pointed to a tall longleaf pine. It would be a shot of about thirty meters. "You and Dessart grab the guard when the dog falls.

"Oh," Schiller said, turning to Krueger. "Leave the dart gun with Cao. You won't need it."

"*Bon. C'est bon,*" Dessart shrugged as he whispered through a frown.

"Doc, you'll stay with Cao, and Mr. Calloway," Schiller said. "Inform me by radio when the dog is destroyed and the guard subdued. Withers and Barry will go with me to the rear entrance near the swimming pool."

"A different wrinkle, sir?" Cao, half Vietnamese-half African American, took a few moments to absorb the changes then turned to Krueger and Dessart. "No moving about, you two. When you think I've got the shot, the bullet's already gone."

"We'll move on Vervoort's command—the word 'go,'" Schiller said, turning to Krueger and Dessart. "Remove the infrared entry key from the guard's pocket, and go inside. Take Mr. Ha in the right front bedroom. Withers and I will clear the pool area and enter the rear of the house."

Then a wry grin curved the corners of his mouth. "Don't shoot me or Mr. Boggs—if you expect to get paid.

"Withers, Barry and I will take Col. Cain. His suite is on our right as we enter the rear of the house. Doc, you cross after giving us the 'go'. Cover Dessart and Krueger then block the driveway." He paused, wiggling two fingers at each man. "I need two healthy hostages. Try not to kill anyone, shall we? Questions?"

"Phones and alarms?" Withers asked.

"No changes. Turn off the alarm as planned. Call forward the villa number." Schiller nodded, twitching slightly as the old familiar chill worked its way down his neck and arms. "Excellent." His eyes panned the circle of men in the darkness, making contact with each pair of eyes. "*Bonne chance, mes amis.*"

Seventy meters away, Cain was spending the evening in his private suite consumed by the M & H expansion plans. The big leather chair was soft and comfortable, but he had been reading for two hours straight and needed a break. He tossed the reports on the ottoman, stood up and stretched. He pulled off his reading glasses, frowning as he rubbed the bridge of his nose where they had been dug in for too long.

"Philippe!" Cain's voice broke the silence as he stuck his head out of the door to his suite. "Double Scotch-rocks. In my room." As always, it was an order, not a request.

"Certainly, sir," Philippe said with a sigh. He had drawn double duty for the weekend, filling in for Regout, the love struck security chief, and the villa's full-time chef. Both had the long weekend off. Despite his fatigue, Philippe was back in a flash. The drink was exactly as ordered. He opened his mouth to ask Cain if he wanted anything else when his pager beeped twice. It was linked to the villa's security system.

"Excuse me, sir." Philippe fumbled with the pager. "I must check this right away."

"Indeed." Cain was sarcastic. "No telling who's out there. A deer eating shrubs the last time—at 2 a.m. Roused those fucking canines, ruining a good night's sleep. Please. Check that right away."

"Yes, sir. Excuse me, sir." Philippe left Cain leaning against the door to his suite, nursing the Scotch, then hurried to a small office near the center of the villa just off the kitchen. It was the security center where video monitors kept constant watch over the grounds. If the motion detectors picked up an intruder, strategically placed cameras would zoom in, flashing the picture up on a screen in the little office.

"Wonderful," Philippe said, watching a monitor display pictures from the fairway side of the villa. One intruder was wearing a black witch's cape. A tall, pointed cap sat atop her head, and a craggy witch's mask covered her face. She straddled a straw broom. Her partner was dressed as a ghost— flowing white sheet, ghoulish mask with hollow eyes and open, misshapen mouth. Escapees from a Halloween party, Philippe assumed. The witch had fallen, and was now sitting up and waving the broom over her head. The ghost was spinning a striped umbrella like a pinwheel.

At least someone was having a good time, Philippe thought, and for a moment, he wanted to join in. "We have two intruders—harmless, I believe," Philippe said, walking past Cain who was standing in the doorway to his suite. "Probably strayed from a party and stumbled into our perimeter. This will only take a few minutes. I'll get Big Red." Philippe walked toward the garage, whistling for the huge rottweiler—a four-legged insurance policy, considering the weekend's skeleton security staff.

"Good," Cain snapped without looking up. "I'll have steak and eggs when you've finished out there. Medium rare. Soft-scrambled."

"Certainly, sir." Philippe wondered if his workday would ever end. "If I'm not back soon, you may wish to ask Vinh. He's a better cook than I am, anyway. He's out checking the property around the pool house. He should return in a few minutes." At least he was supposed to be surveying the rear areas. Philippe had no respect for Mr. Ha's two bodyguards. They behaved more like playmates than security professionals.

"Just hurry." Cain sipped his drink, walking toward the ottoman where a pile of reports was waiting. He frowned as he brought the tortoise shell half-glasses up to his eyes. He picked up the document he had abandoned a few minutes earlier, but quickly tossed it down. His craving for steak and eggs was stronger than his hunger for corporate knowledge—for the moment, at least. He walked out of his suite into the huge living area that ran the width of the house, heading for the kitchen to freshen up the Scotch and wait for Philippe.

Cain rarely showed interest in household security matters—particularly on Hilton Head. He relied on Regout for such things. But tonight, he paused outside the little office with the video monitors. He saw the two costumed intruders and Philippe on the screen and leaned inside for a closer look. They pranced around, twirling the broom and umbrella and making fools of themselves. Cain could not hear the conversation, but the silent video belied any problem. Philippe was guiding the intruders back into the fairway. They were waving and nodding in apparent agreement but clearly keeping their distance from Big Red. Cain could understand that; he was uncomfortable around the guard dogs as well.

"That's that," Cain said, turning away from the monitor and satisfied Philippe had things under control. Behind him, a sudden bright blip appeared in the dark gray field of the video screen. It was the muzzle flash from Cao's rifle thirty meters across the fairway. Big Red recoiled from the bullet's impact as it shattered his skull. The dog's collar fell from its near headless neck, landing at the feet of the stunned bodyguard. He still had a tight grip on the dangling leash when he turned toward Dessart and Krueger, his puzzled face searching for an answer. The only thing—the last thing—Philippe heard was Dessart's rock-like open palm striking him squarely on the ear, reeking havoc on his equilibrium, and rendering him helpless.

"Trick or treat, *mon ami*," Krueger said as he blindfolded Philippe. Dessart bound and gagged him.

"Go—repeat—go." Vervoort whispered into the tiny microphone as Philippe went down. "Nice shot," Vervoort said, patting Cao on the shoulder as he slipped out of the tree line and scampered across the fairway toward the villa.

Krueger and Dessart were heading for the front of the house before Vervoort reached the other side, and he watched them long enough to see that a second security guard had not trailed out after Philippe. Convinced they were safe, he veered off to their right to cover the driveway and garage.

Schiller, Boggs and Withers had crossed the fairway before the others engaged the security guard and were hiding in the rough just outside the villa perimeter. When they got the "go", they slipped between two clumps of pampas grass into the manicured garden at the rear of the compound. Seconds later, they were behind the pool house, shielded from the lights at the rear of the luxurious home.

Vinh was unarmed, sprawled across a chaise lounge on the patio between the pool and the raised rear deck. He had just taken a drag from his third marijuana cigarette of the evening, holding his breath for the full effect. Surprisingly good weed, he thought, considering the source—an enterprising young bartender he always over-tipped at a bar in Sea Pines.

Another giant rottweiler sat on the fieldstone steps and had just raised his head and began to growl, sensing something might be wrong.

Schiller had also taken a deep breath, waiting to experience his own morbid kind of high. It came in that dead calm between inhaling and exhaling when he gently squeezed the trigger on the H&K, hitting the huge rottweiler in the head. The big dog tumbled down the steps to the patio beside the pool, collapsing in a bloody heap of black and tan fur.

"Go," Schiller whispered. Withers and Boggs rushed the stoned security guard who was almost cooperative as they bound, blindfolded and gagged him.

"The rear is clear." Schiller whispered into the headset mike.

At that instant, Cain bolted through the patio doors, spraying automatic pistol fire across the patio where Boggs and Withers had subdued Vinh.

Cain cut hard right, jumped the four-foot patio wall and rolled through a low hedge of Indian hawthorn. As startling as it was, Schiller barely flinched. "Doc," he said calmly into the microphone, "primary target heading your way. Careful. Withers is behind him."

Schiller moved cautiously toward Boggs and the security guard.

"Jesus!" Boggs muttered as blood trickled down his arm. "I didn't need this."

"You okay?" Schiller asked.

""It's my left arm," Boggs said. "I think it went right through."

"There's more blood," Schiller said.

"It's the guard's," Boggs said, reaching under Vinh's chin in search of a pulse that was not there. "He caught a round in the head. Cain killed his own man."

"Leave him, Barry," Schiller said in a calm, businesslike tone. "The cleaners will handle this. Let's get inside—through the patio doors. Can you watch my back?"

"Let's go," Boggs said as he pulled the Colt from its holster and held his wounded left arm close to his side.

Schiller stepped inside as Krueger and Dessart burst into Ha's bedroom suite. There was a single, deafening pistol shot followed by two quick rounds of suppressed fire. There was one loud scream then moaning.

"Clear," Dessart said, panting into his microphone. "All clear."

"We're inside," Schiller said, moving cautiously toward the front of the villa then looked into Ha's bedroom. "Are we all right here?"

"Yes, sir." Krueger's tone was almost apologetic. "Unless we shot the wrong one."

The acrid smell of gunpowder clashed with fragrant cut flowers in a tall crystal vase on the bedside table. A frail Asian man with thick gray hair was leaning against the headboard, gripping the bedpost for dear life. He wore nothing but a blood-spattered white silk pajama shirt. His face was twisted into an expression of fear like a macabre photograph from a Vietnam scrapbook. The naked body of a younger Asian was sprawled across the bed. The top of his head was missing. A 9-mm automatic dangled precariously from the corpse's bent right forefinger.

"I'm not sure what those two were up to," Krueger said, winking at the same time. Then the smile disappeared. "The young one nearly got me when we rushed in, but Dessart capped him, thank God.

"The old man's not hurt—physically, anyway," Krueger said. "Pretty shaken, though."

"Doc?" Schiller asked, speaking into the headset mike.

"We have Cain, sir," Vervoort said.

"Good." Schiller spoke without emotion. His eyes darted from Krueger to the mess in Mr. Ha's suite. "Get some trousers and shoes on Mr. Ha. Locate the spent shell casings. Meet the others out front and look at Mr. Boggs. He's been hit."

Withers bounced through the patio door, pulling on surgical gloves as he walked toward the security office. He quickly removed the videocassettes from the recorders, then cleared and reset the alarm system. The telephone rang a few seconds later, and Withers answered as if he expected the call.

"M & H International," Withers said in his best fake French accent. "Philippe speaking."

"Hilton Head Police Department," the caller said. "Your alarm sounded. What's your code and do you need assistance?"

"It is three-five-five-seven-three, and *non, monsieur*," Withers said. "*Merci*—thank you—but we need no assistance. Some partygoers entered our grounds by accident, but they have left. I was slow in resetting the alarm—I am so very sorry. Our supervisor, Mr. Regout, is on holiday. I would be most pleased if he is not told about this."

"Don't worry, son." The compassionate dispatcher spoke with a slow southern drawl. "You boys just remember, now. The city'll fine y'all for false alarms."

After Withers hung up, he call-forwarded the villa telephone to a predetermined cellular number. "All finished lads," he said, smiling as he walked briskly toward the front door. "Golden Globe performance, if I say so myself."

Vervoort was waiting with Cain at the bottom of the steps where the colonel was handcuffed, gagged and blindfolded. "I tripped him as he dashed between the corner of the house and the garage. He dropped his pistol. Not much fight left after he hit those cobblestones. Just bumps and bruises," Vervoort said. "He'll be sore tomorrow. I suspect the biggest injury is to his pride." Vervoort motioned for Schiller to step away from their prisoner.

"Mr. Boggs should be okay," Veorvoort whispered. "The round went through his forearm, but missed the bone. Bleeding's about stopped. I've patched him up, but he'll need to see a doctor at some point."

"Let's move out, then," Schiller said. "I allowed seven minutes once the guard went down," he mumbled as he looked at his watch. "Remarkably, we are still on schedule."

—⚋⚋—

"Ready." Schiller whispered into his headset.

The message was for Cao, who was waiting impatiently for his commander's words. Cao scanned the fairway to his left and right and the villa property across from his position in the tree line. "All clear," he whispered back.

Krueger and Dessart double-timed across the fairway with Mr. Ha between them. When he showed the slightest sign of stumbling, they lifted him off the thick turf without missing a step. It seemed like an eternity to Cao on the one side and to Schiller on the other, but it took just seconds for the trio to cross and disappear in the tree line.

Vervoort and Schiller were next, with Cain between them and Boggs covering their rear. When the colonel stumbled the second time, Vervoort simply slung the man over his shoulder in one smooth motion and double-timed toward the trees.

Only Withers remained on the villa property, finishing the last bit of security work. Once he stepped outside the invisible electronic fence, he used the remote control taken from Philippe to reset the system. When he finished, he placed it and the infrared key next to the dead guard dog. The cleaning crew would expect to find it there.

"Okay, ready." Withers whispered into his microphone.

When Cao gave the appropriate response, the Englishman sprinted across the fairway to safety.

Cao chuckled when the breathless Withers rushed into the woods just a few feet from his position.

"You all right, son?" Calloway asked.

"Yes … sir," Withers said, bending over with his hands on his knees, trying to catch his breath. "A little winded … That's all … Bloody hate … being the … last man out."

"Let's hit it, then—if you're up to it." Cao smiled. "The others are down the trail. We'll cover the rear."

"Let's go," Withers said, his breathing having slowed to near normal. Then the three slipped into the darkness of the woodland head. "If Krueger spooks another deer," Withers said, "I just hope it's at the front of the column."

The three reached the team halfway between the fairway and the boats, walking up as Vervoort prepared to give Cain and Ha injections. "Just a little cocktail to relax you," he said.

Cain resisted, but he was no match for his captors. Mr. Ha remained silent when Vervoort took his arm, barely flinching when the needle went in.

"It won't knock them completely out," Vervoort whispered, "but they'll be very pleasant to be around for the next hour or so."

Schiller walked over to Boggs. "How's the arm?"

"Bleeding's stopped," Boggs said. "I'll be fine."

"Let's move out," Schiller said, glancing at his watch. They had made good time through the trees on the high ground, but it was slow going when they hit the marshy area near to the creek. Cain and Ha had also slowed them down, but the leader had allowed for the condition of his hostages.

Krueger had taken the point, as usual, stepping out ahead of the team. He did not expect to be surprised by another deer, but would bet his paycheck Spencer was waiting out there somewhere with the dreaded little clicker. Krueger had vowed not to let it startle him again, but Spencer had the advantage. Not only did he blend into the woods, he could see the team in his night scope. But there would be no clicker this time. Spencer was already with the boats, busily attaching new South Carolina boat registration numbers, along with the round, tri-color decals of the S.C. Department of Natural Resources.

Schiller and his men pulled on the green jackets worn by state game wardens and donned the baseball-style caps with the department's tri-color seal. There was a photo identification card and badge, along with a South Carolina driver's license, for each man—Boggs and Calloway included.

With the game warden disguises covering the tiger stripes, and with Cain and Ha lying prone under blankets on the floor of each boat, the team moved silently into the creek. Chances were slim they would see anyone on the water at this late hour, but the professor had convinced Schiller the disguises were a necessary precaution. As the sputtering outboards fired up in the darkness, he crossed himself and prayed the costumes would not be put to the test.

CHAPTER TWENTY-THREE:
STARK REALITY

PROFESSOR LYLE PACED NERVOUSLY IN THE damp grass between the small barn and Calloway's cabin, stopping when the whine of the outboard motors fell silent in the darkness. Moments later, the rubber boats thumped against the creosote poles supporting the dock, and Lyle looked in its direction, hoping for a glimpse of his team and their prisoners. Twenty paces closer, their identities became shockingly clear.

"Jesus Christ," Lyle said as he stared at Cain and Ha. They were blindfolded with their hands zip-tied behind them, shivering as they shuffled along in the cool night air. The wind chill from the twelve-mile boat ride and their wet, mud-splattered clothes had made it worse. They had fallen several times, stumbling through the woods and marsh between the villa and the island creek. Both were cut and scratched from briars and the switch-like tree branches, waiting in ambush along their forced march.

"Pathetic," Lyle mumbled, as he stared at the Vietnamese. His once white silk pajama shirt was a mass of rips and pulls and covered with blood. His blue jeans and sport shoes were muddy. Lyle raised his eyebrows, shaking his head at what he had created. It was a real-life drama, far from the abstract embedded in a computer disk, and this could not be erased.

As for Cain, the professor had expected a much larger man. Standing about five-feet-nine, the retired colonel was slim and mostly bald. His expensive sports clothes—impeccable just two hours earlier—were snagged and tattered. He said nothing as he looked straight ahead with his head held high. Arrogant to the end, the professor thought.

"Captain? Step over here please." Lyle spoke politely to Schiller as the column turned toward the little barn fifty feet from the cabin. "There are dry clothes inside for these gentlemen. Please see that they are cleaned up and changed. You'll find blankets in there as well."

"Yes, sir," Schiller said and motioned for Krueger to handle the professor's request.

"Maybe some coffee or a soft drink for our guests would be nice. No doubt they've had a somewhat stressful evening."

"Somewhat!" Cain shouted as he looked in the direction of the kind voice. "You shoot my people and drag my partner and me through a swamp! You call that somewhat stressful? Skip the bullshit!" His lip quivered at the failed attempt to restrain himself. "Get to the goddamned point."

"Please, Colonel." Lyle spoke in the same gentle tone. "If we skip the bullshit, as you've characterized my attempt to keep things relatively civil, you and Mr. Ha might just get a bullet through the head. And while there are those among us who would gladly pull the trigger, we're all committed to a different outcome. Now, if you'll excuse me, the captain will look after your immediate needs. A medical officer will treat any injuries you may have sustained. I'll return later to explain why you're here. And, please, let me ease your fears." Lyle was smiling, although his captives could not see it. "Your prospects of getting out of this alive are quite good. With some cooperation, you'll be back in your lovely beach house in a day or so."

Cain was ready to blurt out another angry comment, but stopped short. The precision of the assault at the villa assured him his captors were not amateurs. Had they wanted to kill Cain and Ha, they would have been dead in a matter of seconds. Cain believed they were especially shrewd as well; the kidnappers had grabbed both partners. The object had to be money, and Cain knew the corporation would give it up gladly—millions if necessary. M&H International had a strategy in place for that. The kicker was the partners' ability to survive. Even he knew most kidnap victims were murdered, with or without a ransom payment.

"I'd like some coffee," Cain said, taking a few moments to calm down and try to clear his head. "I think Mr. Ha would prefer tea—if you have it."

"Yes, yes please." The shivering little man spoke for the first time since his abduction. He turned his head left, then right, toward his partner's voice, but he saw nothing but darkness from behind the blindfold.

At the very least, Cain knew his partner was alive. He also knew Ha was terrified. It reminded him of their risky business during the Vietnam War. It was decades ago, far away and, ironically, far less dangerous than this deadly little predicament. Then, like now, Ha was the nervous one while Cain prided himself on being the steady, driving force. He was determined to reprise that role tonight.

"We have coffee," Lyle said. "We'll have it for you shortly, along with the dry clothes. You'll be inside—out of this chilly night air—and those blindfolds may come off, eventually."

Schiller and Boggs had walked away from the group, and Lyle motioned them toward him.

"How'd we do back there, Karl?" Lyle nodded toward the big island beyond the marsh and Calibogue Sound.

"We can add murder to our list of potential charges," Boggs snapped before Schiller could answer.

"Uh…quite well, sir," Schiller whispered in a polite tone. "Two guard dogs shot dead. Regrettably, we killed one bodyguard. A second died as result of friendly fire."

"Friendly fire? Are you kidding me?" Lyle asked in amazement. Then he turned to Boggs, spotting the bloodstain on his camouflage shirt. "And what the hell happened to you?"

"Cain shot one of his own men while shooting at us," Schiller said. "Barry was wounded as well."

"What?" the professor asked. "Where?"

"Left forearm. It's nothing," Boggs said. "Let's move this thing along."

"The third man was taken without incident," Schiller said. "He was bound and gagged and placed in the kitchen pantry awaiting the cleaners."

"Our cleaning crew has already checked in," Lyle said. "They were on the job minutes after you crossed the fairway—damned professional. Cost us out the ass—fifteen grand to stand by, plus ten grand a head. By now, they've hauled the dead away to God knows where, but they're gone forever—guaranteed. They'll release the third guy when we tell them to. Now, we've got a lot of work to do.

"Very good work Captain," Lyle said, patting Schiller on the shoulder. "We'll talk later. Needn't discuss this with Barry's old Rangers. He'll handle that."

Schiller nodded and walked off to check on his men.

After the mercenaries guided the prisoners toward the barn, Boggs placed a friendly, but firm grip on Lyle's arm just above the elbow, steering him away from the others.

"I had fair warning Graydon," Boggs said, "but the killings take this thing to a new level."

"I agree," Lyle whispered. "One man dead is one too many. I'm truly sorry, Barry. But it could've been you or Calloway. You almost got wacked, for God's sakes. That would've been a son of a bitch to explain. Anyway, we knew the risks."

"I know," Boggs said. "But we're in too deep to get weak now, so let's get on with it."

"We'll do our best," Lyle said. "Pretty much logistics and finance from here on out. We do have to get home safe and sound, of course." He smiled at Boggs, zipped up his field jacket and turned toward the cabin. "Guess it's the chill—maybe the excitement and those two beers, but my bladder's working overtime. After I pee, we'll convene our legal proceeding."

Boggs walked to the barn where Vervoort and Krueger were guarding the prisoners. Once satisfied they were in good shape, he walked back through ankle-high Bermuda, found Calloway and headed to the cabin where the old Rangers were waiting.

Johnson and Vasquez sat on the front porch of the cabin. Vasquez sat with his painful legs dangling over the edge and resting his back against the cedar posts that supported the cabin's porch. Each man was poker-faced, masking any emotions or memories dredged up by this tense and troubling scene. They were too far away to have heard the conversation between Lyle, Schiller and Boggs.

The Rev. Macdonald had found a comfortable, creaky old rocking chair inside the cabin. He pulled it up to a propane gas heater whose warm, gentle purring took the edge off the room. He was there for Boggs if, and when, he needed him.

"Those guys looked pretty rough coming in," Vasquez whispered as Boggs climbed the weathered pine steps to the porch. "How'd it go out there?"

"Cain and Ha seem to be okay. None of our guys got hurt." He paused a few moments. "The M&H men had a real bad night."

After a long silence, Johnson spoke first. "What happened, Barry?"

"Worse than I'd hoped." Boggs's tone was matter-of-fact. "We had to kill one of Mr. Ha's bodyguards. Cain accidentally shot and killed one of his own men. That's where I got this scratch on my arm."

Two sets of wide, inquisitive eyes stared right through him—the same eyes that he had seen years earlier during a very real, very public war. Now their very private, almost surreal war of retribution had exploded into the stark reality of death, danger and culpability. Each man had lived with such risks before. Ironically, the stakes could be even higher on this short tour decades later.

"Too bad," Johnson said, "But we knew it could—knew it would. So, what does it do to the mission?"

"Nothing," Boggs said. "Nothing at all. We're on schedule—if anything, a little ahead. Schiller's men are setting the camp perimeter as we speak. Cain and Ha should be cleaned up in a few minutes. Keep quiet when we get inside the barn. We can't afford for those two to hear our voices—especially yours, Calloway. It's a long shot, but Cain might recognize you." Boggs took a step back and eyeballed the old Rangers from their black berets down to their green canvas and black leather jungle boots. "Costumes look damn good, don't they?" A nervous smile worked across his face. "Tomorrow's Halloween."

The old Rangers remained silent.

Boggs shrugged. "Poor attempt at humor. It's all in the timing, I guess."

CHAPTER TWENTY-FOUR:
JUSTICE DELAYED

"H EY! Y'ALL BOYS LOOK LIKE SHIT!" The Southern accent was an oddity coming out of Krueger's mouth, and the big German laughed out loud, taking pride in his twang as he hustled his prisoners across the damp grass. Seconds later, the soft Bermuda stopped, and Cain and Ha stumbled against the edge of a hard, gritty concrete slab.

"Step up, please." Krueger switched to his German-accented English. He led the bound and blindfolded men across the slab then slipped a commando knife from its sheath just above his right boot.

Ha moaned when Krueger slid the cold steel blade between his tattered shirt and his cool, damp skin.

"Not to worry, Mr. Ha," the soldier said. "Just cutting away your filthy clothes." Krueger guided the razor-sharp blade through Ha's pajama top and jeans in smooth, swift strokes. In seconds, Ha stood shaking in the darkness, wearing only the blindfold, zip ties on his wrists, and muddy sport shoes.

Cain sensed what was happening. When he got the same treatment moments later, he accepted the humiliation without comment.

"*Desole messieurs.*" Krueger threw in a little French to add to the confusion. "Your new clothes will feel better after a shower," he said, turning a garden hose on both men and smiling as the stream hit them. Although the water was warm, they gasped as it splashed over their bodies, struggling to keep their balance as Krueger switched the hose from one man to the other.

"Get on with it, Sergeant," Schiller said as he raised his eyebrows and sighed. Like everything else, he knew hosing down the prisoners had been part of the professor's plan—calculating, often brutal, in his orchestration of each scene of the mission. This crude shower where hunters dressed freshly killed deer was just another insult on a night that would be filled with them.

After the shower, Krueger cut the zip ties, hurriedly dried off the blindfolded hostages, and helped them into orange prison jumpsuits. Each was marked with a large white "P" on the back and a smaller one on the breast pocket. He bound the prisoners' hands with new zip ties and led them toward the barn door.

"Where… are… we?" It was Ha's first coherent sentence since the mercenaries burst into his bedroom suite two hours earlier. No one answered. He cowered as he was pulled along, taking the short, uncertain steps of a suddenly blinded man.

—ᴍ—

Cain held his head high as Schiller led him into the barn. He was boiling inside, but asked nothing of his captors. He was determined to maintain his dignity, even in the face of hopelessness. He felt the hard-packed dirt floor under the flip-flops they had put on his feet. He flinched as the creaking door snapped shut, and he took his first deep breath of the musty air inside. The old barn had smells of its own: hay bales stacked to the rafters in stair step fashion, burned tractor oil mixed with the dirt floor, and the acrid odor of fertilizers. Within seconds, Cain's self-confidence gave way to unexpected fear that rushed in from long, long ago.

"My God," Cain whispered. "Not this damned place. Not now." Although blindfolded, his brain converted the smells to memories, taking him to a place that still struck terror in his heart. For a few moments, he was back in the old barn of his boyhood in southern Nebraska. It was not a nostalgic visit, but a nightmarish flashback to the place where three generations of Cains had taken their children to the proverbial woodshed. The conduct of his forbears was only hearsay, but the scars from his father's thrashings were real. Although he never set foot in that barn after he left for college, it still haunted him. How could his father—a decorated World War II veteran and pillar of his church—beat a child for no other reason than family precedent?

Cain's mind was still stumbling through the Nebraska barn when rough, hard fingers loosened the blindfold, jolting him back to his real-life nightmare. The light appeared as bright as a camera flash, and he dropped his head and turned away, squeezing his eyes shut to avoid the glare. Then he blinked furiously as he regained his distorted vision.

Ha reacted slowly to his first encounter with light since the abduction. He simply hung his head and closed his eyes, shielding them from the naked hundred-watt bulb hanging from a rafter. It was the only illumination in the barn. He was still groggy from the injection, but he managed to babble, "Where…am…I?"

"You're safe, Mr. Ha, quite safe." It was the polite, southern voice again.

Both Cain and Ha looked up. A man was sitting behind a sparse table twenty feet away.

"Sit, gentlemen. Please." The professor pointed to ancient, wooden folding chairs that had been placed behind the prisoners. He nodded to Schiller. "Captain, you may free their hands."

Cain rested his elbows on his knees and rubbed his wrists where the zip ties had dug into his skin. His vision cleared slowly, like a developing picture from an instant camera, and it was a troubling sight. The polite voice came from a figure clad in tiger stripe camouflage and a black beret. An expressionless hockey mask hid his face. When Cain's eyes adjusted, he thought he saw a red and black Airborne Ranger scroll on the man's left shoulder. Was the costume simply coincidence—something grabbed from an Army-Navy surplus store—or was there a message here? The answer came when he looked to his right where four men sat motionless on a wooden bench. Each was dressed exactly like the man with the polite voice—tiger stripes, black berets and Airborne Ranger scrolls on their left sleeves. Hockey masks in black, yellow, white and brown, hid their faces. Cain never had wartime flashbacks or nightmares, but in the silence of a musty barn with blacked out windows and masked Rangers, he knew he was in the middle of one. He sensed this was more than a kidnapping, but why? The military uniforms and the prison clothes suggested some kind of tribunal, but what did they really want?

"Gentlemen—Colonel Cain, Mr. Ha—you may address me as General." Lyle was smiling behind the mask as he ran his fingers along the collar of his camouflage shirt, stopping to rub the embroidered black star. He had never been a general before and liked the idea, even if it was just a brigadier. He stood and walked around in front of the table. "I hope you'll be returning to your lovely villa soon." Then he turned, nodding toward the four men sitting on the bench. "There is, however, business to attend to first, and we'll get right to it. I'm not much on formalities, but this is, in fact, an inquiry of sorts. And my apologies for the primitive accommodations, but I assure you justice will be served." With his hands clasped behind his back, Lyle walked slowly toward his two defendants. "Colonel, your are James B. Cain, are you not?"

Cain was puzzled, taking a few moments before he answered. "I think you know very well who I am."

"And you, sir." Lyle turned to Ha. "You are Nguyen Ha, are you not?"

Ha looked up and finally spoke. "Yes, General. I am Nguyen Ha."

"Very well, and it's true you served together during the Vietnam War?" Lyle did not wait for an answer. "Colonel, you in intelligence, and Mr. Ha—Captain Ha at that time—you were an ARVN liaison officer serving in a U.S. Army infantry brigade. The Ranger unit associated with the brigade at that time was Tango Company, 75th Infantry. You two officers worked closely for a number of months, including the entire month of December 1970. Is that correct?"

"That is basically correct." Cain's will and voice were getting stronger, but he was not about to elevate this character by calling him general.

"Yes, General," Ha replied, without hesitation.

"Well then. Now that we've established who you are, I'll proceed with the charges against you."

"Charges!" Cain jumped up from the folding chair, only to be yanked back down by Krueger who was standing directly behind him.

Boggs and his former Rangers shifted uncomfortably on the bench.

"Who the hell do you think you are?" Cain asked. "Charges! What charges?"

"Colonel," Lyle said in a condescending, professorial tone. "I know this is traumatic, but y'all are gonna hear me out, so restrain yourself. Another outburst and we'll gag you. You may speak when I've finished. Do we have an understanding?"

Cain spoke only after a long pause. "We do."

Ha slowly nodded in agreement.

"Thank you, gentlemen." Lyle returned to his polite voice, then the barn door creaked as it opened. "Good. I believe there's coffee, Colonel. And I'm happy to see we've actually found some hot tea for Mr. Ha."

CHAPTER TWENTY-FIVE:
REFRESHING MEMORIES

"E LEVEN DECEMBER, 1970." THE PROFESSOR SPOKE reverently as he cut his eyes toward Boggs and the old Rangers on the wooden bench. "More than four decades ago." He sighed and shook his head, then looked straight at Nguyen Ha.

"Was there anything unusual about that day?"

"It's difficult to remember, sir." Ha spoke clearly; the drugs were wearing off. "It was a very long time ago."

Cain glanced at his business partner, shrugged, and said nothing.

"But there was something unusual." The professor continued, playing to the men on the bench. With his arms folded across his chest, he turned slowly to Cain. "Colonel? Who insisted on changing orders for Ranger Teams 3-1 and 3-2?"

"I don't know what you're talking about." Cain was annoyed. "Orders were changed, patrols cancelled, all the time."

"Indeed," the professor said. "Last-minute intelligence—concocted by you and Captain Ha—forced the change of orders that day."

"What are you're talking about?"

"It'll come back to you, Colonel. Captain Ha—your buddy, right there—said he got a tip from one of his spies. According to his intel, the original LZ's were too hot for teams 3-1 and 3-2. Intel from you two guys—brigade level intelligence and liaison officers—moved those Rangers a couple of kilometers south of their original LZ. It was just enough to protect your illicit operation and get those boys clobbered."

Cain slouched in the chair, folding his arms across his chest and crossing his legs at the ankles. "Nothing unusual. Situations changed. Plans had to change."

The professor turned away from Cain and Ha, clasping his hands behind his back. He walked slowly toward the table and chair twenty paces away. "Plans… had… to change." He shook his head then faced the business partners. "Seems you boys got a touch of amnesia. May I refresh your memory?"

"Will it speed up this charade?" Cain had regained his arrogance.

"I'll keep it simple." Lyle spoke coldly, but never raised his voice. "You were handling drugs and military equipment in those days. Because of your self-serving lies, the teams' orders were changed. The next day, those brave men were dropped damned near on top of the enemy. Four died. Every other soldier was wounded. Some still suffer today."

"Officers issue tough orders. Soldiers die." Cain sounded like a military lecturer. "We were not smugglers. Besides, no court will listen to this garbage."

"Excuse me, Colonel." Lyle remained calm. "That's bullshit where I come from. A soldier heard you two bragging about the switch you pulled. He'd been tracking you for years since the war. You're damned lucky he didn't kill you himself." Lyle tapped his forefinger on papers stacked neatly on the pine table. "It's all right here. It all checks out.

"As a matter of fact, intelligence agencies are watching you now. You may look clean on the surface, but I'm betting there's plenty of dirt. Your people spend a lot of time around bad guys in the Middle East and, more recently, in South America. Arms deals, military computers, high tech gunrunning—stuff like that. Somebody close to M&H is always sniffing around the edges. Your big shot friends have helped keep the heat off, but I've got a tip for you: your gook buddy's freelancing in Africa and Asia's gonna catch up with y'all real soon."

"That's preposterous!" Cain sat up straight, clinched his fists, and glared at his interrogator. "You're nuts, and don't insult Nguyen Ha like that."

"Fuck you, Colonel!" Lyle screamed, rushing over to Cain and getting right in his face. "There's nothing politically correct about this proceeding!" Pigeons roosting in the rafters took flight, searching for a safer perch near the peak of the tin roof. Lyle was still screaming. "Never thought about the lives you ruined—families left behind. They're still hurting. You bastards ought to be shot!"

"Sergeant!" Lyle walked straight to the Rangers on the bench and put his hand on Johnson's shoulder. Then he pulled a .45 from the holster on his hip, cocked it and began working the room like a wild-eyed tent evangelist. Instead of the Good Book, he waved the Colt over his head. "African Americans paid dearly in that war. Two young brothers died on that December patrol, and these…these *businessmen* are to blame. If I give the order, will you pull the trigger?"

The barn fell silent, save the gentle cooing of pigeons still settling down after the professor's outburst. He had posed his question to Johnson, but the other old Rangers pondered Lyle's chilling words, answering the question in their own hearts.

Vasquez leaned over to Johnson, put his arm around his shoulder and whispered in his ear.

Calloway swung his legs around and over the back of the bench, stood and glared silently at Cain and Ha. He walked toward one of the barn windows covered with thick burlap, pulled it back, rested his arms on the windowsill, and peered out.

Boggs cut his eyes from Johnson to the professor and back, wondering just who would have to be restrained—an old Ranger or the professor, himself? And what a surprise, Boggs thought. He had never seen Lyle's emotional side. With all the professor's brilliance and bombast, could a soul be banging around in there somewhere? Or could his old college friend be even crazier than he had imagined?

Tears welled up in Johnson's eyes, ran down the inside of the hockey mask, and merged into streams of sweat that soaked his shirt collar. He stood and faced Cain. Feelings for friends lost in the war and decades of pent-up frustration overran rational thought. He could hardly believe he was about to say the words. "I'd shoot them both, sir… shoot 'em dead. *All* those Rangers were my brothers."

"Thank you, Sergeant. Thank you." Lyle spoke softly, tapping Johnson on the shoulder. "It's all right. You can sit down now."

Lyle turned away from the Rangers and walked back toward Cain and Ha. "You're probably right, Colonel," Lyle said. "We are nutty enough to kill you, particularly the four guys on that bench. They're here on behalf of the four dead Rangers and those who were wounded. Their poor families thought they died for their country. Sad truth is you put 'em to death. Makes me sick to my stomach." Lyle turned around, walked toward the table and chair and sat down.

"By the way, Mr. Ha." Lyle's comment came as an afterthought. "How is your freelance business? Africa? Syria?"

"My only business is M&H International, General."

"Come on, Mr. Ha." Lyle's mask showed no emotion, but there was a smile in his whining voice. "You lied about Tango Company. Aren't you lying about cutting Cain out?"

"I never betrayed Colonel Cain—never!" Ha's lip quivered. His voice turned angry for the first time since his capture. "We have made millions together. Why would I steal from my partner?"

"Damned if I know." Lyle shook his head and sighed. "But we've got to get on with this.

"Y'all probably figured out why we grabbed both of you," Lyle said. "We grab one; the other ignores our demands and lets his partner die. The survivor gets it all."

Boggs, his Rangers and the prisoners sat quietly, listening to the professor's presentation. No one knew exactly what Lyle was doing. Krueger and Schiller were in the dark as well, but neither hesitated when Lyle motioned them away from the prisoners. Cain and Ha watched nervously as the mercenaries stepped away, leaving them alone in the center of the barn floor.

"Not looking for a confession with crying and carrying on," Lyle began. "And I'll repeat my earlier statement: I don't want to order executions for treason. But I want the truth about Tango Company—the orders. You know you conspired to do it—using those boys as pawns in your little game. And there's a price to pay. The good news is you shouldn't have to pay with your lives."

There was a long silence. Cain shifted nervously on the folding chair.

Ha looked around the barn, turning his head in quick jerks from the professor, to the Rangers, then to Schiller and his men. When he looked at the professor again, the big Colt was in the holster. He held a Ruger .22 automatic in his left hand and a slender metal tube in his right hand, slowly screwing the two pieces together.

"Very interesting," the professor said, admiring the slim little weapon. "Light. Silent. Accurate. Damned deadly. The choice of many professionals, I'm told."

"Excuse the digression, gentlemen," Lyle said. "You've got one minute—no, take two minutes since there are two of you—to tell the truth about Tango Company. If you don't, I'll shoot one of you. Of course, I'm not saying which one. It'll be a surprise."

"This is insane!" Cain stood up. He saw Krueger move toward him and sat back down.

"Insane? Absolutely." Without looking up, Lyle cocked the Ruger, checked his watch and walked slowly toward the prisoners. "One minute, thirty seconds."

Lyle stopped five feet in front of Cain and Ha and raised the pistol. Both men covered their faces and ducked. Seconds later, there was a spitting sound from the handgun. The bullet zipped over their heads, slamming into a galvanized washtub hanging on the barn wall. The professor checked his watch again. "Sixty-second warning, boys."

"Please, General!" Ha was shaking. "Please…don't kill us. "It …It was like you said. I—we—lied about the orders for the Ranger teams, but we meant to harm no one."

"Shut up, Nguyen!" Cain grabbed his partner by the arm. "They're going to kill us anyway."

"No, James. No!" Ha was ready to talk. "We were just protecting our business. We didn't know where the Rangers would be sent. We meant no harm. It was an unfortunate event."

Cain sat up straight in the chair but said nothing. His eyes were fixed on a dusty bridle hanging from a nail on the wall beyond the professor. He was unfazed by Ha's confession, but the Colonel had come to grips with the gravity of the situation. His life could end in a musty old barn that conjured up nightmares from his youth.

"This is your chance, Colonel," the professor said. "Speak up."

"This is no trial. There is no justice here. You've used murder and intimidation to force confessions from us." Cain turned away from Lyle, looking first at the old Rangers on the bench, then at Schiller and Krueger. "I refuse to dignify this kangaroo court with any statement. Get on with whatever it is you're going to do."

"Very well." The professor's tone was business-like. "It is the finding of this tribunal that James B. Cain and Nugyen Ha intentionally provided false intelligence to Tango Company, 75th Infantry, United States Army, the Republic of Vietnam on or about 11 December 1970. By providing said false intelligence, orders for Ranger Teams 3-1 and 3-2 were changed. By changing the orders, said teams were needlessly placed in harm's way on 12 December 1970. Four Rangers—Washington, Brown, Sigwald, and Sciavo—were killed on or about 12 December as an indirect result of criminal acts by Cain and Ha.

"Therefore." Lyle paused. "It is hereby ordered that James B. Cain and Nugyen Ha be executed—"

"What!" Cain sprang to his feet. "This is outrageous!"

"You had your chance to speak, Colonel." The professor's voice was especially calm. "Sit down. I'm not finished. Considering how long it's been since the incident, it is also my ruling that the sentence may be suspended, upon payment of $300 million dollars when banks open Monday morning, London time."

If Boggs's Rangers were surprised by the amount, Boggs was stunned. He was expecting less than one-tenth the amount. The unpredictable Professor Lyle had struck again.

Schiller, the stoic mercenary, looked at the professor, struggling to hide the smile tugging hard at the corners of his mouth. "Great God," he whispered through his teeth. "I really love this guy."

"Crazy," Cain said, as the number sank in. "You're nuts—all of you. We don't have it. If we had it, the company wouldn't pay it."

"Oh, I think M&H has the cash," the professor said. "And they'll pay."

"Might as well photograph the Colonel and Mr. Ha," Lyle said after a long silence. He looked at his watch. "They'll want fingerprints, too, along with Mr. Ha's left footprint. He's missing half of his little toe. Must've tripped over a Jeep he stole during the war."

"What the hell's going on?" Cain was almost polite when he asked the question. "What are you planning to do with us?"

"We began negotiating with your London office soon after you were captured. Your third in command wants proof you're still alive before he'll transfer the money. We're giving it to him."

"So," Cain snarled. "It was just the money all along."

"For the most part." Lyle was blunt. "Can't help banged up old veterans without cash. Rotten as you two are, you're no good to us dead…unless, of course, your underlings don't release the funds."

"We'll be ready in a flash, General." Withers strutted through the barn door with his computer gear and a fingerprint kit under his arm. Like the rest of the team, his face was painted in three-color camouflage. A black mask covered his eyes and he wore a tiger-striped boonie cap. He walked straight to Lyle's table, set up his laptop and camera then faced the prisoners. "You'll need to stand up, lads. Look at me, please. It's going live to your London office. Smile—wave if you wish."

Ha stood up, following Withers' instructions and turned toward the tiny egg-shaped camera.

"You'll never get away with this." Cain was not impressed with the cheery Englishman's attempt at humor; he showed his displeasure by covering his face with his hands and slouching in the folding chair. Seconds later the full force of a karate sidekick landed squarely in the back of the Colonel's chair. The blow sent him sprawling headlong across the dirt floor. When he rolled over and looked up, Schiller was staring down at him. The mercenary clicked his heels and he bowed slightly. The Colonel was too busy spitting dirt to appreciate the gesture.

"Stop the childish behavior, Colonel." Schiller spoke softly as he knelt beside Cain. "Please understand. I don't need your money, and I'll gladly kill you if you don't cooperate. We're on a tight schedule. Now, if you will oblige my sergeant?" Schiller was a man of few words, and his timing impeccable.

The stunned business executive struggled to his feet and, without saying a word, brushed the dirt from his face and jumpsuit, and was ready to have his picture taken.

"Could we have some coffee, Captain?" Lyle asked.

"*Oui, mon General,*" Schiller replied as he stepped closer to the professor. "Sorry," he whispered out of earshot of the prisoners. "I was tired of listening to that condescending bastard. You have my apology."

"None needed, Captain." Lyle was smiling inside the mask. "We do have a schedule to keep."

"I'll check the perimeter while I'm out," Schiller said. "I'll spend a few minutes with the reverend as well. His feelings were hurt when you kept him away from the barn."

"Jesus, man," the professor whispered back. "If I'd been Barry, the old boy'd still be standing on that runway in the mountains."

"But, of course, you're not Barry."

The professor shook his head and sighed. "Ain't that the truth."

"Besides, General, we'll all be old guys one day—if we get out of this line of work." Schiller smiled, his white teeth gleaming in contrast to the dull, dark swirls of camouflage distorting his face. "And we'll want someone to be nice to us."

"Only if she's young and beautiful." Lyle smiled. "And brings lots of beer."

Schiller thought for a moment, his arms folded and resting his chin between his right thumb and forefinger. His mind drifted back to Cape Town where Sylvie was waiting—at least he guessed she was. Then he sighed and whispered, "And she must wear only emerald green bikini pants."

"Like 'em dressed up, do you?" The professor laughed out loud, slapping Schiller on the back as they walked toward the barn door.

All eyes in the barn stared in disbelief at the self-proclaimed general and his captain. To a man, they were dying to know: what could possibly trigger such a humorous exchange between such dangerous men at such a tense time?

CHAPTER TWENTY-SIX:
CONTACT!

"Ow GOES IT, LAD?"

"Very well, Reverend." Schiller smiled as he walked up the steps to the cabin where the Padre had been told to stay put. "The business in the barn should be over soon—an hour, at most."

The Padre knew not to ask for details and changed the subject. "And your lads on the perimeter?"

"They've had a long day." Schiller checked his watch. "Two hours until first light. Fortunately, things have been quiet."

"Let me take something to them, sir. I'll be quiet as a cat."

"A nice gesture, Reverend, but I can't risk it."

"Good Lord, son. I've seen more action than the lot of you put together." The Padre begged to get into the game. "Besides, it's been a cakewalk so far. Please, let me help?"

Schiller pursed his lips, looking around the bean field bordering the hunting camp. It had been quiet. They were miles from nowhere, and, after all, this was America. He also reflected on his conversation with the professor a few minutes earlier, and he would let the Padre play, even if the role was nothing more than the water boy.

"They have MRE's," Schiller said. "But I'm sure they'd like some fresh water or hot coffee."

The Padre broke into a wide smile.

Then the mercenary put his hand on the Scotsman's shoulder and looked him straight in the eyes. "I'll tell them you're coming, but stay in the shadows along the tree line. Vervoort's on the edge of the dirt road behind the cabin. Stop there first. Then follow the trees along the field around to that finger-like tip of woods out there." He pointed to the tiny woodland head, snaking through the bean field but barely visible in the thickening fog. "Cao is positioned in the tip. Dessart is directly across the field to the left—that's nine o'clock from here. When you leave Cao, walk quietly over to Dessart. Continue circling around the tree line. It will bring you back to where we're standing. Don't worry about our man watching the boats. I'll take care of him. We should be finished in the barn when you return."

"Thanks, lad," MacDonald said. "It'll be a nice jaunt around the perimeter, and I'm glad to help."

Schiller walked away, then stopped and looked over his shoulder. "Oh…Reverend, do you have a weapon?"

"Just this sapling I've been whittling on." He held up a five-foot piece of scrub oak, about the diameter of a garden hoe handle. "It's all I need."

—⁓—

"Don't turn there, W.J." Dinky Betts was calling the shots for the deer-poaching trip. "Don't want to get close to Calloway's cabin. Somebody might be out there. You never know." W.J. Jones nodded as the Toyota bounced along the dirt road behind the bean field. Jones had been recruited for one reason; he owned a four-by-four pickup. "Pull off the road—up there about a hundred yards to the right. We'll go in the woods where that long head juts out in the bean field. I'll put you and Earl about a hundred yards either side of it. I'll ease right up the middle. If there's a deer in there, I'll get him with the crossbow. If we don't jump one going in, we'll just sit and wait. We'll get a shot."

"You mean you'll get the shot," Earl smiled. "Asshole."

"Hey, man." Dinky held up the crossbow. "I learned to use this thing in 'Nam. It's damn quiet. Don't shoot the guns unless you have to. Start shootin' shotguns and somebody's liable to come lookin.'"

"Damn, W.J." Earl wrinkled his nose, sniffing loud enough for W.J. to hear him. "When you gonna fix the exhaust on this piece of shit. It's about to gag me."

"If you don't like it, walk." W.J. eased the old pickup off the road onto a logging trail and rolled to a stop, squealing brakes and all. "We're about fifteen miles from the nearest paved road. With the looks of your big fat ass, it'd take you two days to find your way out."

"See this fuckin' cell phone?" Earl pulled the flip phone from his jacket pocket. "My brother's just a call away."

"Y'all shut up!" Dinky's whisper was stern. "And don't slam the doors getting' out. Sound carries out here. Let's get in the woods while it's still dark." He looked down both ends of the sandy road then signaled his men to follow him across. When they reached the other side, he raised his hand, and crouched low. "Hear that?" he whispered.

"Hear *what*?" Earl's tone was sarcastic. "Still got them Vietnam snakes in your head, Dinky?"

"Listen, godammit. Choppers comin' in."

"Choppers, my ass," Earl said.

"Listen. I'd know that sound anywhere," Dinky said. "They're a ways out, but I'll bet they come in close."

—⚒︎—

"Mother of God." Spencer looked east over the wide marsh between the hunting camp and the sound. The deep bass thump-thump of helicopter rotors was unmistakable. "Surely they're not coming for us."

"Don't flatter yourself," Schiller said, handing Spencer a plastic bottle of water. "Americans rarely use the military on their own soil." Still, he kept his eyes on the choppers as they rumbled overhead, pushing further inland over the bean field and beyond. "Blackhawks—six total. There's an Army Ranger battalion in Savannah. Just training."

"How do you know?"

"First," Schiller said. "If they were after us, they'd have sent a recon team—probably by water. Second, you and I would probably be dead by now."

"A comforting thought." Spencer cracked the seal on the water bottle and raised it high in the direction of the choppers heading inland. "To their mission—far the fuck from here, I hope."

Schiller keyed the mike button on his radio, alerting his men on the perimeter. "Stand easy. Those birds are headed elsewhere."

—m—

The professor looked up, smiling as Schiller stepped through the barn door. "Damned masks were too hot. We put the blindfolds back on the prisoners. Your boy's watching them in that horse stall over there. Ah, coffee," he said, taking the insulated bottle from Schiller. "Where'd you have to go? Hilton Head?"

"Spent some time with the Reverend."

"How is the old boy?" Boggs stepped closer to Schiller.

"Happy," Schiller chuckled. "I sent him around the perimeter with coffee and water for my men. He was eager to help."

"Just as long as he stays out of trouble," Lyle said. "By the way, what was all that racket? Sounded like helicopters."

"Blackhawks—Army Rangers out of Savannah, I suspect. They kept going inland. No problem."

"Good," Lyle said, glancing at Cain and Ha sitting quietly in the horse stall. "We're almost finished here. The info went to London without a hitch. We heard from our man over there, too. M&H senior management is burning the midnight oil and we have an agreement on the terms. No doubt we've ruined their Sunday. He also said there's no indication the police have been called in—no delays either. No problem with us holding up here till the banks open in Europe Monday."

"Full of surprises, aren't we, *General*?" Boggs pulled the professor aside for their second private conference of the evening. "Three hundred million? That's ten times the original figure."

"Meant to tell you sooner," Lyle said. "Guess I forgot in all the excitement. You'll get a proper explanation when this is over. Bottom line is your needy vets will get more—much more than you imagined. Besides, if the Somalis can get that kind of cash, why can't we?"

"Can I have a word with you, Captain?" Boggs asked, holding his left arm as he walked toward Schiller.

At the same time, the mercenary pressed his headset against his ear and turned toward the door then looked over his shoulder at Boggs.

"Let's step outside," Schiller said. There was concern in his eyes for the first time since the mission began. "Cao reports intruders moving into his position."

"My God," Boggs whispered, pulling the barn door shut behind him. The chills shot down his arms like an electric shock. "How many?"

"He's not sure," Schiller said, motioning Lyle to join them outside. Then he spoke into the mike. "All positions. Number Two reports movement, but no contact. Report."

"One is clear, sir." Vervoort was on the road closest to the camp.

"Three is clear, sir." Dessart reported from the tree line across the bean field from Cao's position.

"Four, clear, sir." Spencer checked in from the boat dock.

"Sir, it's a deer." Cao was excited, but there was a sigh of relief in his voice. "Two—maybe."

"Where's the Reverend?" Schiller was trying to account for everyone.

"Crossing the field toward Number Three," Cao said, standing up for the first time since he reported the noise.

Dinky Betts' arrow was already in flight, launched from the crossbow toward a big buck, its faint silhouette barely visible in the shadows. When Cao stood, he was directly in the arrow's path and took the bolt meant for the whitetail.

"Jesus Christ! I'm hit!" The razor-like arrow had gone under Cao' left collarbone, continuing its deadly flight through shoulder muscle before slamming into a pine tree.

Startled by the commotion, the deer bounded from the narrow strip of woods into the bean field, cutting right toward the tree line between Cao and Dessart. W.J. Jones, infected with buck fever, was nervous and waiting. Seconds later, a shotgun blast exploded in the tree line, sending the deer head over hooves into an awkward acrobatic spin. He was dead when he crashed in the soft, rich dirt between two rows of beans.

"I got him, Dinky!" W.J. screamed, charging out of the trees through the smell of gunpowder hanging in the air. "Son of a bitch! I got him! Worked just like you said. I got him!" Winded from his run, W.J. pulled up when he saw the big whitetail sprawled between the bean rows. He stared silently at the carcass for a moment, then tiptoed up to the buck and nudged its thick neck with the gun barrel.

"Dinky!" Jones called out, dying to share the excitement of the kill. "Where the hell are you?"

"Right here, you stupid arse!" The stunned poacher whirled to face the angry voice only to catch the full force of the Padre's walking stick. Stinging fingers, smashed between the stick and the shotgun stock, dropped the weapon as if it were on fire. Before W.J. could fully appreciate the pain of three crushed digits, the Padre landed another sweeping blow across his back—kidney high. He moaned as he hit the ground. Fueled by fear alone, Jones struggled to his feet and trotted toward the tree line—staggering and stumbling along the way.

"Run, you bloody coward! Run!" The defiant old warrior screamed at the poacher, waiving the walking stick above his head. Moments later the Padre touched the stream of blood running down his forehead and into his right eye. With his finger, he followed it up to its source under his matted hair. "For goodness sake," he muttered as he fell unconscious in the soft dirt between the rows.

Gasping for breath and reeling from the Padre's blows, Jones dropped to his knees ten yards from the tree line. His vision was blurred by sweat running down his forehead, but the poacher saw nothing when he looked back across the field through the first mottled light of day. "Thank you, Jesus," he said between deep, painful gulps of air.

As W.J. struggled to his feet for the last steps to safety, he heard it—the unmistakable crack of a small caliber rifle. He screamed as the round slammed into his hip. With swollen, broken fingers, he tugged at the burning hot projectile that punched through his faded camouflage pants, burying itself deep in muscle. When he pulled it out, he saw two slender darts in two hands. The trees at the forest's edge appeared to double as well. The drug in the tranquilizer dart had done its job. After a few stumbling steps, his legs crumpled beneath him.

—⁂—

"Hold your positions," Schiller said, barely raising his voice when Cao went down. The order was too late for Vervoort. He was running to Cao's aid in the narrow finger of woods jutting out into the bean field.

"I can see Cao," Vervoort said into his radio microphone. "He's down… but alive. There's no one else here."

"The shooter is down." There was an eerie calmness in Dessart's voice. "And the Reverend."

"Hold your position," Schiller replied.

Boggs hung his head for a moment, thinking about his adventure that had just gone wrong. His best friend was lying wounded—maybe dead—in a bean field. He looked at Schiller. "How can we help?"

"Krueger will stay with the professor and the prisoners," Schiller said. "If we must, we can take them to our alternate rendezvous point by water. We'll also need a man in Vervoort's position near the road behind the cabin."

"This is my place. I know every inch of it." Calloway stepped into the middle of the discussion. "Those guys out there got to be poachers. Probably parked a vehicle behind that bean field and slipped in. If we were really under attack, all hell would be breaking loose by now. Those boys are shakin' worse than we are." Calloway turned to Schiller. "Give me your toughest guy. We'll take a shortcut and cut 'em off."

Schiller pursed his lips and looked at Calloway. "I'm that guy." He turned to Boggs. "Take over here, Barry. Send a man to help retrieve Cao and the Reverend then stand by the radio."

"Roger that, Captain." Then Boggs looked each old Ranger straight in the eye. It had been decades since he had given an order, but he swore to God this mission would not end like the ill-fated one that had brought them here. "Vasquez, you'll cover the road behind the cabin. Johnson, help with the wounded across the field."

Both men touched the corner of their black berets in a casual salute and popped clips in the old Colts the professor had given them.

"And," Boggs warned, sounding more like a father than a commander, "be careful with those damned weapons."

The old vets moved out in the predawn silence like they had done many times, many years ago. Without question or comment, each man slipped obediently into the shadows. Much later in life, in this different, but no less dangerous place, these veterans were on all too familiar ground.

CHAPTER TWENTY-SEVEN:
MOPPING UP

"Trail's in good shape," Calloway said, hurriedly painting his face and hands with black, brown and gold camouflage. "Scouted it for deer twice this month. It's pretty clear through there and the footing's good." He stretched a black bandanna over his thick gray hair, tying it against his neck just above his shirt collar. "If we're lucky, that boy'll hunker down in the woods, and we'll beat him to his vehicle. It can't be but one or two places." He snapped a banana clip into a Chinese SKS carbine, pulled back the bolt and locked the first round in the chamber.

"Where did you get that?" Schiller's eyes widened, watching how easily Calloway handled the rifle.

Calloway, the dealmaker, smiled. "Bought ten of 'em before the assault ban took effect. Eighty-eight bucks a piece. Great deer rifle in the thick stuff. Gave 'em away at Christmas. Let's move out." Confident as a twenty-year-old, Calloway stepped off at a brisk rout step with Schiller close on his heels.

Two hundred yards later they stopped at the tree line. The sixty-five-year-old used car dealer never broke a sweat and was breathing normally. He glanced over his shoulder, making sure the mercenary was still with him. "You all right, son?"

"Very well." Schiller smiled. The old Ranger's stamina surprised him. It was as if Calloway had been at war or in the woods all his life. "Mike," Schiller whispered. "Remember to wear the mask. I'll do the talking—if it comes to that. This person—or persons—may know you."

"Hell," Calloway said. "I'd bet on it." He sliced a strip of chewing tobacco from a rectangular brown plug, never looking up. "Used this stuff in the war. I only chew when I hunt now. Want some?"

Schiller furrowed his brow, catching a whiff of the tobacco's strange sweet smell then shook his head. "No, thank you."

Calloway paused, working the tobacco from one cheek to the other. "It'd be nice... real nice if we don't have to shoot anybody else."

"Nice?" The question caught Schiller by surprise. He pondered it as he followed Calloway into the shadowy trail where the predawn light was creeping in, reaching for the foothold it would surely gain. "Nice, indeed," the mercenary whispered softly, but he promised nothing.

—⚓—

"How are you feeling, *Mon ami*?"

"Old and stupid." MacDonald winced as he touched his scalp where the buckshot had literally parted his hair. He sat up, with Dessart's help, but was still unsteady. "Can't believe I passed out. I've had whiskey hit harder than that over-sized BB."

"Keep low," the mercenary said. "We are sitting targets." He examined MacDonald's wound, then wrapped it with a field dressing. Dessart turned to the tree line, focusing his binoculars on the dark crumpled heap at the edge of the field. "Do not move, Reverend. I'll be back soon."

Dessart keyed his mike and reported to Boggs. "He was grazed by a shotgun pellet. Some bleeding, but he's conscious. He should be fine. I must attend to the shooter near the woods. He is down and has not moved."

Dessart slipped the Colt 45 from its holster, stepping cautiously toward W.J. Jones who had fallen a few yards from the tree line. He pulled back the hammer on the pistol, then kicked the sole of Jones' hunting boot. "*Dormez-vous, Mon ami*?"

The poacher moaned incoherently but was in no condition to resist.

"*Tres bien,*" Dessart whispered, pulling the hand with the broken fingers behind the poacher's back and lashing it to the other with a zip tie. He blindfolded the drugged man with a wide strip of cotton flannel cut from the poacher's own shirttail. When he left Jones, Dessart retraced his steps past the big whitetail and back to MacDonald.

—᠁—

"There's a blanket in his kit," Vervoort said, never looking up at Johnson as he worked calmly but deliberately on Cao. "Get it out and cover him up. I'll start an IV. You watch the woods behind us." Johnson found Cao's rucksack, pulled the blanket out and covered the wounded man.

"This is One," Vervoort said into his microphone.

"Go ahead, One," Boggs replied as he paced along the edge of the field a hundred and fifty yards away. He stopped and pressed the binoculars against his eye sockets; it was still too dark to detect movement.

"A hunting arrow passed under the collarbone, slicing through shoulder muscle. It went straight through him. He's lost some blood. I'm trying to stabilize him now."

"Roger that." Boggs was pacing again. "Call if you need us. Out."

—᠁—

Dinky Betts was out of breath, battered by the terrain and, worst of all, lost, as he collapsed in a bed of gray-green ferns. It had been a difficult retreat—running, walking, sometimes crawling—four hundred yards southwest of the bean field. Thorns had jabbed him like barbed wire. He had stumbled into a spring-fed branch, falling facedown in the cold water. Worse yet, he had stepped through a rotten tree stump and twisted his ankle. Shivering among the soft ferns, he took deep, painful breaths and rubbed the swollen ankle inside the ancient jungle boot. He needed to rest, but more importantly, he had to gather his wits. It was as if scavengers had scattered them like animal bones in the dark woods.

Once his heart rate slowed and he caught his breath, Betts cocked his head to one side then the other, cupping his hands around his ears to improve his hearing. He listened for things he hoped not to hear—truck doors slamming, dogs yelping, limbs crunching under foot and men calling out to each other. A man on the run listened for such things, but there was nothing, save the gentle breeze and tree branches rustling overhead.

Betts rested his weathered face in his hands, wondering how this simple deer hunt had gone so wrong. He had been stunned when the silhouette in the ghillie suit had stepped into his line of fire with the deer. No one should have been there. He hoped he had not killed that guy. He had already turned tail and run when he heard the shotgun blast—W.J.'s, he assumed, but could not be sure. Betts never looked back. To stay and face the consequences would have guaranteed a return to a North Carolina jail. He had sworn never to get caught again. As for his hunting partners, they would know something was wrong and head for the truck. But, in the end, it was every man for himself.

Betts shook and his teeth chattered from the splash in the creek, but he could not stay in the ferns. He stood to test the sprained ankle, putting weight on it for the first time since he collapsed. He sighed. It was in better shape than he had thought. As he took a few steps, he heard the sound in the distance. "Jesus," he moaned. "Again?" It was unmistakable—the muffled thump, thump, thump of helicopters. Betts swallowed hard. It was the second time he had heard them since this horrible hunt began. Vietnam had never haunted Betts, but this warlike incident gave him pause to reflect. Distant memories from a long lost youth muscled their way into his psyche like a snarling barroom bully. He had not been scared since the Highlands—not until now. He had gone from hunter to hunted in the time it took to release an arrow. He had to get moving, find the trail then the dirt road and reach the truck. He was sure the Army choppers were not coming for him, but his jailhouse mindset assured him somebody was.

—⋙—

Quickly, but quietly, Calloway led Schiller through the shortcut. The car dealer was as confident as a Low Country bobcat prowling his own territory. He knew every inch. They eased down a gentle slope shrouded by brush, crossed a narrow branch under a wax myrtle canopy and detoured around dense briar patches. In a matter of minutes, they were crouched at the edge of the sandy, seldom-scraped road behind the bean field.

"Two logging trails—one fifty yards to the right," Calloway whispered. "The other one's a hundred yards to the left. Fresh tire tracks goin' left. None comin' out. The vehicle's still there. We'll go left."

Schiller nodded in agreement. "Remember, I'll do the talking if we make contact. And don't forget the mask. Anyone who identifies you is a dead man."

Five minutes later, with weapons at the ready, the unlikely partners followed the tracks into the trail bordered by a wall of thick, brown brush under towering longleaf pines. Calloway froze when he saw the silhouette of a small pickup blocking the way. It had been backed into the narrow trail.

A careful inspection of the vehicle produced nothing until Calloway reached under the rear bumper and pulled an ignition key from the tailpipe. "That's where these knotheads usually leave them," he whispered.

Schiller nodded, signaling his partner to hide in the brush on the passenger side of the pickup. The mercenary disappeared into the thick cover on the driver's side.

—⋙—

Fear mixed with Betts's adrenaline to blot out the chill from the branch water and the painful thrashing from the thorns. The twisted ankle was getting worse as he hobbled to the edge of the dirt road. He dropped to one knee, resting his forehead in his shaking, weathered hand. He worried he had lost precious time in the woods, but, finally, he had found his way out. He would have killed for a cigarette, but it was a good thing they were soaked. A match struck at first light could paint a target for anyone.

After the wiry poacher struggled to his feet, he limped along in the shadows on the edge of the sandy road. When he reached the logging trail, he took a deep breath and hobbled across for what he hoped would be a reunion with Earl and W.J. "Thank you, Lord," he whispered when he saw the Toyota sitting in the middle of the trail. "Earl? W.J.? Y'all here?" Betts called out in a whisper. When there was no response, he walked to the rear of the truck and sat on the bumper. Then he remembered; W.J. had put the truck key in the tailpipe. He slid off the bumper, turned around and stuck his fingers inside the exhaust. He flinched when Schiller shoved the cold barrel of the H&K behind his ear and pinned him against the bumper.

"Go ahead," the poacher said with a sigh. "Read me my rights."

"Rights, *monsieur*? You have no rights. Keep your head down unless you want to die this morning. Hands behind your back." Betts complied, and Calloway bound him with a zip tie. "Now the blindfold, Sergeant."

"What the hell is this?" Betts started to look up and Schiller jabbed the gun barrel even tighter behind his ear. Calloway found a soiled tee shirt in the truck bed and blindfolded the poacher.

"You have entered a restricted area." The mercenary's exaggerated French accent had a healthy dose of German in it, but Betts failed to notice. "Cooperate and you may survive."

"Goddamn," Betts sighed. "I thought y'all was cops."

"I can assure you, *monsieur*, we are not *gendarmes*. You are not under arrest. *Vous etes prisonier de guerre*—a P.O.W. as you would say in the English."

"A what? This is America, for God's sake. What damn country y'all from?"

"Certainly not this one," Schiller said. "Now, where is your other friend?"

"Uh, it's just me—by myself—huntin' alone, all night."

"Curious," Schiller said. "We've captured you and shot your friend in the bean field. You called out two names when you approached the truck. Which one remains at large, Earl or W.J.?"

"You shot W.J.? Is he…dead?"

"Not yet, but he could be if you fail to cooperate." Schiller's impatience showed. "Where is this Earl?"

Betts slumped against the truck bumper. "Y'all got a drink of water?"

Calloway held a quart-sized canteen up for Schiller to see. The mercenary nodded in agreement. The car dealer knelt beside him, bringing the canteen to Dinky's mouth, and he took several big swallows.

"Thanks," he said, breathing hard after gulping the water. "Didn't mean to hurt your man—guess he was yours. He popped up between me and that deer right when I let the arrow go. I was scared. Nothing I could do— 'cept run." There was silence, then resignation in his voice when he spoke. "I don't know where Earl's hidin'—in the woods or maybe he just run off."

Calloway stepped away from the poacher and whispered to Schiller. "Ask him where he got that airborne tattoo."

"Your tattoo, *monsieur*. Where did you get it?"

"Fort Benning. Before I shipped out to Vietnam. Nineteen seventy, I guess. Spent some time with the Rangers—fought mostly with the Montagnards up in the Highlands." He gulped down another swallow of water. "It was a long time ago."

Calloway slowly shook his head as he motioned the mercenary to follow him a few yards down the trail. "I'm for this thing a hundred percent," Calloway said. "But if you're thinking about killing this ol' boy, you'll have to shoot me first. Pathetic as he is, he's still one of ours."

Schiller glanced back at his prisoner—bound, blindfolded and lying on his side in the middle of the trail. "I understand." He spoke as if he had expected Calloway's reaction. Then the mercenary looked skyward, squinting as the morning light filtered down through the canopy of long leaf pines. "This old soldier will not die today, but we must find the one called Earl."

CHAPTER TWENTY-EIGHT:
CHANGE OF PLANS

EARL MALLARD STRUGGLED WITH THE TOUGHEST decision of his life as he hid in the brush ten short yards from the Toyota pickup. He followed the brass sighting bead atop his shotgun as it wandered from one soldier to the other like a divining rod with a mind of its own. But in every shot he framed, Dinky Betts was in the line of fire. Then, to Earl's surprise, the soldiers stepped away from his hunting buddy.

To shoot, or not to shoot, and *who*? His heart pounded as he selected his target—the tall soldier with the foreign accent, the one who did all the talking. His hands trembled as they wrestled his nerves for control of the Winchester pump. Finally, he took a deep breath, let it out and squeezed the trigger—cringing in anticipation of the recoil and deafening blast, but there was nothing. It was as if the trigger had been welded in place. Blame forgetfulness. Blame fear. He had failed to snap the safety behind the trigger guard to the *off* position.

"Damn," Earl whispered, fumbling nervously for the safety. When he raised the 12 gauge to his shoulder once again, one of the soldiers had stepped in to give Dinky water. Mallard lowered the shotgun and rested his head on the cool steel of the receiver. Any courage he had mustered floated off in the wake of the missed opportunity and rational thoughts crept in. Maybe they had other plans for Dinky. "He's still alive, and they gave him water," Earl said under his breath. Besides, an arrest could mean a return trip to state prison for Earl. If he killed someone, the stakes would be much higher. They did more than debate the death penalty in South Carolina; they carried it out. Of course, a shot and a miss would virtually guarantee his being cut in half by a machine gun. Mallard would watch and wait and hold his fire.

Earl's choice of discretion over idiocy helped calm his nerves as he hid in the brush, pondering the deer hunt-turned-Halloween nightmare. It had started with the commotion in the finger-like tip of woods extending into the bean field. The shotgun blast followed with W.J. Jones yelling he had he shot the deer. After that, soldiers—foreigners—had come from everywhere. Then there was nothing—no Dinky and no W.J. Maybe the soldiers were linked to the helicopters zooming overhead. They were too quiet for local cops, Earl thought. God forbid, they were government agents. Maybe it was a drug deal. "They sure ain't deer hunters," he whispered. Hunters did not carry machine guns, and he had heard the tall one call Dinky a prisoner of war. Earl furrowed his brow, more puzzled than ever by what had happened. "Whose war is this?"

—w—

"We have one prisoner," Schiller whispered into the headset. "We will bring him in. There's a second man, hiding in the forest, we believe. It would be futile to search for him. Have my men hold their positions. We have the vehicle keys and will disable it before we return." Calloway was already under the hood, removing the distributor cap.

"Roger that," Boggs replied. "Everyone's accounted for here *and* we've got an uninvited guest of our own."

Schiller shook his head and whispered, "Too many guests."

—w—

Our departure plans have to change." The professor spoke quietly to the leadership gathered around the rough-hewned dinner table in Calloway's cabin. As usual, Schiller was the stoic one. Boggs pushed his boonie cap back on his head, quietly rocking on the back two legs of an old oak chair.

His blank stare had turned to a frown. Three hours had passed since the wounded and the poachers had been brought in.

The professor stood up then walked to a window facing the wide expanse of backwater marsh. It stretched for miles, out to the May River and beyond. He leaned against the window ledge, sipping hot coffee and staring into the distant haze where the dark water met the bright blue sky. "Damned beautiful out there, damned beautiful," he said, breaking the silence. "Halloween's arrived on an Indian summer day."

"I believe we were talking about plans." Boggs, still sporting his sour expression and favoring his left arm, got his old friend back on track. "I guess we're leaving soon—considering someone's loose out there."

"He's out there," Lyle said, "but I don't think he's a problem for us. Mike knows him and the other two." He turned to Calloway. "How far's the paved road? And the nearest house with a phone?"

"Fifteen miles to a paved road," Calloway said. "Another six or seven to any house. Telephone? Who knows? Earl—the one who's out there—he's the weakest. Lazy fat boy, as I recall."

"He's scared—hiding somewhere in the woods," the professor said, speaking with conviction. "If he heard anything, it was in French or heavily-accented English. My hunch is we're good here till nightfall. Besides, poachers don't call the sheriff's office for help.

"Karl's team will leave by boat as planned," Lyle said. "The rest of us will leave in two vehicles." He put his hand on Calloway's shoulder. "You're familiar with the Ocean Star Cottages?"

"Am I?" Calloway smiled. "Just this side of the bridge to Hilton Head. Used to be the best whorehouse in South Carolina, well…second-best." He laughed. "So I'm told!"

"I want you to drop Cain and Ha off there tonight," the professor said. "Two high-paid babysitters will be waiting. It's number fourteen, the last cottage way in the back. Pull up to the side door, and they'll come out for the delivery. You won't have to get out of your Suburban."

"Roger that," Calloway said. "Who's goin' with me?"

"Johnson and Vasquez." The professor grinned. "After the drop, y'all go to your beach house. Play golf for a few days. Your original cover story is still good.

"Barry and I will take the Padre with us. We'll all leave at dusk. In the meantime, everybody stays inside. Any questions?"

"I thought Karl was in charge of heavy lifting." Boggs rocked the straight chair forward, banging the front legs against the pine plank floor. He looked his old fraternity brother in the eyes. "My guys aren't on the payroll."

"No choice," the professor said matter-of-factly. "The country boys surprised us. We've got to hold Cain and Ha till after the London banks open Monday. It's risky leaving them at the Ocean Star, but they'll be drugged. It's the best plan we've got." He paused. "Our only plan, really." He looked across the salt marsh again. "Of course, we could kill them all. Lighten the load, so to speak."

"Feed the sharks." Schiller spoke softly, without emotion, and to no one in particular.

Calloway slid off the kitchen counter where he had been sitting during the briefing. As his feet hit the floor, he swung the SKS rifle to a port position. "I thought I made myself clear about any more killings."

"I beg your pardon." The professor's eyes widened as he looked down the barrel of the SKS.

A wry smile worked its way across Schiller's face. "Mr. Calloway is simply restating the position he shared with me in the field."

"Which is?" Lyle was not amused.

"If we plan to kill anyone else," the mercenary explained, "we must kill him first."

"I see." The professor saw nothing but serious and determined faces as he gazed around the room. His off-handed remark had been taken too seriously, and he had to correct it. "Well, then. It's settled," he said as he smiled. "Seems you boys are bound for the Ocean Star."

CHAPTER TWENTY-NINE:
BREAKING CAMP

S UNDAY HAD BEEN QUIET—NO HELICOPTERS, NO sheriff's deputies
and no sign of the third poacher. The hours had dragged by since the
bean field incident. Boggs's bleary eyes worked their way around
the hunting cabin, stopping on each man for a quick, but careful, look.

"Karl," Boggs said as he turned to Schiller, "are your guys ready?"

Schiller nodded and motioned for Boggs to follow him out to the porch
where he leaned against a cedar post and looked across the field where all
the trouble had begun. "We're ready, except for Cao. Our medic stopped
the bleeding, but he has lost a lot of blood."

Cao rested quietly on the well-worn sofa in the cabin's main room. He
watched Schiller and Boggs through the open front door. He could not
hear them, but would bet they were talking about him. He managed a
smile and gave a thumb's up.

Boggs acknowledged Cao's gesture with a nod then turned to Schiller.
"Can he survive the boat trip?"

"He says he can," Schiller said, raising his eyebrows. "He told me not to
worry. He'd lived to spend his share." Schiller looked across the field again.
"I'm not sure he can make it.

"And your Padre?"

Boggs looked at the Padre. He was kneeling beside Cao, acting more
like a chaplain than a casualty.

"Your medic said the buckshot grazed his scalp, and he's lost some
blood. Look's nasty, but not life threatening. There's a surgeon a few hours
from here who will look at him." Boggs stood with arms folded, quietly
watching the Padre minister to each man, doing what he did best.

"God bless you," Padre said, grasping Cao's hand. "You'll make it, my boy."

"Padre's the happiest man here," Boggs said, watching the minister work has way around to every man on the team.

"Karl?" Boggs whispered. "I want to take Cao with us. If he hemorrhages when you cross that choppy water, he'll die for sure."

"A kind offer," Schiller said. "But Cao knew the risks. Besides, it puts your group in a bad spot."

"Jesus Christ, Karl." Boggs forced a smile and slid the boonie cap back on his head. "We've been in a bad spot since we landed on Hilton Head." Then the smile disappeared. "The boat ride will kill that boy. At least he'll have a chance with us."

Schiller shook his head and looked at his watch. "If he lives, you've got to get him home. If he dies?"

"We'll handle it," Boggs said.

Schiller said nothing as he looked out across the marsh. His mind was out there somewhere, too. He only half-heard Boggs's comment. "I hope this will be my last job," Schiller said. "I've been thinking about it—hanging up my six-shooters. That's what the cowboys say, isn't it?"

"In the movies," Boggs chuckled. "And I hope you're right. I know it's my last one." Boggs put his hand on Schiller's shoulder. "Listen, you guys did a fine job...your father would've been proud of you."

"The sad truth is I've hardly thought of him." Schiller's tone was apologetic. "I hardly knew him. Anyway, we'll celebrate when we get home," Schiller said. "And there's still a long way to go."

"Sir." Withers walked up the steps to Schiller. "We've scouted the area for brass and rubbish. Everything's accounted for. We've fetched the poacher's lory from the woods. We're ready to shove off."

"Excellent," Schiller said, stepping back inside the cabin. "There is one change; Cao is staying. Mr. Boggs will fly him out for medical attention. They have a safe place for him to recover." He glanced at Boggs. "They will see that he gets home—somehow."

There was a puzzled look on Cao's face. "I can travel, sir. Really, I can." Then he sank back in the sofa. "I can make it."

"Not this time," Schiller said. "Go with Boggs and the professor. You'll get the care you need. Money is of no use to a dead man. Besides, you happen to be riding with the check writers."

Schiller turned to Boggs. "I guess this is farewell, Barry. The sun is behind the trees. It will be dark when we reach the rendezvous point. Wish us luck," Schilller said as he saluted the American contingent. "*Au revoir,* Professor. We'll meet again soon."

"*Bonne chance, mon capitan.*" Lyle's French was as mushy as grits and red eye gravy. He doffed his boonie cap in cavalier fashion. "May God bless you all," he said, making the sign of the cross. "And may your brokers invest the money well." Lyle walked over to Schiller and put his arm around his shoulder. "Fine fucking job, son. We'll have that little party in France some day. *Bon voyage.* And, uh, my regards to our southern belle."

"Move out," Schiller said, motioning his men toward the boat ramp.

"Damn, Barry. I like that boy," Lyle said, rubbing his chin, raspy with three days' growth. "He'll be out of the game for a while now that he's rich as shit."

"Nobody's cashed a check yet," Boggs said as a chill crept down his spine. "Let's see if we can avoid any more excitement."

Without a word or looking back, the mercenaries boarded the small boats for the trip to the rendezvous point, slipping out of South Carolina as quietly as they had slipped in. There was a feeling of anxiousness in each man longing to escape his stoic façade; they were closer than ever to the biggest paychecks of their lives.

"Dessart?" Krueger whispered as they pushed the boat away from the dock. "A good job, yes?"

"Ask me tomorrow," Dessart said. "If we get our money—a good job. If we get our money and Cao makes it—an outstanding job." He turned away from Krueger and cranked the outboard motor, then opened the throttle to catch Schiller's boat.

Krueger shrugged, turning his face into the cool autumn night. "*Ya, ya,*" he said. "It is always tomorrow."

—m—

"Mike." Boggs spoke softly as he walked toward Calloway. "Time for y'all to hit the road." Calloway, Johnson and Vasquez were leaning against the dark green Chevy Suburban. Cain and Ha were handcuffed, sedated and hidden under a tarp in the back. Vervoort had given them the once over before he left, pronouncing them fit for travel.

"We're ready," Calloway said. The three men had shaved, showered and changed into civvies—expensive knit pullovers, silk trousers and tropical weight wool blazers.

"Never owned clothes this nice," Johnson said. "Fit like a glove. My compliments," he said, nodding to Lyle.

"My pleasure, Sarge," Lyle said. "Y'all look real slick—like three old farts out chasing a little nookie." Lyle grinned broadly and winked at the three old Rangers. Then it was back to business. "Y'all are straight on how the deposits are to be made?"

"Straight, sir," Johnson said. "Bobby goes with me in the Suburban. Mike follows with the poachers in their truck. We dump them ten—maybe fifteen miles out. We drop the honored guests at the Ocean Star before we leave the mainland. After that, it's out to Mike's house on Hilton Head. We're just old Army buddies visiting our rich pal." He paused and his tone shifted. "If we get stopped, we're just cruising around after a little side trip to Savannah."

"And if a cop stops you before you dump the country boys?" Boggs asked the question.

"We'll be fine," Calloway said. "I'll dump them between Pritchardville and Bluffton on Highway 46, then ease over to Highway 278 and on out to Hilton Head. Only thing I'm worried about is messing up my new clothes in this old Toyota."

In Lyle's scenario, the poachers would wake up the next day with terrible hangovers, still wondering just what they had stumbled upon. Cain and Ha would wake up at the motel outside Hilton Head. They would be pre-registered under their own names. A car from their villa would be parked outside the room, and they would be alive.

"Y'all do good, now," Lyle said, warning the three as they climbed into the vehicles. "Keep your mouths shut, and don't contact us. I'm dead fucking serious, now. It'll be a while—months, maybe—but y'all will be contacted." All three nodded, then boarded the trucks in the dusk that was rapidly turning to darkness.

"Those three were good soldiers," Boggs said, watching the taillights fade into the distance. "We were kids in Vietnam, just trying to stay alive. We knew there were protests at home, but we couldn't worry about it. No time for that when a bullet's cracking past your head."

"Well, BB, there ain't no kids out here tonight, just us old farts. But I wouldn't tangle with your guys—including that gimpy boy with one arm. They can still get the job done."

"Yes they can," Boggs said, staring into the darkness where the truck taillights had been. "Now, let's just get this little left over piece of the war behind us and find our way home."

The professor nodded his head. "I'm not a religious man, BB, but I'm praying for them … praying for us all."

CHAPTER THIRTY:
LOOSE ENDS

"DOC? IT'S BARRY." BOGGS SIGHED LIKE a kid calling to say he had wrecked the family car. But this was worse—even worse than the time he pointed the shotgun at the Columbia real estate man, and Dr. Raines had saved his hide that day, too.

"The e-mail said you were hunting in the Low Country," Raines answered. "Where are you, son?"

Boggs swallowed hard, listening through scratchy cell phone reception between Maywood and the coast. "Out of pocket for a couple of days. Hope you didn't need me."

"No, no. We're fine here."

Boggs turned toward the Jeep Cherokee, taking a good look at Jackie Cao. The Padre, with his head wrapped in a field dressing, sat in the back seat. "Doc," Boggs said, "I need your help."

It had been years since Raines heard Boggs use that tone of voice. "Are you all right?"

"I'm okay, Doc, but a couple of my friends need a doctor," Boggs said. "And it needs to be at Maywood—not at a hospital. Sort of a...hunting accident."

"I see," Raines said, weighing the seriousness of the request. "Can I handle this, or do you need someone special?"

"Both guys are stable for now. But we need a trauma guy I can trust, and Walt Guerry came to mind. We're an hour's Jeep ride from my plane, maybe two from Camden by air." He paused. "Hate to involve you in this, Doc, but it's damned delicate."

"Don't give it a thought." The old man forced a smile, lowering his voice to a whisper. "You're not just my partner. You're the son I never had."

Boggs looked out across the marsh, shaking his head and exhaling a long, slow breath.

The old man knew his protégé never minced words and never exaggerated—traits he had learned from his mentor. Raines broke the silence. "Walt's the best around. His horse farm's a few miles back toward Camden. I'll find him when we hang up."

"Walt and I go back a ways," Boggs said. "Tell him he'll be doing me a huge favor," Boggs said. "And Doc, we can't land in Camden. Maybe Freddie can stand by to light up the old airstrip. I'll give you plenty of warning."

Maywood's chairman had a thousand questions, but this was not the time and certainly not on the telephone. Raines spoke matter-of-factly. "We'll talk when you get here."

"Thanks, Doc." Boggs raised his eyebrows then scuffed the damp Bermuda grass with the cleats of his jungle boots and dredged up a pathetic little smile from God knows where.

—ɯ—

"Hope you're comfortable, son." The professor leaned into the right rear passenger window of the Cherokee, checking on the wounded warrior Schiller had left behind. "We'll take it easy getting out of here. Then it's a short plane ride to some medical help. You'll be fine."

"I'll make it, sir." Cao's speech was slurred but he tried to smile. Even with the painkillers, he was uncomfortable, wincing between words. "I know I will. It's the money…my share… keeps me going."

"Me too, son." Lyle patted the young mercenary on the shoulder and looked at Mr. MacDonald. "Reverend, looks like your doing okay. Bleeding's stopped?"

"Aye, Professor. Ready for the last leg of the trip." The shot Vervoort had given the Padre eased the pain, but the minister said nothing about the dizziness. He had taken the pills his doctor had given him but was determined to keep the condition to himself.

Boggs surveyed the camp for a final time. The small cabin and barn were silhouetted against the clear night sky. The mercenaries had checked and rechecked for telltale signs of their visit. In true commando fashion, they had bagged everything and carried it all out to sea. Still, the man responsible for this adventure checked behind everyone as well. Boggs was determined to leave Calloway's camp just as they had found it.

"Ready, BB?" The professor had been watching his old friend survey the camp. He lowered his voice to a whisper. "I think the Padre's gonna be okay, but I'm worried about Cao. That kid definitely needs a doctor."

"Let's hit it," Boggs snapped, as if jolted from a daze by the professor's words. "If we've left something out here, we'll just have to live with it. We're just damned lucky the bean field incident happened after the raid." He pursed his lips and flung an oak branch he had picked up into a nearby thicket. "Still worried about that third guy."

"Listen, Barry," Lyle said. "The guy's on foot. So he runs a few miles. Shit, son, we're fifteen miles from a paved road. How damned far can he get? He's laid up in the woods, scared shitless. He doesn't have a clue what he and his buddies stumbled into. Besides, they didn't get close to the cabin, much less see an American before we drugged them."

"I hope you're right." Boggs turned and walked to the driver's side of the Cherokee. "It's the loose ends. They bug the hell out of me."

—◊◊—

"You have reached the residence of Tommy and Gina Mallard." The message was rehearsed and stilted. "We are sorry we are unable to take your call at this time. If you will leave a message at the tone—"

"Goddammit, Tommy!" Earl Mallard turned off the cell phone, crouching low in the pines beside the longest dirt road he had ever seen. He had hiked eight tough miles since leaving the spot where Dinky had been captured. He pressed the redial button every hour, trying to reach his brother, but no one was home. He looked at his watch then at the distant tree line across the road where the sun had slipped behind the pine tops.

Earl's jaunt had taken its toll—no water, a couple of candy bars he had inhaled during the early hours, and darkness was coming. Thinking the soldiers might be searching for him, he had stayed off the road, slipping through the trees and brush and picking up more than his share of briars. His feet burned where the boots had rubbed huge blisters. His shotgun felt like a boat anchor, but he gripped it like a lifeline. It had been his only companion during this trying ordeal, and the thought of a night in the woods without a weapon terrified him.

"Please, Tommy, please be there." Earl held his breath and pressed the redial button. He had to try again before resuming his long trek toward civilization. There was a click on the second ring. After endless attempts, he recognized the sound as the prelude to the answering machine.

"You have reached the residence of Tommy and Gina." The phone clicked again. "Wait a minute. Don't hang up. We just walked in. Let me turn this machine off."

"Tommy!" Earl had never been happier to hear his brother's voice. "Jesus, Bro'. Where the hell you been? I'm in deep shit—real deep. You gotta come get me. Where you been?"

"Slow down," Tommy said. "Church. We been to church, then to Gina's mama's for Sunday dinner—went to a Halloween party for the kids after that." Tommy paused. "You in jail?"

"Hell no," Earl said. "Worse. We hunted Calloway's land last night."

"It's closed," Tommy said.

"Run up on foreign soldiers."

"Run up on what?"

"No shit, Tommy. They got Dinky Betts." He paused. "I'm pretty sure they shot W.J."

"Earl, if you're in the meth again ..." Tommy's voice dropped to a whisper. "Tell me now, goddammit."

"I ain't! I swear! My phone's about dead, so listen up. Take the dirt road that runs behind Calloway's camp. Stop at that old chinaberry tree on the edge of the second cotton field. I'm in a little pine thicket across the road."

"It's at least an hour from here," Tommy said, "but I know right where it is. I'll flash my brights three times when I get there. You come runnin' out."

"Good." Earl rubbed his chin and sighed. "Bring Hazel if you can find him—Lloyd, too. And listen, Tommy, no cops—no matter what. This shit's got jail time written all over it."

"Should I call the Geneva Convention?" Tommy snickered.

"This ain't no joke, Tommy," Earl said. "It's life and death shit. Just come and get me."

CHAPTER THIRTY-ONE:
TROOPER'S
DISCOUNT

THE POACHER'S OLD PICKUP CREAKED AND groaned as Calloway stopped where the dirt road met the tar and gravel highway. His two-vehicle convoy had put fifteen miles of wide fields and woods between them and the hunting camp. He glanced back at Johnson and Vasquez in the Suburban then stuck his head out of the window. "Y'all okay?"

"Fine." Johnson said with a nod and reassuring grin. "I was afraid you wanted to switch vehicles."

Calloway waved, revved the Toyota's engine, and pulled out on the paved road. When he pushed the pickup past fifty-five, the over-sized tires sang like a bad tenor in a country church choir. The Toyota's sliding rear window glass had been knocked from its frame and the driver's seat was ripped down through the padding. Calloway sat cautiously on the edge of the seat. An errant coil spring could pop up at any time, ripping his new slacks or, worse yet, tear into his backside. At highway speeds, with the windows down, the truck cab still smelled like musty clothes, sweat and stale beer. Fumes from an exhaust leak drifted into the cab through the rusty floorboard, adding to the mix. Oil cans and beer bottles rolled and clanked under the seat. It would have nauseated anyone else, but Calloway had made a fortune buying and selling trashy trade-ins just like this one. For Calloway, it was the smell of money, of working a deal, but he needed little motivation on this strange Halloween night. The lifestyle he had worked so hard for over the years rode on the success of this mission.

And, dangerous as it was, Calloway chuckled as he zipped down the dark, lonely highway, listening to Vince Gill on an after market-stereo worth more than the truck, itself. Old feelings of excitement and fear from his youth crept into his middle-aged body, and, to his surprise, he liked it.

—⁓—

"What a trip," Johnson said, squeezing the Suburban's leather-wrapped steering wheel as he kept pace with the Toyota fifty yards ahead.

Vasquez looked at his Army buddy and smiled.

Here was Johnson, driving an expensive sport utility vehicle with the new-car smell, dressed in the finest clothes, and scared to death. The sounds, smells and fears of combat from decades ago had invaded his senses, and he prayed it would be the last time.

"Firefight to vacation in the same night," Johnson said. "Who'd believe it?"

"It's not a story we'll be telling the grandkids," Vasquez said. "I just hope we'll live out our old age with our families—not in some prison."

"Some conversation at this stage of our lives," Johnson said, fumbling with the FM radio tuner. "That's better," he said, locking in a Savannah blues station. But he cringed as one car, then another, passed in the opposite direction, only to fade harmlessly into the darkness behind them. The blues calmed his nerves a little until another set of headlights appeared in the rear view mirror. Suddenly, the car flashed high beams that bounced off the mirrors and shiny finish of the Suburban, and it was closing fast. Seconds later, pulsing blue and white lights flooded the interior of the big SUV. A piercing siren wailed in what had been a quiet night on a lonely road. Chills raced down Johnson's legs as his foot felt for the brake. Instinctively, he cocked the .45 and slipped it between the seat and center console.

"This can't be happening!" Johnson begged his pounding heart to slow down. He had been here before. And, so what if it was a new century?

He understood the situation as only a black man in the South could. The scenario was bad news on the best of days, even without two kidnap victims sprawled behind the back seat. Would he—could he—shoot, or try to explain the inexplicable?

It would not, however, be Johnson's decision to make.

The big, silver Crown Victoria with its shimmering blue stripes and gold shield sailed around the Suburban and hugged the Toyota's rear bumper. The pickup, not the Suburban, had attracted the attention of the South Carolina State Trooper. And if Johnson breathed a sigh of relief, it was a short one. Tonight, like decades ago, these old Rangers were in this thing together. In his heart, he knew it was a matter of honor and loyalty. Damn the risks, he thought. This time, no Ranger would be left behind.

Calloway wrestled the shuddering Toyota from the pavement to the narrow grassy shoulder with the patrol cruiser nearly touching his bumper.

Johnson drove slowly past, stopping about ten car lengths beyond the Toyota. He stayed in the Suburban, but his eyes were glued to the rear view mirror, studying every detail of the traffic stop. "Is he gonna get out of the car or what?"

Finally, a tall black man emerged from the patrol car—ramrod straight and neatly pressed. He held a long flashlight in his left hand, and his right hand was close to the automatic pistol holstered on his belt. This was no rookie, Johnson thought, watching the trooper move slowly and deliberately toward the pickup.

"I'm sure glad to see you." Calloway spoke before the trooper could open his mouth. "I'm Mike Calloway from Orangeburg," he said, smiling and extending his hand out the window to this striking specimen of law enforcement. He could have been the "Trooper of the Year".

"Sir." The trooper was courteous, but did not take Calloway's hand. "May I see your license and registration?"

"Certainly, officer." Calloway was still smiling when he handed the trooper his license. "I'm not sure about the registration."

"Mr. Calloway, you're probably wondering why I stopped you. You've got a burned out headlight on the passenger side."

"Thank you, sir," Calloway said, "But like I said, I really am glad to see you. "I don't have the registration. This ain't even my truck."

"According to DMV computer, it's registered to a W.J. Jones of Walterboro. Maybe you'd better step out of the vehicle, sir." The officer remained cautious, keeping plenty of space between himself and the driver's door.

"Yes, sir," Calloway said. "I guess this nasty old thing belongs to one of those drunks lying back in the truck bed. Me and my friends—that's them up there in my Suburban—found these boys passed out on the road a few miles back."

The trooper leaned over the side of the pick up for a look. He focused the flashlight beam on the unconscious poachers sprawled in the truck bed. He could smell the liquor the professor had poured all over them. Then he turned to face Calloway.

"Would've called the patrol right when we found them," Calloway explained. "Couldn't get my cell phone to work out here in the boonies. We just piled them up in the back of the truck. Figured the least we could do was get 'em out of the road. Hell, somebody could have robbed 'em— maybe even run 'em over."

"Mr. Calloway, I need to see your registration for the Suburban—your friend's license, too, please."

"No problem." Calloway was still smiling and cheerful. "Hey Robert! I need the registration. It's in the glove box. Better step down here for a minute, too."

Johnson had no idea what was going on, but he followed Calloway's instructions with one exception. He slipped the .45 under his blazer, wedging it between his silk trousers and the small of his back.

"Stay cool, Robert. Stay cool." Vasquez tried to calm his friend, but at the same time, eased his Colt from under the front passenger seat, cocked it, and carefully replaced it.

Johnson slipped off the soft leather seat of the Suburban. The loose stone on the tar and gravel road crunched under his new Italian loafers as he walked toward the trooper and Calloway. The officer directed them to stand in front of his cruiser while he fed their information into his computer. Calloway was calm, but Johnson was fidgeting. The only bright side to this situation Johnson could see was the trooper's young, black face. At least they were not facing some pot-bellied Southern stereotype whose heart was still shrouded in the Stars and Bars of the past.

"Mr. Calloway?"

"Yes, sir," he said, still maintaining his happy tone.

"Are you the Mike Calloway of Calloway Cars?"

"Guilty." Calloway chuckled.

"You know," the trooper said, "my grandparents and my parents bought cars from you. Granddaddy said you gave him credit years ago when nobody else would. I think they still buy from you—Rab and Etta Mae Jamison. James and Althea are my parents."

"You ain't Rab's little grandson?"

"Yes, sir, I'm Marshall Jamison."

"I'll be damned. Your granddaddy's sure proud of you, son." Calloway extended his hand and the officer took it this time. "Appreciate the way you handled this situation—real professional."

"Thank you, sir." The trooper's pleasant smile had replaced the empty, cautious game face so often associated with policemen on duty. "Mr. Calloway—I hate to ask—would you help me get those two into my vehicle? I'll call for a wrecker to tow their truck, then take them to the county hospital for a check-up. They'll wind up at the detention center after that."

"They're pretty messed up," Calloway said, frowning as he looked at the poachers in the truck bed. "Scratched up some. Maybe a fight or something." He wrinkled his nose. "Stink to high heaven, too. What do you reckon they've been drinking?"

"Sorry you had to get involved with trash like this," the trooper said. "You probably saved their lives, but they'll never know it."

"That's okay, Marshall," Calloway said. You know, I'd appreciate it if you'd just low-key this thing. Keep us out of it. Waking up in jail and all, well, they might blame us for getting them arrested. Might even want to kick our asses. We're heading to my house out at the beach. Thought I'd show my old Army pals a good time. The ladies are comin' down tomorrow."

"I think I can keep you gentlemen out of it," the trooper said.

"That'd be real nice of you," Calloway said. "I'll tell your granddaddy I saw you at the beach or some place nice. A story like this might upset him."

"Pleasure meeting you and Mr. Johnson," the trooper said. The three men shook hands, and the Army buddies walked toward the Suburban.

Calloway turned back toward the trooper. "By the way, Marshall, call me if you need a car or truck. Dealer's cost on anything you want—trooper's discount."

"Thank you, sir." The trooper smiled. "I might see you in a couple of months."

"Mike." Johnson whispered as they reached the Suburban. "You know what?"

"What's that?"

"You've got a horseshoe all the way up your ass."

"Well," Calloway said as he managed a little smile. "I can't feel anything back there right now. But if it's a horseshoe, I sure hope it don't fall out till we drop those other two off at the Ocean Star."

CHAPTER THIRTY-TWO:
ROAD BLOCK

"CRITICAL JOB HERE. DAMNED CRITICAL." RANGER SFC Willis Wilson sounded convincing enough.

Two young Army Rangers narrowed their eyes, showing their best game face to their platoon sergeant. He expected nothing less, and they knew it.

"No civilians beyond this point." Wilson pointed to a sawhorse with an orange sign—Military Exercise No Thru Traffic. "If that don't work, get on the horn to me. Individuals disregarding this order will be considered opposing force. Rangers in that treeline up ahead will take appropriate action."

"Roger that, Sergeant Wilson." Corporal Randy Hickson gave his best lip service with the snappy response. He had other plans after Wilson left.

"No mental lapses, Corporal." Wilson pointed his forefinger between Hickson's eyes as if it were a pistol. "Stay alert. Stay awake. Opposing Force is everywhere. Let me down and I'll smoke your asses. You got blanks—flashbangs, too. But I doubt you'll need 'em. No fixed bayonets, either. They may be OPFOR, but they're our guys." He laughed. "These riot sticks should scare the ghouls and goblins. See you at dawn. Happy Halloween!"

Hickson smiled, chuckling under his breath as he slapped the riot stick against his open palm. He was convinced guys like Wilson kept modern psychology running wide open.

The sergeant climbed into the Humvee and sped off toward the tree line, leaving his two young Rangers alone in the intersection that neatly quartered three hundred acres of cotton.

Hickson pushed the Kevlar helmet back on his head and turned to his single subordinate—PV2 Mark Green, fresh from the Ranger Indoctrination Program at Fort Benning, Georgia. He had reported three days earlier to the First Battalion, 75th Ranger Regiment at Hunter Army Airfield in Savannah.

"Fuckin' mental lapses," Hickson mumbled. "It's why I'm here." Then he dropped to one knee, rubbing his left ankle. He had sprained it playing basketball with the legs—the Rangers' not-so-nice nickname for a unit of 3rd Infantry Division ground troops, also stationed at Hunter. The injury had landed Hickson on a light duty medical profile—no parachute jumps, chopper rides or fast roping.

"What'd you say, Corporal?" Green spoke for the first time since Wilson left. Young Rangers kept their mouths shut. First days in battalion were worse than basic training—constant hazing by the unit veterans—getting smoked.

"Mental lapse. Wilson checked my room this afternoon looking for guys for this detail. I was on my bunk when he grabbed me—busted ankle and all. Said I could sit on my ass out here just as easy as in the barracks. Fuckin' ruined my weekend. Had just met this college chick from downtown—goddammit. Knocked me out of a cool Halloween party. So, here I am. Stuck out here in God knows where. How long did we ride, anyway?"

"About an hour and a half, Corporal. Wilson said we're in the South Carolina backwater between Beaufort and Hilton Head Island." Unlike Hickson, Green had expected the guard detail. The new guys always got it.

With painted faces and combat gear, Hickson and Green looked like the be-all-you-can-be boys in the recruiting ads. In reality, they were all dressed up with no place to go and nothing important to do while their platoon was in the middle of a war game. At least someone was having a good time, he thought.

"Hey, Green." Hickson unscrewed the cap from his canteen, wrinkling his nose as he sniffed the cool water in the plastic container. "I'm taking a pill the Doc gave me and taking a nap. Watch the road for a while, would you?"

"No problem, Corporal." The muscular nineteen-year-old from Washington, D.C. nodded. "Ankle bothering you?"

"Fuck, yeah." Hickson gulped down the medication. "Gotta get off it. See that tree?" He pointed to a scrub oak a few yards from the sandy intersection. "That's my pillow. Just whistle if you see headlights."

"You expecting anybody?"

"A local or two, maybe." A broad, toothy grinned spread across Hickson's face. "And you better stand ready. These backwoods guys don't like outsiders. Chances are they've never seen a Black Ranger either. Hell, the Army hasn't seen many. In fact, you're an enigma. Know what I mean?"

"I've been to college." Green returned the Corporal's smile. He was comfortable with Hickson, relaxing for the first time since arriving in the battalion. "Don't know about that enigma stuff. I'm just proud to be a Ranger."

"Cool," Hickson said, his smile fading. "Some folks out here still think the "N' word's a proper noun, but don't worry. It'll be real quiet. All we'll see is woods and bean fields. We'll be damned lucky to see the Blackhawks coming in." Then he turned and limped toward the scrub oak without looking back. "You're in command, Ranger Green."

CHAPTER THIRTY-THREE:
RIDING AROUND

"Took y'all long enough," Earl said, lifting the tailgate on his brother's Chevy K-5 Blazer and sliding his shotgun into the cargo hatch. "Thought y'all said an hour. Must've forgot where the cotton field was."

"Took a while to find Hazel," Tommy said. "And if we weren't brothers, I wouldn't be here. Had to give Gina some bullshit story just to get out of the house. Won't be gettin' any when I get home tonight—thank you very much."

"Can't believe I'm here either." Hazel Knight chimed in. "You and Dinky lied to me. Now, you see what it's got you?"

"I'm damned glad to be here." Lloyd Jones, Hazel's part time pulpwood worker and W.J.'s oldest brother, put in his two-cents' worth. "I love shit like this," he said, popping the tab on another cold Budweiser. "Of course, my main concern's about W.J. and Dinky."

"Listen Hazel." Earl walked up to the front passenger door and climbed into the old Blazer. "This is serious shit. Foreign soldiers got Dinky and W.J.—killed 'em, for all I know. If I'd gone straight back to the truck like Dinky, they'd have got me too."

"Foreigners?" Tommy laughed. "What y'all been smokin'?"

"It ain't funny, Tommy." Earl shook his head as he raised his right hand like a witness in court. "I ain't high and I ain't drunk—I swear to God.

"First, we slipped in the big field behind Calloway's camp. Didn't hear nothin'. Didn't see nothin'. Hadn't been in the woods an hour when all hell broke loose—commotion from the narrow head where Dinky went in. Then gunshots from where W.J. went in, and he starts yellin'. Soldiers comin' out of no where—painted up with camo, speakin' somethin' foreign. French, I think."

"Now you're a language expert," Tommy said.

"They carried machine guns, Mr. Wiseass," Earl said. "They sure as hell didn't come to hunt deer. Didn't need no interpreter to figure that out.

"I was too scared to move at first," Earl said. "I just stayed where Dinky put me—crouched down in a stand of little pines. A few minutes later, a soldier run past me—damn near stepped on me. I waited a few minutes, jumped up and worked my way back to W.J.'s truck. Two of 'em had already caught Dinky when I got there. A couple of minutes sooner, and I'd be a prisoner too. Damn, I need somethin' to drink."

"Sodas' in the cooler on the seat," Hazel said.

"No beer?"

"Lloyd drank the last one. Anyway, this story don't need no alcohol." Hazel grinned as he pulled a canned drink from the cooler and handed it to Earl.

Earl pulled the tab on a Pepsi, taking a big gulp before continuing his story. "One soldier had the drop on Dinky—put the damn gun to his head. The other one blindfolds him and ties him up. Had him on his fuckin' knees, for God's sake. Then he asks him who else is with him besides W.J., and Dinky gives them my name. Then they pull the distributor cap and drag him away. "Thought about shootin'," Earl said, "but I was outmanned and outgunned, and I mighta hit Dinky." He paused for another gulp of Pepsi. "Plus, shootin' somebody could get me another scholarship to 'pen state'. Y'all do know what I mean."

"I believe we do." Tommy raised his eyebrows as he looked around at Hazel.

"After they hauled Dinky off, I started walkin' out," Earl said. "Kept in the woods mostly, stayin' off the road. Oh, I didn't tell you about the helicopters. That was last night. I'm bettin' there's still soldiers out there—watchin' us right now. I was scared shitless. Don't feel too good now either."

"We'll just ride a while," Tommy said. "There's that bean field cross-roads a few miles up ahead. W.J. might be wandering around out there. If we see somebody, we can ask if they've seen any hunters or W.J.'s truck."

"Y'all do know Dinky's wanted in North Carolina," Hazel said.

"So?" Earl asked.

"You're a stupid shit, Earl." Hazel was heating up. "Don't mention Dinky's name to anybody. If the sheriff ties us to Dinky, we could all get in trouble. I love him better than any of my relatives, but he's on his own out here."

Tommy eased the clutch out and the big Blazer groaned forward. "Nobody'll arrest us for ridin' around," he said. "Besides, it's about all we can do right now."

"Might run into those foreigners," Earl said as he rubbed his arms briskly and folded them against his chest. "I'm still shakin'. And it's been almost a day since all this started." He turned to Hazel. "I'm real sorry, man. Dinky was gonna hunt come hell or high water. Shoulda said no—I know it now. We just thought it'd be a lot of fun. I'm real damn sorry." He turned his eyes back to the sandy road ahead, washed by the Blazer's headlights. For a moment, he thought he saw a yellow light flicker in the distance. He blinked furiously and looked again. "See that, Tommy?"

"Yeah." Tommy took his foot off the accelerator, pushed in the clutch, and let the Blazer to coast to a stop. He turned off the headlights and reached for the pair of battered binoculars.

"What's up Tommy?" Hazel leaned over the seat.

"Don't know," he whispered, bringing the field glasses up to his eyes. "Somethin's out there—some kinda light." There was a long pause, and Tommy lowered the binoculars.

"Come on, Tommy, what is it?" Earl was anxious. "Give me the damn glasses." Earl looked through the binoculars then slumped back in the seat. "See for yourself, Hazel. Y'all thought I was drunk—doped up, maybe. It's a damned roadblock. That's a soldier standin' by that barricade with a flashing light."

"Don't necessarily mean nothin'," Tommy said. "There's military all over. Marines at Beaufort. Army down Fort Stewart. They got shit goin' on all the time."

"Maybe," Earl replied. "But they don't go around talkin' French and kidnappin' civilians."

"Let's go talk to him," Hazel said. "Keep it nice and everything. Ask him if he's seen any hunters. We ain't done nothin' wrong—at least not you and me, Tommy." He smirked as he looked at Earl.

"This is for you, Hazel." Earl frowned as he gave Hazel the finger.

"Y'all knock it off," Tommy said. He switched on the headlights, eased the Blazer into first gear and pulled off in the direction of the faint, flickering light. "Got my forty-five in my lap, just in case." He looked at Earl. "Don't touch that shotgun. I'll handle this. You've done enough out here already."

CHAPTER THIRTY-FOUR:
AMBUSH

THE SHRILL WHISTLE SLICED THROUGH THE darkness, jolting Corporal Randy Hickson from his dreams of coeds, costume parties and any place but here.

"Corporal!" PFC Green focused his binoculars on a faint glow at the end of the huge cotton field and whistled again. "Headlights—two hundred meters out."

"Who taught you to whistle like that?" Hickson rubbed his eyes then scratched the Mohawk-like strip of brown hair running down the middle of his scalp. "I'm coming. I'm coming," he moaned.

"They're headed straight for us." Green continued to watch the distant light through his field glasses.

"Jesus!" Hickson cringed, putting weight on his bad ankle for the first time since he had fallen asleep. He hobbled toward the barricade, using his riot stick as a cane. "Just look serious—like a cop pulling somebody over, but don't say anything. I'll do the talking."

Minutes later, an old K5 Blazer, riding on over-sized tires, rumbled to a stop at the roadblock. Both Rangers stood in front of the black and white-striped sawhorses, their weapons at a low port position. Hickson raised his open hand, slung the assault rifle over his shoulder and walked toward the driver's door.

"Evening, sir," the corporal said, smiling as he touched the corner of his Kevlar helmet.

Tommy Mallard smiled back.

"Military exercise ahead, sir." Hickson pointed down the long road bisecting the cotton field. "This area's restricted tonight. I'm afraid you'll have to turn around."

"We been huntin' here for years," Tommy said, cutting his eyes toward Earl. "Never seen soldiers out here. What army y'all with anyway?"

"Yours, sir." Hickson grinned. "Sorry for the inconvenience. No civilian traffic beyond this point, sir."

"Uh-huh." Tommy adjusted his cap, rested his elbow on the window and lit a Marlboro. "Y'all seen any hunters tonight? We're missing two of our guys."

"No sir," Hickson said. "Have you reported them missing?"

"Too early for that," Tommy said, gazing back at Hazel. "They drink too much sometimes. Could be sleepin' it off in the woods."

"Actually, I'm familiar with that program, sir." Hickson's white teeth gleamed in contrast to the dark camouflage swirls painted on his face.

"They're driving a blue Toyota—beat up old four by four," Tommy said. "One's a skinny old boy. The other's a big young one."

"Haven't seen them, sir. You're the only folks we've seen." Hickson glanced down the long sandy road where Green first spotted headlights. "Another vehicle's coming. Could be your guys."

"Maybe." Tommy looked at Earl who had wriggled into a comfortable position against the front passenger door.

"Wait around if you like, sir," Hickson said. "You can back up and pull off the road over there. And please stay in your vehicle."

"No problem." Tommy nodded and smiled as he shifted the Blazer into reverse.

"Ranger Green?" Hickson turned to the young PFC.

"Yes, Corporal."

"Step back with these gentlemen while I wait for the next vehicle." The corporal motioned the private toward the big Chevy. "Don't get friendly with them," he whispered. "It's a long shot, but they could be OPFOR."

"Roger that, Corporal." Green turned on his flashlight as he walked toward the Blazer. "Jesus," he whispered as the narrow beam of light danced across the truck's front license plate. He raised his eyebrows, shook his head and sighed. It was the Confederate battle flag, a relatively discreet furled version, but the message was not lost on the African American soldier. Love of a lost cause dies slowly, if at all. The theme continued with stickers on the rear bumper. The one on the left read: "We don't care how y'all did it up North." The one on the right said: "If I'd known it was gonna be like this, I'd have picked my own cotton."

Green took a deep breath and let it out slowly. His Baptist preacher-father would have recommended counting to ten. He recalled his father's old stories about turning the other cheek, but that had been years ago. Cheek turning was not in the curriculum at the Ranger Indoctrination Program. Rangers were taught they were better than the rest. Converts were the most zealous, and Ranger Green had been freshly baptized into the warrior brotherhood. Add to that his special status—an African American in a mostly white Ranger world. He adjusted his helmet, set his jaw and walked toward the front of the Blazer, pointing his M4 at the ground then stopping at the right front passenger door. Earl was dozing against the window frame. A sly smile crossed Green's lips as he looked across the sea of southern cotton.

"Suh." Green slipped into a dialect somewhere between the mini-series *Roots* and Foghorn Leghorn of cartoon fame. "Y'all is welcome to practice if'n you gonna be here a while."

"What?" There was a puzzled look on Earl's tired face.

"Practice suh—y'all know, practice yo' cotton pickin'."

"Do what?"

"Your bumper sticker, suh." Green struggled to hold an innocent, wide-eyed expression. "Don't it say somethin' 'bout pickin' yo' own cotton?"

"Oh…" Earl finally got it and was not smiling. "That ain't what it means."

"My goodness, I'm so sorry, suh." Green laid it on extra thick. "What do it mean, suh?"

"Well." Earl furrowed his brow and pursed his lips, inhaling and exhaling short, hard breaths. Counting to ten was not a consideration. When he finally spoke, his face wrinkled into a sour expression and his lip quivered.

"What it means, soldier boy, is if we'd known you spear chuckers were gonna be such a pain in the ass, we'd a turned you loose a long time ago."

The latch clicked on the Blazer door. The hinges creaked loudly as it flew open and Earl's right foot hit the ground with a thud.

A split-second later, Tommy stretched across the front seat, grabbing his brother by his jacket collar. "Earl," he whispered. "This ain't the time or the place. You're the one said the woods were crawlin' with soldiers. You gonna fight 'em all?"

"No, no I ain't," Earl said, scowling as he jerked away from his brother's grasp. "But I know they're out there waitin'—waitin' for us to make a move." He glared at the smiling soldier, swung his leg back up into the truck and slammed the door. He stuck his head out of the window and called to Green: "Another time, another place, homeboy."

"Any time, any place. I'll be there, Mr. Peckerwood, sir!" Green spoke without a hint of an accent, squeezing the M4 grip as he backed away from the Blazer. Earl's only response was a trembling hand thrust out the truck window, middle finger raised in the defiant gesture of ill will.

Green knew his conduct had crossed the line, and while it felt good— really good—he broke off the taunting exchange with Earl. He may have been a member of one of the world's elite fighting forces, but on this night he was armed with nothing more than high-tech fireworks. His assault rifle was loaded with blank ammunition. He would have bet a month's pay the country boys were locked and loaded with live rounds, and ready to use them.

"Evening, sir." Green came to attention, giving a perfect salute as the Jeep Cherokee pulled alongside him.

"Stand easy, son."

"Uh, yes sir," Green stammered. "General, sir."

"Relax, son." As usual, the professor was enjoying the privileges of his self-appointed rank. "They didn't tell you the brass was coming. That's the way I operate. I'm down from the Pentagon—poking around. A few days over at Stewart, then over to Benning. I'll stop off at Bragg on the way home. You're in command here?"

"No sir," Green said. "Corporal Hickson is, sir. He's heading this way, sir."

The idea that an officer would show up at Hickson's desolate roadblock was bad enough. Coming face to face with a brigadier general in the middle of the Carolina backwater was a real shocker. This was supposed to be a simple, boring detail near the coastal marsh. "Good evening, sir." Surprisingly, Hickson did not stumble through the greeting and salute.

"Now," the professor said, "who's that over there?" He nodded toward the Blazer on the side of the road.

"We're stopping all traffic here, sir," Hickson said. "They're looking for their hunting buddies—got lost or drunk, sir. Supposed to be in a blue Toyota pickup. Haven't seen it. Have you, sir?"

"Afraid not," the professor replied then leaned over the front seat and tapped Boggs on the shoulder and raised his eyebrows. "How about you, Colonel?"

"Not tonight, General." Boggs glared at the professor. As usual, his old college buddy was having entirely too much fun.

The professor turned back to Hickson. "Son, we've got to pass through—cross these fields and move on to the main highway. Any fireworks expected out here in the next few minutes?"

"I'm not sure, sir." The soldier stepped closer to the Jeep window and lowered his voice to a whisper. "There's Ranger ambush set at a bridge—a mile or two up the road. I'll call Sergeant Wilson. I'm sure he'll pass you through."

"Thank you much," the professor said. "We'll miss our flight if we have to double back."

Moments later Hickson was on the radio to SFC Wilson, telling him about the one star in the Jeep. "You're cleared all the way, General," Hickson said.

"Thanks, son." The professor tossed him a regulation salute. "I'm real proud of the job you Rangers are doing. Country should be damned proud, too."

Boggs glanced at Cao who seemed to be resting comfortably for the first time in hours. Then the Padre leaned forward, tapping Boggs on the shoulder.

"I'm sure the Lord God Almighty is proud as well," the Padre said with a smile. Then he lowered his voice to a whisper. "As for the general, well, I'm not so sure."

Boggs nodded in agreement as he guided the Jeep past the Blazer and around the barricade. "Good thing we haven't changed clothes yet, and he's still 'General' or we'd never have made it out."

"I'm sure the guys in the Blazer are looking for our county boys," the professor said.

"No doubt at all," Boggs said, never looking up from the long stretch of sandy road that lay ahead. "Wonder which one is Earl?"

—ɯ—

"Let's follow that Jeep, Tommy." Earl leaned over, slapping his brother's shoulder with the back of his hand. "You saw those soldier boys salute whoever was in there. It's officers. Maybe they'll help us find Dinky and W.J."

"It'll mean runnin' this roadblock—"

"Fuck it!" Lloyd's six beers spoke loud and clear. "We're the only ones with real bullets. Them GI Joe's are shootin' blanks. When I was in the Reserve, they never gave road guards live ammo."

"That was twenty years ago," Hazel said.

"That kind of shit don't change," Lloyd said.

"Maybe the DEA and the Army's cooked up somethin' out here," Tommy said.

"Bullshit," Lloyd said, leaning across the seat. "County cops would be out here with 'em. "Look, my brother's out there, and I'm gonna find him."

"Hit it, Tommy." Earl buckled his seat belt. "This truck'll cut through those sawhorses like cardboard."

Hickson walked to the driver's door of the Blazer. "Sorry, sir. Just military personnel in the Jeep. Guess you'd better turn around now."

"No Problem, Sarge." Tommy smiled, touching the bill of his camouflage hunting cap as he gently revved up the big V8. He looked around at his passengers. "Everybody buckle up." He shifted into first gear, pressed the pedal to the floor and the Blazer roared into the middle of the crossroad.

Hickson jumped off the road as the truck fishtailed, spraying sand in every direction.

Green had walked toward the barricade, but he looked back when he heard the big engine whine. He was trapped between the Blazer and a sawhorse, and, at the last second, he sidestepped the right front bumper with the skill of a bullfighter.

Hickson watched in amazement as Earl flung open the door, slamming Green across the back and launching him into the sawhorses.

"How you like me now, spear chucker! How you like me now!" Earl screamed with laughter, slapping his palm against the door of the Blazer as it sped after the Jeep.

Hickson ran to his fellow Ranger's aid, firing short bursts of blank rounds at the Blazer. "You okay, man!"

Green gasped for breath as he crawled from under the broken sawhorses. He was still gasping as the corporal helped him to his knees. "Got the...wind... knocked...out of me." He threw his helmet to the ground and brushed the sand from his face. "God damn! What was that all about?"

"Roadblock one to base. This is Hickson. We have contact! Over."

"Corporal!" Sergeant Wilson screamed into the radio. "What's going on down there? How can you have contact? Over."

"Happened after we passed the general through, Ranger Sergeant. Four guys in a Chevy Blazer ran the roadblock and knocked Green down."

"Is he hurt? Over."

"Had the wind knocked out of him. He's sitting up now."

"How many enemy, Hickson?"

There was a silence, then the corporal spoke. "Enemy, Sergeant Wilson? Four, but they looked like rednecks to me."

"Sound's like OPFOR infiltrators, son. Could be after that general. But it's my problem now. Stay put. I'll send a medic to look at Green. Out."

—⁂—

Boggs squinted as headlights appeared in the rearview mirror. "We've got company."

The professor looked over his shoulder and shook his head. The headlights seemed to be gaining on the Jeep. "They're coming fast, Barry. Better kick this thing."

Boggs checked the odometer. "The bridge should be about a mile ahead. Don't want to spin out in this sand or hit the bridge running wide open."

"We're gainin' on 'em," Earl said. "Probably catch 'em just across that irrigation ditch. Flash the lights and blow the horn, Tommy. Maybe they'll stop. We just want to talk."

"They're flashing their headlights," Boggs said.

"Might have to shoot our way out of this one." The professor shook his head.

"What a comforting thought." The Padre spoke without emotion, unconcerned with the chase that was underway or the prospects for a firefight.

"They're about two hundred yards and closing." Boggs swerved to the right as he spoke.

"Drive, don't talk," the professor said.

"Got to slow down for the bridge." Boggs eased off the gas pedal. "Can't out run them. I'll do a one-eighty after I cross the bridge. Padre, you and Cao stay down."

"I'll take care of myself, laddie," MacDonald replied. "Calloway gave me this shotgun, and I'll use it."

"Please, Reverend," Lyle said. "Hold your fire—your water, too, if you can."

Seconds later, the Jeep nosed up as it climbed the short ramp to the bridge. For a split-second, the four passengers were weightless, as if riding a roller coaster. Boggs fought the steering wheel for control as the Jeep skidded and swerved on the other side of the bridge. Then he hit the brakes, putting the Cherokee into a spin. When it stopped, the Jeep had completed an almost perfect one-eighty and was about one hundred yards beyond the bridge. Everyone except Cao piled out, each aiming a weapon in the direction of the headlight glow on the other side.

"Don't fire," Boggs yelled, "unless fired—" If Boggs finished his sentence, no one heard it. There was a massive thunderclap, and the ground shook on either side of the irrigation ditch. Pieces of wood, tons of sand and water sprayed skyward.

"Take cover!" Boggs shoved his passengers back into the Jeep as bits and pieces of debris fell around them.

Tommy Mallard's Blazer was about forty yards from the bridge when the C4 exploded. The truck swerved from one side of the road to the other, finally coming to rest on its side in the cotton about twenty yards from ground zero. The Blazer appeared to be the only casualty. A piece of four by four bridge support had slammed through the grill and into the radiator. Hot, green coolant was spewing out. Dazed by the blast, Mallard and his passengers crawled out through the tailgate and stumbled toward the road.

"God, I love this job!" Wilson shouted, then he tossed the detonator on the ground and stood ramrod straight, peering through binoculars at his handiwork. Combat engineers had built the bridge three days earlier, specifically for this mission. Now—a bit earlier than originally planned— he had blown it to bits. He was relieved, but still smiling, when he saw the occupants moving under their own power. "Fire at will!" His deep voice broke the brief, eerie silence. Instantly, Rangers hidden in the treeline fifty yards from the bridge opened up with M240 machine guns and M4 assault rifles.

Tommy and Hazel dove headlong into the tough cotton stalks.

"I told y'all!" Earl screamed as he ran across the cotton field away from the muzzle flashes. "I told y'all! Goddammit!"

Lloyd Jones' service as a cook in the Army Reserve had done little to prepare him for the Halloween night ambush set by the Rangers. The six beers he drank earlier in the evening—the source of his false bravado—only exposed his fear and added to his humiliation. When he finally stopped running he was hopelessly lost, and that unmistakably wet, warm feeling was rushing down his legs and into his boot socks.

—⁓—

Boggs and his passengers had scrambled into the Cherokee when the Rangers opened up from the tree line. The professor smiled as he sat back in the seat satisfied the gunfire fire was directed toward the other side of the bridge. "Time to go, gentlemen. As granddaddy used to say, 'we ain't got no dog in this fight.'"

Boggs smirked as he turned the Jeep ignition key to the start position. "I didn't think you knew your granddaddy."

"Well," the professor stammered, caught in on of his fictional anecdotes. "If I had known him, I'd bet that's what he would have said." He paused. "What the hell. I always wanted to use that line. It just seemed to fit."

"Bullshitter." Boggs laughed as he pressed the accelerator, powering the Jeep's four wheels through the sand.

Then the Padre chimed in. "Confession, my dear Professor, is good for the soul."

Lyle leaned over to the Padre. "Speaking of worn out old lines…"

CHAPTER THIRTY-FIVE:
GOING HOME

STRAINING TO SEE IN THE DIM light, Freddie Jones aimed a beer bottle at the last slot in the six-pack on the deer stand floor. When it clanked into the carton beside five empties, he grinned like a kid who had beaten a hustler in a carnival game. Freddie had found two beers in the cooler, downing both after climbing the twenty-foot-high press box-sized structure. It had been built for gentlemen hunters, but, when necessary, it doubled as the airstrip tower. Freddie leaned against the smooth pine railing and sighed. Day or night, the view was spectacular, and November First was no exception. Neither clouds nor city lights blemished the star-filled sky. Not a single highway sound from distant Road 276 penetrated the woods and fields. It was a typical, beautiful autumn night at Maywood.

"This here place, dear Lord—and it ain't the beer talkin'—is home," Freddie said. "Ain't no other place I'd want to be."

"Freddie." A clear, calm voice spoke over the walkie-talkie he clutched in his left hand.

"Yes sir, Dr. Terrill."

"Switch on the lights, Freddie," Raines said. "They're ten minutes out."

"Yes sir." Freddie turned to the gray metal power box on the tower wall, lifted the cover and flipped four black circuit breakers. Bright white lights came to life, outlining a long rectangular airstrip on the dark grassy landscape. He cocked his head to one side, looked south and listened for the drone of the Cessna.

Fifteen minutes later, Boggs was on the ground at the north end of the field, making a tight one-eighty before taxiing to the deer stand.

"Doc?" The man sitting next to Raines in the Ford Expedition spoke softly. "Even if I didn't owe you one, I'd still be doing this."

"You're a good man, Walt, and a great doctor." Raines patted the younger man on the shoulder. "That's why I called you."

"Freddie!" Raines called out as Jones descended the tower steps. "We've got a couple of injured men. We'll need your help."

Boggs was helping the Padre off the aircraft when the SUV pulled up. He noticed the minister was a little unsteady and held on to his arm.

"Jesus, Laddie." The Padre grumbled and pulled his arm free. "A little wobbly from the plane ride, that's all. I'm perfectly fine."

"We've got doctors here to make sure." Boggs nodded toward the Expedition. "And we're not taking off again unless they say it's okay."

Freddie pitched in, helping get Cao off the aircraft. The drugs Vervoort had given him had long since worn off and he moaned softly with each step.

Doctor Walt Guerry skipped the introductions, moving directly to Cao and pulling open his camouflage shirt for a quick look at the wound. "What the hell happened … and when?"

"Hunting arrow." Boggs answered matter-of-factly. "About twenty-four hours ago. A field medic cleaned it up the best he could. He's had some morphine."

"And the older man?" Guerry looked at the Padre, still wearing the field dressing on his head.

"Buckshot pellet grazed his scalp." Boggs smiled as he glanced at Mac-Donald. "Says he's okay, but he was a little dizzy getting off the plane."

"Were you guys hunting or in a firefight?"

Boggs looked at Dr. Raines, then back to the younger physician. "Come on Walt. It's just a hunting mishap," Boggs said.

"Let's get these injured men to the duck pond cabin," Dr. Raines said, stopping the game of twenty questions. "We'll examine them there."

An hour later, the doctors walked out the front door of the cabin. Guerry's stethoscope hung from his neck, his black bag dangling from his left hand.

"Well?" Boggs asked. He and the professor had been pacing outside the cabin like expectant fathers.

"They both seem okay." Guerry dropped his bag and pulled a Winston light from a half-spent pack in his coat pocket. "I gave the young guy something for pain. Whoever treated him in the field did everything right. I changed the dressings and gave them tetanus shots—Tylenol for the old guy's headache. Get the young one to my clinic tomorrow—after six o'clock. I'm pretty sure he'll be fine, but I want an X-ray to be sure. If the pictures look okay, he'll need at least a week of rest before he travels

"And…" The younger doctor paused and turned to Dr. Raines. "It might surprise you, but I'm no cherry when it comes to something like this. I'll keep it off the record books. You sure as hell don't need Deputy Barney out here snooping around.

"As for the Scotsman." Guerry lowered his voice. "The scrape on his head's fine, but his blood pressure and heart rate worry me a little. Might just be what ever the hell went on where ever y'all were." He cut his eyes toward Boggs. "Anyway, I asked him about his history, but he was vague—intentionally, I think. Make sure that old fart sees his physician when he gets home."

"I'll try," Boggs shook his head. "But the Padre's got a mind of his own."

"Freddie?" Raines asked. "Can you stay the rest of the night?"

""No problem, Dr. Terrill. Flora's in Charlotte with her sister. Nobody's gonna miss me."

"Walt? Stay the night—what's left of it," Dr. Raines said. "Plenty of room here."

"Thanks, Doc," Guerry said. "It's been a long weekend. Better get home—re-introduce myself to my wife." Guerry climbed into his Toyota Land Cruiser, cranked it up, then lowered the window and smiled. "Hey Doc? Any chance we'll shoot ducks when the weather changes?"

"You've got a standing invitation." Raines reached in to shake Guerry's hand. "Thanks Walt," he said and walked toward the cabin.

"Don't mention it," the surgeon said, raising his eyebrows. "And I really mean don't mention it—ever." Then he turned to Boggs and Lyle. "Guess we've got a second secret to keep."

"Another little one, too," Boggs said.

"Another one?" Guerry asked.

"I got shot in my right forearm. Went clean through," Boggs whispered. "They cleaned and bandaged it in the field. Can't remember when I had a tetanus shot. Don't want Doc to know about this."

"What in the world's going on?" Guerry asked.

"Nothing for you to worry about," Bogg said. "Like we said, just some unfortunate things happening on a hunting trip."

"I'd love to believe that," Guerry said. "But you guys look like you've been in some serious shit."

"Walt," Lyle said. "We've all shared a secret for years. Nothing's been said about our little raid that night at Carolina. Let's just say this is another one—albeit unexpected—we'll have to keep."

"Unexpected. Just another little one," Guerry said, shaking his head. "What choice do I have?"

"None," Boggs said. "And just so you know, it's a hell of a lot more honorable than stealing final exams."

Guerry sat quietly for a few moments, then reached for his medical bag. "Okay, Barry. Walk around to the passenger's side. Let's take a look at your arm before Doc comes out of the cabin."

Twenty minutes later, Dr. Raines walked out the front door of the cabin, buttoned his hunting coat, and walked slowly toward Barry and the professor.

The two men shifted nervously from one leg to the other, like teenagers caught in the act and waiting to face the music.

The professor broke the silence. "It's been years since I was out here, Dr. Raines. Good to see you looking so well." He paused. "Of course, we're sorry about the, uh…unusual circumstances."

"Unusual? Indeed, Professor." The old doctor smiled. "Things were simpler when you were college boys. You'd just steal my whiskey and take girls down to the duck cabin."

"Yes, sir." Lyle shrugged, maintaining a sheepish grin.

"But spare me the details of this adventure," Dr. Raines said. "I'll just assume there's something honorable in it," he said, turning to Boggs. "God knows, you two have everything to loose."

"It's all about honor," Boggs said. "Maybe we can talk about it someday."

The professor weighed in. "With all due respect, Dr. Raines is in deep enough already. It all stems from a matter of honor, and let's just leave it at that."

"Graydon," Dr. Raines said. "I regarded you as a rather benign bullshit-ter in your college days, but it's clear you've elevated that art form to new heights."

"No disrespect intended, Dr. Raines." The sincerity oozed out with the professor's words.

"None taken, Graydon." The old man put his arms on the shoulders of both men. "If there's something I need to know, I'm sure you men will tell me."

CHAPTER THIRTY-SIX:
HOLD HARMLESS

JACK CANNADY COULD WRITE A BOOK on Halloween pranks, playing them as a kid then policing them for twenty years as sheriff of Beaufort County, South Carolina. He was convinced, however, the story just laid out before him was the genuine article—a bona fide nominee for his personal hall of fame.

"So," the sheriff said, leaning back in the old oak chair that had served his father and grandfather before him, "you say you were..." Cannady paused. "Attacked...by state game wardens...possibly foreign soldiers and by U.S. Army Rangers. All in the same night?"

Earl Mallard leaned across Cannady's desk. "The God's truth, Sheriff. I think they shot W.J. Jones over near the Calloway tract. Who knows what happened to Dinky Betts when they took him prisoner."

"Took him prisoner?" The sheriff sipped a diet soda, spun his chair around, and looked out the window across the salt marsh.

"Yes, sir, Sheriff. Like I said, I was hidin' in the brush when they grabbed Dinky—two soldiers wearing masks...with machine guns. Only one did all the talking—in French. I'm pretty sure it was French."

"With machine guns." The poker-faced sheriff kept his eyes on the marsh, never changing expression. "Speaking French."

"Listen, Sheriff." There was frustration in Earl's voice. "I ain't on drugs, and I ain't been drinking. I passed your blood alcohol test. Now, I want to press charges—file a lawsuit against my attackers—the government or whoever did this."

"Whoever?" the sheriff asked. "That's probably the best place to start." Then he swiveled the chair around to face Earl. "Your brother Tommy and Hazel haven't said much."

Tommy pursed his lips and shrugged.

Hazel raised his eyebrows and shook his head, then broke the silence. "Except for that—that misunderstanding with the Rangers, we didn't do anything wrong. We were just trying to help Earl find the other two boys."

"Earl told us the same story he's telling you," Tommy said. "I know it sounds crazy, but he's my brother. I had to go see about him."

"Okay," the sheriff said, placing his palms flat on the big oak desk then leaning over, eyeball to eyeball with Earl. "Y'all listen up. I'm not taking this cock and bull story to a magistrate. He'd love to get a good laugh at my expense. And Earl, my friend, you've got things backwards. It's you boys facing charges. Trespassing, interfering with a federal agency, and assault. Could've killed that Ranger at the roadblock."

Earl jumped to his feet. "But they done it to us, Sheriff! It was them interfered with us."

"Sit the fuck down, Earl," the sheriff said in a calm, weary voice. "Now, since nobody got hurt, the United States Army's willing to forget the incident. And they checked; there were no foreigners with the Rangers. They'll also pay to fix Tommy's truck."

"Fix my truck?" Tommy sat up straight in the chair.

"And drop all the charges?" Hazel asked.

"I just talked to a JAG officer from Hunter Army Airfield over in Savannah," the sheriff said. "They've already put it in writing. All he wants is a hold harmless from y'all—no talking about the incident and no lawsuits against anybody regarding this mess."

"Where do we sign," Tommy said.

"What about W.J. and Dinky?" Hazel asked.

The sheriff stood, still nursing the diet soda. "Their story doesn't square with Earl's. They say nobody got shot. Nobody got kidnapped. They just got drunk, pulled off the road and passed out. They don't remember anything else. No soldiers. No game wardens. No foreigners. A state trooper found them on the side of the road, picked them up, and brought them here."

"Got bought off," Earl muttered. "Somebody bought 'em off."

"You letting them go?" Hazel asked.

"Jones can go," the sheriff said. "Betts is wanted in North Carolina. He stays locked up till that's straightened out. Sorry.

"Now, boys, what'll it be?" the sheriff asked, drumming his fingers on the oak desk. "State and federal charges—and did I mention you'd have to go before a federal magistrate? And those boys got no sense of humor—zilch. Or, you'll sign off and forget anything happened."

"Like I said." Tommy spoke up. "Where do I sign?"

"It's all or none," the sheriff said. "If Earl, in his infinite wisdom chooses to sue this whoever person or the government, then all y'all go before the state and federal magistrates. It's simple. Everybody signs or everybody gets charged."

Earl folded is arms across his chest and frowned. "I got a case," he said, "but I ain't going back to jail. So, I'll sign, dammit."

"Excellent choice," the sheriff said. "The government's already emailed your papers. Y'all can sign and be out of here in a little bit."

—⚬—

Sheriff Cannday leaned back in his swivel chair, pinching the bridge of his nose and waiting for the headache powder to kick in. Two hours had passed since he helped the poachers see the light and stay out of jail. He knew something had happened out there in the backwater—Halloween or no Halloween—but he was relieved there would be no state or federal investigation—particularly with his bid for re-election at stake. No reporters. No television. No bullshit.

"Sheriff?" Cannady's chief deputy spoke softly, trying not to interfere with the headache healing process. "Might want to see this."

Cannady shook his head, pulled his chair up to the old desk and rested his elbows on the glass top. "Okay, Ralph. What is it?"

"It's shrimp boats, off Hilton Head. They ran up on two rubber boats—half sunk. Both are registered to the state wildlife. And listen to this."

"I'm all ears," the sheriff said, pinching the bridge of his nose again.

"The wildlife says it's their numbers, but it ain't their boats. Theirs are safe and sound. Locked in the impound in Columbia."

"They're sure?" the sheriff asked.

"A guy was looking out his window when he talked to me. Their boats are there—safe but with the same numbers as the ones sunk."

"No shit," the sheriff said.

"Want to know what was in those boats?" the chief deputy asked.

"I'm sure you're gonna tell me."

"Game warden jackets, caps, camouflage uniforms and a couple of Halloween masks."

"No machine guns?"

"No, sir," the chief deputy said. "Not a one, but...there was a pack of foreign cigarettes—French, maybe."

"French?" The sheriff never looked up. "Do tell."

"Yes, sir," the chief deputy said. "And a golf ball with a big slice in it. Smiling, like a smiley face—without the eyes, of course. Sounds like something to do with those old boys who just left—foreigners, game wardens—"

"Ralph?" Cannady looked up at his chief deputy. "Stop right there. Get those boats on a trailer. Bag up all that clothing and any other loose shit on those boats. Bring everything over here and cover it all up."

"Then what, Sheriff?"

Cannady pinched the bridge of his nose again. "I don't want to hear anything else about it. Maybe we'll have a look—after the election."

That's it, then?"

"That's it," the sheriff said.

CHAPTER THIRTY-SEVEN:
INTENSIVE CARE

BY THE THIRD RING, BOGGS HAD reached a semi-conscious state, straining to read the red digits on the clock across the room: 3:20 a.m. He stretched an arm toward the nightstand and groped for the telephone. When he found it, he paused, resting his hand on the receiver while wishing for a wrong number. He knew from experience that bad news traveled best in the predawn darkness, and waited for the fourth ring to answer. "Hello."

"Barry?"

"Yeah."

"It's Ann, Sweetie."

Boggs sighed. "Do you know what time it is?"

"It's Rev. MacDonald," she said. "It's his heart. They've taken him down to Hickory by helicopter. He wants to see you."

"Which hospital?" Boggs asked as he pulled a sweater and a pair of khakis from his closet.

"Ridge General," she said. "I'm about fifteen minutes from your place. Shall I pick you up?"

"Yeah…yeah," Boggs said as his mind filled with whys and what ifs Ann Johnson could never know about. "That's fine. I'll be ready."

Boggs and Ann stepped off the third floor elevator at Hickory's Ridge General Hospital and walked straight to the nurses' station. "Where's Reverend MacDonald ma'am?"

A plump, middle-aged nurse was glued to her cell phone, but finally looked up when Ann tapped her perfectly manicured fingernails on the pale green desktop.

"Are you two family?"

"I'm one of his parishioners," Ann said with a smile that really was not a smile.

Boggs pursed his lips, rested his elbows on the nurse's desk, got at eye level with the nurse and smiled. "Ma'am we're all the family he's got. Where is he?"

Boggs's was out of patience, and the nurse sensed it.

"ICU is through those double doors, sir." She pointed down the hallway to her right. "Please see the nurse at the desk."

Boggs walked to the doors of the ICU, stopped and took a deep breath. He had not seen the Padre since Thanksgiving—a week ago—but his thoughts drifted back to the time they had spent together. There had been food, a few glasses of wine and conversation that inevitably had turned to the mission at Hilton Head.

"I told everyone I cut my head on a barbed wire fence—good white lie," the Padre had said with laugh. "Even Dr. Daley over in Boone fell for it."

"And he's given you a clean bill?"

"Indeed, Laddie." The Padre winked and raised his glass. "Said I'm good for a glass or two on special occasions as well—and it's Thanksgiving.

"What about Cao?" The Padre was serious. "Safely back where he came from?"

"Safe and sound, according to Doc Raines. Only problem was he wanted to stay at Maywood—for good. Said things are too unsettled in South Africa. But he knew he had to go—for now, at least. He left with perfectly forged papers, a plane ticket and plenty of cash—all courtesy of our own professor."

"What a bugger your old pal is!" The Padre laughed and slapped his knee. "I've got to hand it too him, Laddie. He put together quite a mission. One I'll never forget. I know you were pissed at my tagging along, but I wouldn't have missed it for the world."

—⁂—

"Are you okay?" Ann touched Boggs on the arm. "Shall we go in?"

Boggs saw the puzzled look on her face. "I'm fine. Just thinking about my last visit with the Padre."

The automatic doors to the ICU opened, and two men walked up to Boggs and Ann. The man in a dark tan hunting jacket identified himself as Dr. Daley, the Padre's regular physician. The other wore bright blue surgical scrubs with a nametag identifying him as Dr. Ames.

"The Scotsman's a candidate for surgery if he can survive it." Ames skipped the pleasantries. "He's pretty weak, but we don't have much choice. Without surgery, he'll have a short, miserable life."

"The Reverend's known about his heart disease since last spring. He knew something like this could happen at any time," Dr. Daley said. "A heart cath is a good bet. Open-heart surgery's more likely, depending on how strong he is. Dr. Ames'll make that call. Can't tell you much more until then. Unless there's something else…"

Boggs, the executive, was involved now. "Can you guys handle this?"

"Dr. Ames is an excellent surgeon."

"Listen, Doctor." Boggs was curt. "If there's any question about the diagnosis, call in the best. The top guys at Duke—send him to Houston if necessary."

"Mr. Boggs." Dr. Daley spoke apologetically. "We'll do our best, but the Reverend's health insurance may not cover all that."

"No offense, Doc." Boggs remained calm. "I won't stand for any insurance bullshit. I'll write you a check or give you a bankcard tonight. Mark Thorne at Bank of America in Charlotte will cover anything I write."

"I think we'll be fine here," Dr. Daley said.

"Rev. MacDonald knows all this?"

"He knows." Dr. Daley folded his arms across his chest and leaned against the wall. "I tried to get him down here in October—before something like this happened—but he wouldn't do it. Said he had to help an old friend first. So, here we are."

"The Padre's like that." Boggs walked to a window, staring silently into the early morning light. He turned to the doctors. "Can we see him?"

"Sure." Dr. Ames smiled. "He's been asking for you."

Boggs stood at the foot of the bed, his arms folded and his chin resting between his right thumb and forefinger. Good drugs, he thought, watching the Padre sleep while wired to monitors, an IV and oxygen.

"Go ahead. You can talk to him," Dr. Ames said.

"It's Boggs, Padre." He walked to the side of the bed. "Ann Johnson's here, too. Can you hear me?"

"Barry? Glad you're here, Laddie. And you've brought...an angel with you." The minister's voice was weak. "There's a note... in my desk at home. It's got instructions for my funeral."

"Please," Ann said, as she leaned over and kissed the Padre's forehead. "I won't listen to that kind of talk."

"For God's sake, Padre," Boggs said. "You'll be out of here in no time."

"Listen, Barry...there's something not in the note. I want to be buried in the MacDonald plaid—as a highlander. The clothes are hanging in my closet. And my shoes. Don't forget my shoes. And find a piper—*Abide with me* for Evelyn and *Amazing Grace* for me."

"Enough of this funeral talk," Boggs said. "You've got fine doctors taking care of you. I'll send for the best in the country if they need help."

"Save your money." The Padre managed a thin smile and reached up to touch Boggs on the arm. "I prayed for you and the lads—Professor, Schiller, Calloway, Johnson—prayed for them all. It was one of the best missions ever. But I've had it, Laddie, and I'm at peace. Scrape the snow from my little plot on that hillside. I'm ready to join my dear Evelyn."

Boggs shook his head and chuckled. "Padre, the only thing getting scraped this morning is the plaque in your arteries."

Ann, stepped closer to Boggs, put her arm around his waist, and whispered, "What's that mission stuff he's mumbling about?"

Boggs raised his eyebrows and managed a faint smile. "Probably something from his warrior days, I guess. If he says any more, he'll probably have to kill us."

CHAPTER THIRTY-EIGHT:
HONOR AND REMEMBRANCE

BOGGS STOOD AT THE FIELDSTONE ENTRANCE to Scots Cemetery, gazing silently at the white peaks across the gorge. His sad eyes followed the ridges down to the old maple at the back of the graveyard. Picked clean by the changing seasons, its bare branches cast a thin shadow over the MacDonald burial plot. He sighed, watching in disbelief, as two workmen scraped the snow away.

Forty-eight painful hours had inched by since the Padre had fought his last battle and lost. Was it just the coronary disease? Was it the excitement of the mission? Was it a broken heart? Whatever it was, Boggs believed the Scotsman had lacked the will to fight and was anxious to join his beloved Evelyn on this mountainside. No one in this life would ever know, but Boggs blamed himself. "Why," he whispered, "did I ever mention Carter's name?"

Unfazed by the morning chill, Boggs continued to brood as emotionless gravediggers plied their trade, making room in the cold ground for the Padre's earthly remains. Boggs thought of his phone calls to the old Rangers from the Hilton Head mission. To a man, they had expressed shock and sadness. The professor and Calloway would try to attend. Johnson and Vasquez would send flowers. Contacting Schiller would have been far too risky, and Doc Raines was in too deep already.

Boggs had telephoned his daughter with the bad news, but the reason for the call went beyond that. He had to hear her voice, tell her how much he missed her and that he loved her more than life itself. There was nothing like watching someone die to sharpen the focus on one's own mortality. When the Padre slipped away, it was as if the dark angel had brushed Boggs's shoulder as he drifted from the hospital room, leaving a chilling reminder: Boggs's time would come, and the dark prince would know where to find him.

Only the whining ignition of the gravediggers' backhoe jolted Boggs from his reflections on the events of the past two days. He glanced at his watch, surprised a half-hour had passed since he had walked to the cemetery gate. Reluctantly, he had agreed to say a few words at the graveside service and had come to this peaceful place searching for the inspiration he would surely need. He had six hours to find those words and put them together.

Sunlight filtered through the broken clouds as the backhoe chugged away, scooping red clay from a rectangular hole in the hillside. Boggs smiled for the first time in two days as the warming rays touched his shoulders. He pulled a pen and small notepad from his leather jacket, leaned against the stone wall and scribbled a few lines as the sunshine worked its way into the gorge. He had time. The Blowing Rock Library was just minutes from the cemetery.

—m—

A lone piper stood at the high point of the gently sloping graveyard, sending the plaintive strains of *Abide With Me* over the mourners and across the gorge. When he finished playing, the senior minister of Scots Presbyterian Church turned to those gathered around the oak casket. "One of Reverend MacDonald's friends will say a few words."

Boggs fumbled with his notes, but stepped forward with confidence, looking at those assembled and nodding when he recognized a neighbor or familiar face from the mountain community. He was surprised to see the professor, dressed in banker's gray, standing next to a solemn Mike Calloway dressed in a fitted Armani suit with a fresh haircut.

"I first met the Reverend MacDonald when he ran his old MG off a mountain road near my house. He called me a Good Samaritan when I gave him a lift. When I called him 'Padre', he told me he wasn't a Catholic. But he looked like a fatherly character from a John Wayne or Pat O'Brien movie, and I called him Padre ever since.

"I know he was a minister to many of you here today, but he was one of my best friends. We have—we had—some things in common." Boggs paused and shook his head. "I'll have to get used to talking about him in the past tense.

"Both of us loved the mountains. He'd say the Blue Ridge was the closest place to Scotland this side of the Atlantic. I'd tell him it was as close to Heaven as a sinner like me could hope to get. But he never stopped praying for me. The first verse of Psalm 121 probably sums up our thinking on the subject. 'I will lift up mine eyes unto the hills, from whence cometh my help.' But he would say the second verse was more important: 'My help cometh from the Lord, who made heaven and earth.' We both found strength up here.

"In his other life, as he called it, he'd served in the British Special Air Service. He was decorated for gallantry, though he rarely talked about it. But he believed in honor and remembrance—not unlike Shakespeare's Henry the Fifth. Please bear with me as I read a few of those lines.

> By Jove, I am not covetous for gold,
> Nor care I who doth feed upon my cost;
> It yearns me not if men my garments wear;
> Such outward things dwell not in my desires:
> But if it be a sin to covet honour,
> I am the most offending soul alive."

Boggs looked up from his notes, making eye contact with the mourners. "I learned the lesson of honor from my Vietnam service. Padre and I shared that bond and belief. He was a man of honor."

Boggs's lip quivered, and he paused to regain his composure. Then he caught a glimpse of Ann Johnson who had stepped within a few feet of him. She nodded her approval and smiled. "Go ahead, Barry," she whispered, taking his arm. "You're doing fine."

"King Henry had a difficult task—inspiring his outnumbered lords who were about to fight the French on Saint Crispin's Day, and he wanted them to know they'd be remembered." Boggs read:

> And Crispin Crispian shall ne'er go by,
> From this day to the ending of the world,
> But we in it shall be remember'd:
> We few, we happy few, we band of brothers;
> For he to-day that sheds his blood with me
> Shall be my brother...

"The Padre was my brother, and he will be remembered."

Boggs walked to the grave and pulled a tattered Airborne Ranger scroll and a faded photograph from his topcoat pocket. He had found them in Carter's lock box. It was a picture of six young Rangers—Boggs, Calloway, Richardson, Johnson, Vasquez and Carter. They were mugging for the camera on a dusty Vietnam landing zone a lifetime ago. He knelt down and dropped both items into the grave then whispered, "Something to remember us by." He picked up a handful of red clay, sprinkled it over the corner of the coffin, turned and walked away.

The senior minister nodded to the piper, and the gentle notes of *Amazing Grace* drifted down the hillside and across the gorge. Everyone knew; it had been the Padre's favorite hymn.

CHAPTER THIRTY-NINE:
YOUR BEST WORK

P ROFESSOR LYLE OPENED THE FRONT DOOR and sized up the short, olive-skinned man standing on the porch. "Mr. Sciavo, I presume?"

The man looked up at Lyle, raised his eyebrows and smiled. "Peter J., in the flesh," he said. "Caught you at a bad time?"

"In the nick of time," the professor said, grinning as he shook hands with his visitor then looked at his watch. "You're cutting it close, though. Got a plane to catch."

"Europe?"

"Eventually." Lyle bowed slightly, extending his left arm toward the living room in a welcoming gesture. "Come on in."

"Sorry for the short notice," Sciavo said, his eyes darting around the room as he stepped inside. He had called from the Atlanta airport early that morning, asking for the meeting. "It's an honor to finally meet you, Professor. I promise this won't take long." He walked over to a brown leather chair and sat down. He leaned forward, rested his forearms on his knees and wrung his hands. "Our friends in Northern Virginia seem pleased, more or less." He looked around the room again. "Possibly your best work, they said."

"They're not exactly friends, but I'll accept the compliment." The professor folded his arms across his chest and glanced at the clock above the fireplace: three p.m. He turned away from his guest and stepped into the hallway. "Too early for a beer?"

"Beer's good, thank you," Sciavo said. Then he rubbed his face with both hands before calling out to Lyle. "They got your message about the money." He paused and leaned back in the chair. "Guess you're aware there's a problem."

There was silence, save the gentle clanking of beer bottles and the *whoosh* when Lyle popped the caps with his old Greek-letter church key. "Yeah," he said, sporting a sheepish grin as he walked back into the living room. "Figured we'd have to discuss that. Kinda sad, too. Always comes down to money. You'd think a hundred and a half would make 'em happy, for God's sake. I suppose you're down here to …work things out."

"Believe me, Dr. Lyle. I'm on your side, but the deal was ten percent— thirty million for you and the old Rangers. The rest goes to the Virginia group. Right now, it appears you're keeping half."

"Listen, Sciavo." Lyle wagged his finger at his guest. "We did what they couldn't do—wouldn't do. We blocked the M&H merger without upsetting a political apple cart. Put the fuckin' quietus on that weapons syndicate. Maybe even saved some of our boys in the next piss ant fight somewhere. Jesus, son!

"And M&H is out for now, at least 'til they replenish their cash. Plus, their Beltway cronies don't get their feathers ruffled. You see, the Virginia boys got what they wanted and then some."

Sciavo sat patiently before rejoining the debate in a calm voice. "I believe the ten percent commission was your number, Dr. Lyle."

"Indeed." The professor paused. "Indeed, it was…but on reflection, thirty million's not near enough. My guys risked it all for honor. None of them knew they were helping government renegades, even if it was for a good cause. Besides, it'll take twice that to get a veteran's foundation going. Those guys are in their early sixties, some older. The more I think about it, they deserve all the money."

Lyle walked to the full-length front window and stared out. It was early December but unseasonably mild. Children in shirtsleeves laughed and played in the sunny street.

Sciavo stood and stretched then joined him at the window. "It was freezing in Jersey when I left. Is it always this nice down here?"

"Usually a lot cooler by now, but you never know. Weatherman says a cold snap's coming. Another beer?"

"No thanks," Sciavo said. "So...what do I tell them?"

"Tell 'em the job's done. I've handled the laundry run as well—flawlessly, I might add. Their cash is safe, stashed in banks between the Caymans and Zurich. It'll bankroll their sneaky-snake shit for awhile—pure gravy compared to our crippling M&H. But...to show good faith, I'll move twenty million more to their account in three weeks." The professor paused. "And a final thirty million six months later—plus some interest. That way, I've got a little insurance policy, if you know what I mean. Of course, our friends in Virginia must behave. That's two hundred million for them and an even hundred for our side."

Sciavo kept watching the children, raising his eyebrows as he ran the math in his head. "I guess they'll get over it...or they'll get you."

"Shit, son! They'll get over it." The professor walked slowly toward the front door, then looked back at Sciavo. "Who those wackos gonna tell? The CIA? The President? Congress, for God's sake? A hundred and a half now and fifty million more over the next nine months—with interest. It's a great deal and they know it."

Sciavo shrugged. "I hope you're right."

"You can be proud, too," Lyle said. "You've helped avenge your brother's death and help some old Vets for years to come." The professor turned up the long neck for the last swallow. "Too bad you can't tell your family this story—the good part, at least. The bad part would make 'em sick."

Sciavo pursed his lips and leaned against the doorsill. "I am proud. I was a little kid when Sonny went to Vietnam, but he was my hero—the best big brother in the world. It almost killed my parents when he died. My old man's got Alzheimer's now. At least he doesn't talk about Sonny anymore. Mother still goes to the cemetery—Memorial Day, Christmas, birthdays. She never misses."

Sciavo changed the subject. "Word's out that Cain's security staff quit—took off in a huff. Left Hilton Head and haven't been heard from since."

"Imagine that." Lyle shook his head. "Good help is hard to find."

"All your people make it out?" Sciavo asked.

"Nothing serious. Boggs is okay, I guess, but one of his guys died last week—heart attack. Nothing to do with our little trip, but he took it real hard. Anyway, he's meeting one of my contacts soon to pick up some stuff on the foundation. And I've got a surprise for him, too. Kind of a Christmas present."

"A surprise?"

"Yeah. He's got all the dough in the world, but there's more to life, and he knows it, too. He's been suffering for a long time. The present I got him should pick him up—push him in a new direction. There's something for you, too."

Sciavo wrinkled his brow. "Me?"

"Yeah, you. Couldn't have done it without you. You took a big chance helping ol' Buddy Carter—God bless him—and running interference with those Washington weirdoes. Anyway, I've got a little consulting job for you. It's perfectly legal, working through a foreign bank doing business here. But first, there's a crusty old paratrooper sitting in a North Carolina jail you've got to spring. Work through the locals; pay off a victim or two. You'll be getting a file at your office in a few days. And don't tell me your practice doesn't need the work."

"I can't take money like that!"

"Bullshit. It's got nothing to do with M&H. You'll be working for a legitimate foundation. Behind the scenes for the most part. It'll help you take care of your folks. Do something for your kids or run naked in Costa Rica, for God's sake. Anyway, no one will question it." The professor opened the door. "Sciavo, you're a patriot and a damned good man. I bet you visit your mama whenever you can."

Sciavo chuckled. "Every week."

"Good," Lyle said. "Now, get goin'. A white Jaguar's gonna pull up in a minute with a beautiful blonde behind the wheel, and you don't need to be here." Lyle flashed his broad, conquering smile and glanced at his watch. "She'll want to spend some quality time with me. Like I said, I've got a plane to catch, and the clock is ticking away."

The lawyer turned back to the professor as he walked out the door. "You watch your back."

"Thanks for the reminder," the professor said with a smile, "but let me assure you this ain't my first trip to the amusement park."

CHAPTER FORTY:
REGOUT'S RETURN

"YES, COLONEL CAIN." MICHEL REGOUT WHISPERED into the telephone receiver. "I am still in the Washington area—northern Virginia, actually.

"The information I have received may—I repeat, may—help us locate this special person. My source believes this person could have knowledge of the type of operation we are interested in. He may also know of individuals capable of pulling it off."

"Interesting," Cain said from his comfortable South London office. "But far from certain."

"I am hopeful," Regout said, standing at the pay phone in a cluttered convenience store outside Alexandria.

"What else?" Cain was terse.

"There is, Colonel." Regout paused, shifting his weight from one foot to another. "There is the matter…of finances."

"Meaning?"

"There is travelling involved—if I am to find and talk to this certain person," Regout said. "Lodging, food, payment for information, among other things."

"Among other things?" Cain's frown traveled the phone. "How much?"

"Five…five thousand now," Regout said, glancing at two young men who were sizing him up as he used the phone. "Of course, it may take more as things progress."

"Of course," Cain snapped. "Same bank account?"

"Yes, Colonel. If you would be so kind."

"And just where is this certain person, as you call him?"

"All that I can say is that I will be heading back to the Carolinas," Regout said. "I will call you promptly as things develop."

"I'm sure you will," Cain said. "Anything else?"

"No, sir." Regout had barely spoken the words when there was a sharp click on the end of the line. Then he turned his attention to the two men stalking him from the front of the store.

An East Indian clerk stood motionless behind the counter, cutting his eyes nervously between Regout and the two men—the store's only customers at the time.

Regout sighed as he turned toward the two men standing near the front door. "Is there something you want?"

"Yeah," one of the men said, with a smile full of gold-capped teeth. "We'll take your spare cash. You know, as a Christmas gift for needy brothers."

"Spare cash?" Regout replied. "I have no spare cash, but I do have this." As if by magic, Regout produced a Glock 40 caliber automatic from inside his topcoat. He exposed just enough of its stubby snout to command the full attention of both men. "Surprised?" Regout spoke in an almost maniacal chuckle. "The amazement is written on your faces. And you, Mister Gold Teeth, where is your golden smile now? Too bad I am pressed for time. It could have been an entertaining afternoon, but you must leave— now. If not, I will share this weapon's contents with you both. And I must tell you, its bite is far, far worse than its bark."

"Easy my man, easy." One of the men raised both hands where Regout could plainly see.

Gold Teeth mimicked his companion, hands raised and shaking his head. "Easy brother, easy," he blurted out as they stumbled backward toward the door, demolishing a rack of potato chips in the process.

"I want no trouble," the clerk said, watching nervously as the Glock vanished inside Regout's coat. "I-I must live with these people."

Regout stared into the clerk's eyes. "You, my pathetic friend, you should find another place to live."

"But America is now my home," the clerk said.

"What I mean," Regout said, looking around the walls and ceiling of the store, "is you should find a better place than this.

"Now, one last thing. Let's step into your storeroom and retrieve the cassette from the security camera."

"I-I am not to leave the front unattended," the clerk said.

"I understand," Regout said, producing the Glock again. "If you don't accompany me, you will leave with the coroner. *N'est-ce pas?*"

"I-I don't understand," the clerk said.

Regout sighed. "Let's go, or I will blow your brains out."

The clerk rushed from behind the counter, waving his hands in front of his face. "I-I-I understand."

—⫯—

Cain leaned against the massive desk in his South London office, fumbling with a green envelope postmarked Hilton Head Island, South Carolina. It was mid December, and holiday cards were trickling in. While generally displayed in the M&H lobby, the hand-written note on this envelope had caught the mail clerk's eye, and he sent it up to the executive suite. Cain scowled as he tapped the flat side against his outstretched palm. His feelings were far from festive as he reread the note; there was the burning fire of anger and the coldest chills of fear.

"Personal—from your Ranger buddies." The words were neatly printed at the bottom of the envelope.

"Open it, James." Ha grew impatient, lighting an unfiltered Gauloises as he walked to a window for a view of the city. "What could they want now?"

"Probably rubbing our noses in it." Cain frowned as he sliced the flap with a silver letter opener. "Just as I thought. It's that maniac—the self-proclaimed general of Hilton Head." Cain's voice shook in a kind of post-traumatic reaction as he read: "Wish you boys were here. Remember, now. We're just like Santa. We're everywhere, so y'all be good…"

Cain crushed the card into a ball and tossed it toward the fireplace. He sighed, shaking his head as he slumped into his leather desk chair.

Ha showed no emotion, puffing his cigarette while staring into the streets below. When he broke the silence, he spoke in a soft voice. "Has he contacted you today?"

"Regout?"

"Regout," Ha whispered.

"This morning—very early," Cain said. "He met with a Washington source—an old CIA renegade. He may have a lead on our so-called general."

"And?" Ha turned to face his partner.

"He was vague, very vague, which troubles me. But we'll go along with him. It could all be bullshit, but we have little choice." He paused to rest his head in his hands and rub his eyes. "He wanted more money, which I arranged. No traceable link to M&H, of course."

"He is holding out on us," Ha said.

"I'm not sure," Cain said. "He's been loyal to us, and we've bailed him out a time or two."

"Come now, James." Ha furrowed his brow. "Security failed on his watch. Except for this final business, we are finished with Mr. Regout. *N'est-ce pas?*"

Cain shrugged. "Absolutely."

"He was lucky to escape his captors in Morocco, but Mr. Regout is not stupid," Ha said. "He knows his days with M&H are numbered. So, what he brings to us will have a pretty price."

Cain spun his chair around and gazed into the London skyline. "You're probably right. Payback for our general will not come cheap." A nasty little sneer worked its way across Cain's face. "And I'll gladly pay if Regout slits his throat."

"Indeed," Ha said, "but the woman is the key—the southern belle, the one who humiliated Regout. It is our best hope that she and our general are together." Ha inhaled the Gauloise then exhaled the smoke in a sigh.

"Killing the general is just business. Finding the girl, now that is Regout's obsession. It is the thing that will keep him going."

—⚋⚋—

Regout sat on a park bench outside the South Carolina State House with his collar turned up against the December chill. He saw two young women out of the corner of his eye—a brunette and a redhead—walking in his direction. He stood as they passed. "Pardon me, *Mademoiselles*," he said.

Intrigued by his accent and confident in the safety of their numbers, they stopped. "Yes, sir?" the brunette asked, looking over her shoulder.

Regout removed his wool hat, pressed it against his chest, and spoke in a polite tone. "Could you please direct me to what is called 'The Horse-shoe'?"

The redhead pointed toward the University of South Carolina campus several blocks away. "Down Sumter Street on the left. Old buildings around a grassy area. It's U-shaped. That's why they call it The Horseshoe."

"*Merci, merci beaucoup.*" Regout replaced his hat and walked toward Sumter Street. He hoped to visit a professor known for his writings on military intelligence from the Vietnam era. Regout's Washington contact had suggested he tell the professor what happened at Hilton Head. The professor loved a good story, the source said, and, with a little encouragement, may be willing to help.

Twenty minutes later, Regout stood at the basement entrance of an old classroom building on The Horseshoe. He checked the note he had scribbled on a napkin then opened the door.

A young woman sat at a desk behind a long counter, transfixed by a computer screen.

"*Mademoiselle*," Regout said.

"Sorry," the woman said. "Didn't hear you come in. May I help you?"

"Yes, please." Regout clutched the hat against his chest, repeating the humble and sincere routine used on the State House grounds. "I wish to speak to Professor Graydon Lyle."

"Gone for the holidays," she said. "His graduate assistant is here. Maybe she can help."

"I doubt it." Regout frowned, tapping his fingers on the counter as he pondered his next move.

At the same time, an office door opened in the hall behind the counter. A woman wearing a fisherman's sweater and faded jeans stepped into the long corridor.

Regout could not see her face, but he watched her bend over to lock the office door. Very nice ass, he thought.

"Goodnight, Jane," the woman at the computer said.

"Goodnight," she replied, never looking back as she walked down the long hall toward an exit.

Regout raised his eyebrows and smiled as he turned to face the clerk. Then it hit him—the fisherman's sweater, that terrific figure, that walk, and the soft voice when she said goodnight. Could she be Caroline Deschamps, the treacherous would-be lover who sold him out to the old Frenchman? He could never be that lucky.

"The young lady leaving the building," Regout said softly. "Did you call her Jane?"

"Jane Bennett. Professor Lyle's assistant. The one I mentioned. Should I catch her before she leaves the parking lot?"

"No, no," Regout said. "An imposition at this late hour. But...will she return tomorrow?"

"I suppose so," the clerk said.

"Thank you, *mademoiselle*." Regout's fingers nearly clawed the countertop as he backed away. "May I also leave through the rear exit?" He nodded toward the door Miss Bennett had used moments earlier.

"If you like," she said, returning to her computer screen.

Regout wanted to run, but he walked down the hall at a moderate pace. He stopped at the door and looked through the sidelight. If this woman was Caroline, the last thing he wanted was a confrontation at her office. Satisfied she had left, he stepped outside and slipped behind a tall hedge alongside the building, hoping for a better look at this Miss Bennett. He got his wish moments later when she lifted the trunk of a VW Jetta and placed her briefcase inside. It was the sweater, the figure and, most importantly, the face. The hair color and style were different, but Miss Bennett was Regout's Caroline. He was sure of it now. The blood raced through his veins. His muscles tensed. Sweat popped out on his forehead. He closed his eyes and opened his mind to the memories of the nightmare in Charleston harbor. He could smell her perfume and the salt air. He could taste the deadly Scotch that had taken him down, and it sickened him. His psychotic side screamed inside his head: kill her—now.

Regout had a practical side, and it weighed in as well. If Caroline is here, can Cain's general be far away? If so, why flee the scene a penniless murderer when one could wait on the paycheck of a lifetime and then kill the girl?

He stood motionless behind the prickly holly hedge, battling his emotions as Caroline or Miss Bennett or whoever she was drove away. By the slimmest of margins, Regout's practical side had won.

As he calmed down, Regout began to sense the opportunity before him. He wanted to call Cain and taunt him with his discovery, but that would have to wait. Regout's location would also remain a secret as well. First, he would take time—a day, a week, whatever—to learn everything about Miss Bennett. If she led him to the general, Regout would contact Cain and set a price for the general's life. If he had to torture Miss Bennett to get to the general, Regout would gladly oblige. He owed her something special for the pain she had inflicted, and even now, strolling through the cold dark shadows of a dying December day, his psychotic side ran wild.

CHAPTER FORTY-ONE:
THE CHRISTMAS
GIFT

IT WAS COLD IN COLUMBIA—ESPECIALLY COLD for the week before Christmas. Light snow had blanketed the city during the afternoon, camouflaging the shabbiest neighborhoods with a serene white layer while lifting the beautiful places to new heights. When Boggs eased the Cadillac into Professor Lyle's driveway, he knew it was a place worthy of a holiday card. He stepped out of the car he had borrowed from Maywood, shivering as he pulled on a navy cashmere topcoat. Seldom more than a fashion statement in the South Carolina Midlands, the coat provided a welcomed layer of warmth on this cold, still night. It was a striking contrast to the balmy weather when he had visited last April. Boggs shook his head and sighed; so much had changed since then.

Swags of blue cedar and boxwood draped the lamppost at the driveway's edge, and a large evergreen wreath trimmed in deep red and gold ribbon decorated the front door. Boggs peered through the full-length living room window at a lush Frazer fir that nearly touched the ceiling. Tiny white lights filled each bough, illuminating gold and silver ornaments and velvet bows. He reached for the doorknocker then paused, remembering happy, but distant, family Christmases at Maywood. He turned up the collar on the topcoat, longing for the holidays past and those he had missed with his daughter. Standing in the lonely silence, he inhaled the crisp clean smells of evergreen and snow, absorbing as much of the season's spirit as his sad heart could bear. The professor may have traipsed off to France, but it appeared his house sitter had made the cottage her home—a real home—for the holidays.

Boggs sighed again, forced a melancholy smile and grasped the cold brass ring, rapping it twice against the striker then stepped back. He slipped his hands into the silk-lined coat pockets then turned to look at the sparkling lights decorating yards and houses along the wintry street. He was glad the house sitter was slow to answer the door; in those few nostalgic moments, he had almost forgotten why he had come. Then there was the sound of muffled footsteps. The door squeaked open, and to Boggs's surprise, he turned to face an attractive young woman. She was dressed in a white silk blouse and flowing black silk pants. A single strand of perfectly matched pearls circled her neck, and strawberry blond curls fell gently to her shoulders.

"Uh, yes…good evening," Boggs said, stumbling over the greeting. He had expected a student with stringy hair in jeans and a sweatshirt, not the elegant woman who had opened the door. "I'm Barry Boggs. I believe Professor Lyle left something for me."

"I've been expecting you, Mr. Boggs." She smiled, extending her hand. "I'm Jane Bennett, Dr. Lyle's graduate assistant. We—my mother and I— are house sitting while he's on holiday. Please come in. It's quite cold."

"Thank you," he said, trying not to stare as he stepped across the threshold. "It is a bit chilly." He had the feeling he had seen her before but quickly dismissed the idea. "Middle-aged wishful thinking," he whispered under his breath. She was young enough to be his daughter, and, after all, Graydon Lyle liked them that way.

"May I offer you a drink—coffee or something stronger?"

Boggs smiled, pointing down the hallway toward the kitchen. "Graydon always kept a well-stocked liquor cabinet. Bourbon—straight, please—if he left a bottle."

"The cupboard's just as he left it," she said in a cheerful voice as she turned into the hallway.

"Please sit down, Mr. Boggs. I'll get your drink and the package Dr. Lyle left for you."

Boggs was intrigued by the house sitter—she was poised, pretty and very British. He wondered if she was another of Lyle's grad school babies, but quickly ruled that out. After all, the girl's mother was here. Anything less than a student-professor relationship, and she would probably have been in Europe with Lyle.

When she returned, she had the Bourbon in one hand and a soft, black leather satchel in the other.

"Beautiful decorations." Boggs nodded toward the Christmas tree and the mantel covered with holly boughs and cedar.

"I can't claim the credit," she said with a smile. "Mom's the decorator. "I'm the helper. Although we're just house-sitting, she insists on the full holiday treatment. Wouldn't be Christmas without it, she says."

"Have you known Dr. Lyle for a long time?" She changed the subject.

"Since college. Fraternity brothers," Boggs said. "Pretty wild back then, I'm afraid. Hope he hasn't told you about our exploits." His conversation was polite, but his eyes were fixed on the satchel.

"Oh, no," she replied. "He first mentioned your name when he left the briefcase. He said you were a client. That's all."

"So, you didn't help with my research?" Boggs wondered what, if anything, the professor had told her.

"No, Mr. Boggs," she said, handing him the satchel. "He keeps much of the outside work to himself." Then she slipped a small folder from behind the briefcase. "He also left this." She smiled. "He said to tell you it was from Santa Claus."

Boggs raised his eyebrows as he accepted the folder. Her face, mannerisms and voice—except for the accent—seemed strangely familiar. He sipped the Bourbon as he studied the dark green folder she had given him. It was eight by ten inches and tied up with a cream-colored ribbon.

"He asked that you open it while you were here." Her voice was pleasant, but there was a curious look on her face. "Can't imagine why."

Boggs eased the satchel to the floor, then pulled the end of the silk ribbon tied around the folder. He sat quietly for a few moments, staring blankly at the black and white photograph inside.

"You know, I remember someone taking a picture, but I never saw it... 'til now." His sad eyes never left the photograph as he leaned forward on the sofa, holding the picture in both hands. "It was graduation day. Graydon's on the left. I'm on the right." He nervously tapped the edge of the folder with his right forefinger. "Katherine—Katherine Rutledge is in the middle."

"Mr. Boggs?" She walked to the sofa and sat down beside him. "May I look at the photograph?"

Her words were lost on him as his mind glided into the past. "I'd forgotten just how beautiful she was. We lost touch when I went to Vietnam—my fault, really. I never saw her again."

She touched him gently on the arm. "May I see it? Please?"

He looked up, but said nothing as he handed the picture to the young woman beside him. His smile was a melancholy one. "Just a snapshot from a lifetime ago."

"I've never seen this one." She ran her slim fingers along the picture's scalloped edge. "Now I know why Dr. Lyle wanted me to see this. She was beautiful." She turned to Boggs. "She's even more beautiful now."

"Now?" He furrowed his brow. "You know Katherine Rutledge?"

"Indeed," she said softly. "She's my mother."

The hairs on his arms stood on end. Sweat beads formed on his forehead. An unsteady hand brought the Bourbon to his lips. This was the closest he had been to Katherine since graduation day. He had often wondered how he would handle it if they ever met. What would he say? Now it all tumbled through his mind, along with the quiet, self-confidence he had cultivated over the years. "But," he said in disbelief. "You-you're British, aren't you?"

"Not exactly." She sank back in the sofa. "Dad was teaching at Colorado State when I was born. Three months later, he accepted a position in London. Our family home is still there, just outside the city."

"And your father?" Boggs had to know.

"Dad died two years ago. He was wonderful. We loved him very much." She paused, still looking at the picture. "I know Mom will be happy to see you after all these years."

"She's here? Now?"

"Not at the moment. She and my date are running an errand before we leave for dinner. He's scrambling to send gifts to family overseas. Mom insisted he send them air express. She's very big on the family thing."

"I see," said Boggs, whose heart, mind and body were in full retreat. He had already stood up and was walking toward the front door. "Please tell her I'm sorry—sorry I missed her." Boggs knew that son of a bitch Graydon Lyle set this whole thing up. He wanted to kill him.

"Won't you wait?" Miss Bennett asked. "She'll be walking through the door any moment, I know she'd love to see you."

"You've been most kind, but I've intruded enough." He reached for the doorknob. His heart pounded down to his fingertips as he looked into that beautiful face—her mother's face. He breathed a sigh of relief as he opened the door. Escape was at hand. He paused and smiled, still looking at Katherine's daughter. "Thank you, Miss Bennett. A Merry Christmas to you...and to your mother."

"And a Merry Christmas to you, too." The cheerful greeting came from a woman standing in the threshold. She was even more surprised than Boggs. At least he had had some warning.

The chills racing up Boggs's spine did not come in from the cold. After all these years, he recognized the voice. He had heard it in his dreams and carried it secretly in his heart for years. Now the day had arrived, a day he had feared but subconsciously hoped for much of his adult life. There was nowhere to run. When he turned around, he was face to face with the first woman—the only woman—he had ever really loved. And her daughter was right; she was more beautiful than he had remembered. He sighed in surrender and smiled, searching his heart for the right words—any words. "Hello, Katherine," he said. "Graydon left some stuff...uh, research he was doing for me. I had no idea... It's been such a long time—much too long."

"Barry," she said as a tear formed in the corner of her eye. "What a surprise," she said, holding her arms out to him.

Awkward at first, Boggs was like a twelve-year-old who had been scraped off the wall at his first school dance, but he took her in his arms. "I can't believe you're here," he whispered, trying to rein in a heart that was hurtling across a lifetime of memories.

"No one told me your were coming," she said. "That's just like Graydon. Thank God I'm dressed and wearing makeup!"

"You look terrific, Katherine." Boggs gushed, knowing he sounded like a fool the instant the words left his lips, but he meant it.

"I'm sorry to interrupt the reunion, Mother," she said with a smile. "We do have plans for dinner, and where's my date?"

"Oh, I almost forgot," Katherine said. "I left him downtown—still shopping. He said he'll take a cab and be here shortly."

"Besides, you two can go without me—if Barry will stay and talk for a while."

"Maybe you could join me for dinner," Boggs said, turning to Katherine.

"I am dressed to go out," she said, "and it would save me from being the odd one out with Janie and her date."

"Maybe we could catch up on things after all these years," Boggs said, feeling a little more comfortable about their surprise meeting.

"We could start with the mail service from Vietnam," Katherine said.

CHAPTER FORTY-TWO:

REGOUT'S REVENGE

THE LANE BEHIND LYLE'S COTTAGE WAS smooth and snowy white, save a set of lonely footprints that meandered about a block then slipped between a hedge and a garden house on the professor's property. From there they continued to the door of the old structure, disappearing from the crisp night into its dark and musty interior.

"Excellent." Regout 's whisper came from snarling lips on breath that spread like smoke as it collided with the chilled air. From his hiding place, he could see the side and the front entrance of Lyle's cottage, and he flinched when a light came on in the kitchen. Instinctively, he stepped deeper into the shed. When he looked out, he saw a woman framed like a portrait in the window over the sink. "She is here," he muttered, clinching his cold fist as he stood in the old shed. "She is here."

Regout had been patient, watching the man arrive in the Cadillac, followed by a woman about a half-hour later. He smiled as the pair left together, leaving Jane Bennett alone in the professor's house in this quiet neighborhood. He had taken a week to find her apartment and observe her route to and from the university. Although surprised when she left her townhouse to house sit for the professor, this was an even better place for what he had in mind. Unlike her large and busy apartment complex in Columbia's Forest Acres section, there was no gated entrance and no security staff. His plan was simple enough; he would overpower Bennett and force her to tell him if Lyle was the general, and, if not, who was. He would then contact Colonel Cain and negotiate a handsome fee for identifying the mastermind of Hilton Head. If Cain wanted him killed, Regout would gladly finish the job, but the price would go up. After all, it was just business—the part about the so-called general. The woman was an entirely different matter: she was Regout's obsession.

Bennett stood at the kitchen sink, washing Boggs's bourbon glass and enjoying the quiet moments since he and her mother had left. She was happy that Lyle had reunited the two; it seemed to be a pleasant surprise for her widowed mother. She reached for the switch to turn off the kitchen light when the cell phone rang. It was a special phone the professor had given her for emergencies only, and it was untraceable.

"Yes?" She had been trained to give that simple, one-word answer.

"Just listen." It was Lyle. "Your man from Hilton Head escaped his captors and is in Columbia."

"All right," she said, stunned by the professor's words and struggling to maintain her composure. Then, in an angry voice, she asked, "And how long have you known this?"

"That he escaped? Two weeks. That he was here? Two days."

"And you waited until now to tell me? I am the only one he would recognize, for God's sake."

"Calm down. We've had people watching him," Lyle said. "We had to know if he was working for his old bosses or free-lancing. A number of lives could be at risk here, but it appears he's alone and that he hasn't connected any dots with respect to me."

"But," she said, pursing her lips as she shook her head. "I'm the bait."

There was a brief silence. "Sorry," the professor said, "but you and our man can handle it. It's why I picked you. Where's your mother?"

"At dinner with Boggs. A lovely reunion, though Boggs was as nervous as a cat," she said. "They left after he picked up the satchel you left for him."

"Good. He's not involved in any of this. Keep it that way."

"Of course," she said, as exhilaration began to circle her fear. After all, this kind of work—this clandestine spy stuff—was what she always wanted to do.

"I just spoke to Schiller," Lyle said. He's on the way—ten, maybe fifteen minutes out."

Bennett glanced around the cottage, checking doors and windows as she held the cell phone to her ear. "What else can I do?"

"Just stay put. Stay alert. No cops, of course. It's just the nature of this game." Lyle said. "Are you armed?"

She sighed. "No. It's at my apartment. Didn't want to explain that to Mother."

"Grab something—kitchen knife, fire poker." Lyle's tone was serious. "Regout is one dangerous son of a bitch, and we expect him to make some kind of move. Help is on the way. A cleaning crew is on alert as well."

"Thank you, Professor. That's certainly re-assuring, and just who will they be cleaning up?" There was more than a little attitude in her voice, but she was becoming more focused and confident by the minute. She ended the call and walked back toward the kitchen. She reached for the light switch, but hesitated when she realized the kitchen windows had neither curtains nor blinds. She would navigate the small space in the dark—no need to advertise her search for a big knife, much less present such a clear target. She fumbled through a drawer or two then abruptly ended her search. "The switchblade," she whispered, leaving the kitchen and walking down the hall to the guest bedroom. Schiller had given it to her after the rendezvous with his team off Hilton Head. The knife was in her messenger bag in the bedroom. While she understood the old axiom that one does not bring a knife to a gunfight, this razor sharp pearl-handled beauty may be her only hope until Schiller arrived. Its pearl inlays were ever so smooth to the touch and the stainless steel deadly cool. She pressed the button on the side and the blade snapped forward. Bennett ran her finger down the center to where the two sharpened sides met then she carefully touched the tip. It had killed before, had no conscience, and she knew how to use it. She slipped it in the side pocket of her silk pants, clutched its pearl handle as if her life depended on it and sighed. "This little knife is my only friend for now."

Bennett walked from the bedroom, still clutching the knife inside the pocket of her slacks, when cologne—his cheap cologne—hit her in the face, and as quick as she wrinkled her nose in disgust, Regout grabbed her around the shoulders, pinning her arms to her sides with one arm. With his other hand, he covered her mouth and nose, nearly shutting off her breathing. She gasped for air, managing to take enough breaths to keep from suffocating, but her attempts to wriggle free were futile.

"My darling southern belle, my dearest Caroline or Jane or whoever you are." There was a vile shudder in his voice and stale cigarette smoke on his breath. "We have, I believe, some unfinished business—our time together lost, shall we say, to some very bad Scotch."

Bennett's heart pounded, and when she tried to resist, he tightened his crushing grip and breathing became even more difficult.

"I want to hear your voice," he said. "Want to hear the fear and amazement that your plan failed and poor Regout escaped from his captors." Then he laughed out loud, swinging Bennett's body around like a ragdoll in a bizarre dance of terror. "Poor bastards," he said, shaking his head. "They thought they had it made when they got me to Morocco, but I had all those days on the water to devise a plan. It was after we made landfall that I broke free. I killed them one by one as they slept in some cheap hotel."

Regout pursed his lips, kissed Bennett on her neck and right ear, then whispered, "My dear Miss Bennett, you will not have the pleasure of a quick end to your life as did the Frenchman and his Moroccans. We must talk first."

—ⁿⁿ—

Schiller got out of the cab a block from the professor's cottage. He believed that anyone hoping to surprise Jane Bennett would enter from the back of the property. He stopped when he saw footprints in the snow-covered lane. He pulled a .22 magnum automatic from his top coat, attached the silencer and cautiously followed the tracks as they turned between the hedge and the old garden shed—his own heart racing and hoping he was not too late.

Bennett gasped for air when Regout dropped his hand from her nose and mouth, and shoved it inside her blouse and squeezed her breast.

"Ah," Regout said, "Soft and smooth as I imagined, but business first." He put his face against hers and whispered, "You must tell me who is this 'general'—the mastermind of the Hilton Head plan."

"I-I don't know any general," she said.

"Maybe your Professor Lyle is our 'general'," Regout said as he pinned Bennett's arms even tighter against her waist.

"He's just a professor," she said, struggling to breathe under the pressure of his grip.

"I think he is much more—an expert, I am told, on matters such as these. And if not the professor, my darling, who is your boss?"

"No boss." Her breathing was labored. "Orders came by courier. It was a freelance job—simply for money. Nothing personal."

"Nothing personal!" Regout shouted as he shoved Bennett down on the sofa, releasing his grip on her arms for the first time, but standing over her like a wild animal ready to pounce on his cornered prey.

"Take off the blouse," he said, "and the beautiful lace bra."

He knelt beside the sofa as she followed his orders, but covered her breast with her right arm. She did not resist when he pulled her arm away from her chest, and he smiled as he leaned over to kiss her neck and breasts. Overwhelmed by her apparent surrender, he never saw her left hand slip into the side pocket of her flowing silk pants. His eyes widened when he heard the knife blade snap forward, but it was too late. Her first thrust caught him in the gut, just above his pelvis. She got him a second time just under the sternum, shoving the blade in to the hilt. He tumbled backward with his legs in a grotesque tangle.

"You stinking, pathetic bastard," she said as she watched Regout try to right himself on the living room floor. "You'll not touch anyone again."

In excruciating pain, gasping for air, and bleeding out, Regout still found the strength to pull a pistol from his coat pocket for the first time during this encounter. Though his hand was shaking, and blurry eyes affected his aim, he managed to fire a single round just missing Bennett's head. Stunned by her proximity to the muzzle blast, her ears rang as she got to her feet only to have Regout trip her as she tried to slip between him and the sofa.

No one heard the next shot fire, but it was perfectly placed, leaving a small hole between Regout's eyes. Schiller had been waiting outside the living room window, hoping for a shot to bring Bennett's living nightmare to an end. With no time to break into the cottage, he took the only shot he had—directly through one of nine rectangular window panes, hoping the bullet's trajectory would remain true and stop Regout once and for all.

"Thank you," Bennett said, draping her blouse around her sore shoulders.

"My pleasure." Schiller spoke through the broken windowpane. "If you would kindly unlock the door, we'll take care of this situation."

She opened the front door and fell into Shiller's arms. "I did thank you, did I not?"

"You did," he said, "but you held your own."

"I guess I did," she said. "Now, can we get this mess cleaned up before my mother and her date return?"

"There is a service truck in the driveway waiting to repair your plumbing problem." Schiller smiled. "Maybe they can help."

"Plumbing problem?"

"The cleaners," he said.

"Of course," she replied. "Anyway let's get to it. Mom's with some old flame named Boggs—one of the professor's college chums and a research client. They don't need to stumble in on this disaster."

"Boggs?" Schiller asked.

"I don't know what the professor did for him, but they were college classmates of my mother as well."

"Very interesting," Schiller said. At that point, he realized that the professor had told Bennett nothing about Boggs, nor had he told Boggs that Bennett had grabbed Regout off Charleston.

"I'm just glad they weren't here," Bennett said. "Regout could have killed both of them. Mom would have been defenseless, and an old guy like Boggs would probably have a heart attack if he had stumbled upon something like this."

"Indeed," Schiller said, shaking his head and successfully repressing a little grin.

—⟋⟍—

The cleaners were in and out in a matter of minutes, having removed Regout's body, a puddle of blood from the hardwood floor, along with blood spatter on an Oriental rug and a sofa cushion. The late security chief for M & H International would never be heard from again.

—⟋⟍—

Thirty minutes later Boggs and Katherine Bennett walked into the cottage, having returned from dinner and their conversation about old times. Jane Bennett had just reapplied her make-up along with some special attention to a bruise on her cheek courtesy of Regout. She hoped the four ibuprofen would ease the chest pain she suspected was a cracked rib. Schiller was in the kitchen mixing drinks.

"Dinner was nice?" Bennett asked

"Lovely," her mother replied.

Boggs smiled.

My friend in the kitchen is Karl Schiller," Bennett said. "Karl come meet Mr. Boggs.

If meeting Katherine Bennett had been a surprise, seeing Schiller in Columbia was an even greater one.

"Mr. Boggs," Schiller said, as he extended his hands to Boggs and pretended not to know him. "It is a pleasure to meet you. I've been a guest lecturer for Dr. Lyle for the last few weeks."

"The pleasure is mine," Boggs said, forcing a little smile.

"I am from South Africa," Schiller said.

"I once knew a man from Cape Town," Boggs said. "He was a soldier of fortune—a dangerous breed, I'm told."

"Don't know many of those fellows," Schiller said, playing along with the tale Boggs was spinning. "I'm working on my doctorate in history. I'm here at Dr. Lyle's invitation to talk about the new South Africa. I've had a wonderful time. In addition to being brilliant, the professor is quite entertaining."

"He can be a very funny guy," Boggs said. "As a matter of fact, I believe I've been the butt of some of his best jokes. Too bad he's not here tonight. I'm sure I could learn a lot from both of you."

"The professor is quite the storyteller," Schiller said.

"Indeed," Boggs said with a sigh. "He has had many, many years to perfect it."

"Well, Karl." Katherine Bennett joined the conversation. "Barry and I have had quite an exciting evening—meeting for the first time in many years and going out together. Sorry we're a little late. Are we keeping you two from doing something exciting tonight?"

"No," her daughter said. "I think we're both tired. We'll just stay here for a while. We'll pass on the excitement for this evening."

—⁊⁊⁊—

ACKNOWLEDGEMENTS

Many thanks to: Steve Vassey and SC Writers Workshop Chapter I for their critiques, encouragement and editing help; Carole Garren, Cynthia Wilson, Gibbie Coker, and Rachel Haynie for their thoughts, copy editing, and reading; Susan Olivari, book cover design; and my son, Kent, without whose service with the 1st Ranger Battalion and insight, this novel would not have been written.

Made in the USA
Charleston, SC
17 October 2014